The Sacred Era

PARALLEL FUTURES

Series Editors: Thomas Lamarre and Takayuki Tatsumi

THE SACRED ERA

A Novel

Yoshio Aramaki

Translated by Baryon Tensor Posadas

Foreword by Takayuki Tatsumi

PARALLEL FUTURES

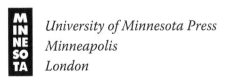

University of Minnesota Press
Minneapolis
London

Published by the University of Minnesota Press
111 Third Avenue South, Suite 290
Minneapolis, MN 55401-2520
http://www.upress.umn.edu

LIBRARY OF CONGRESS CATALOGING-IN-PUBLICATION DATA
Names: Aramaki, Yoshio, 1933– author. | Posadas, Baryon Tensor, 1978–
    translator. | Tatsumi, Takayuki, 1955– writer of foreword.
Title: The sacred era : a novel / Aramaki Yoshio ; translated by Baryon Tensor
    Posadas ; foreword by Takayuki Tatsumi.
Other titles: Shinseidai. English
Description: Minneapolis : University of Minnesota Press, 2017. | Series: Parallel
    futures | "The Sacred Era was first published as Shinseidai. Original Japanese
    edition published by Sairyu-sha, Tokyo" [2015] — Verso title page.
Identifiers: LCCN 2016059302 (print) | ISBN 978-0-8166-9985-8 (hc) |
    ISBN 978-0-8166-9986-5 (pb)
Subjects: LCSH: Science fiction, Japanese | BISAC: FICTION / Science Fiction /
    General. | FICTION / Science Fiction / Space Opera. | GSAFD: Science fiction.
Classification: LCC PL845.R29 S3513 2017 (print) | DDC 895.63/5—dc23
LC record available at https://lccn.loc.gov/2016059302

The University of Minnesota is an equal-opportunity educator and employer.

Naked I came from my mother's womb,
and naked I will depart.
The LORD gave and the LORD has taken away;
may the name of the LORD be praised.

—Book of Job 1:21

CONTENTS

APOCRYPHA NOW!

Welcome to the Quintessence of Japanese Speculative Fiction

Takayuki Tatsumi

Like the strange peregrinations in his works of speculative fiction, Yoshio Aramaki's career might be described as an exploration of currents and countercurrents. Born April 12, 1933, in the town of Otaru on the northernmost island of Japan, Hokkaidō, where his father, Aramaki Yoshi, managed a quarrying company, the young Aramaki, like so many of his generation coming of age in the immediate postwar era, left his hometown to pursue his education and fortune in the booming metropolis of Tokyo. He studied psychology at Waseda University between 1954 and 1957 and then worked for a publisher in Tokyo for a few years. He did not remain in the metropolis but returned home in 1961, in the wake of the student protests of the renewal of the Japan–U.S. security treaty that had rocked the city of Tokyo in 1960. Aramaki renounced his ambition of becoming a professional writer along with the ideals of post-Marxist revolution promulgated around the student protests. Instead, intent on taking over the family business, which had expanded to include several companies, Aramaki returned to Sapporo to pursue a degree in architecture within the Department of Civil Engineering at Hokkai Gakuen University in 1962. His interest in art persisted, and even as he began to run one of his father's construction companies, he also established an art gallery, serving as a patron for a number of talented artists in the area.

His diverse interests and talents found a common focus in his passion for science fiction. In 1965, Aramaki joined the Hokkaido SF Club. In the pages of its fanzine *CORE* (1965–67), Aramaki would publish a series of essays on such renowned writers as Arthur C. Clarke, Philip K. Dick, and Alfred Bester as well as the Japanese writers Mayumura Taku and Tsutsui Yasutaka. It was Tsutsui, already well regarded as a pioneer of Japanese metafiction, who discovered and promoted Aramaki's literary and critical genius. Thus Aramaki entered into debates with key figures within the rapidly transforming world of Japanese science fiction. The New Wave movement dominated the conceptualization of science fiction in 1960s Japan. This movement sought to challenge and to overturn the conventional science fiction emphasis on "outer space," promoting varieties of speculative fiction with a radical, countercultural, and sometimes surrealist orientation toward "inner space," inspired by authors such as Stanislaw Lem, J. G. Ballard, and Philip K. Dick.

One important voice was that of Yamano Kōichi, writer and editor for the first commercial speculative fiction quarterly, *NW-SF* (1970–82). In 1969, Yamano published a highly influential essay, "Japanese SF: Its Originality and Possibility," in which he espoused the radical new view of the speculative mission of science fiction while taking Japanese writers to task for merely imitating the works of their Anglo-American colleagues.[1] In the pages of the fanzine *ŪCHŪJIN* (Cosmic Dust) between 1969 and 1970, Aramaki engaged in a heated debate with Yamano; while Aramaki largely agreed with Yamano's vision of the possibilities of science fiction, his take on the state of Japanese science fiction was less bleak. Indeed, the result of the New Wave movement was not mere imitation but a new era in Japanese science fiction, of which Tsutsui, Yamano, and Aramaki were the heralds.

In the context of these debates over the inner space of speculative fiction, Aramaki made his professional debut as a writer in 1970 with a highly speculative short story, "Ōinaru shōgo" (The awesome noon), published in *S-F Magajin* (Hayakawa's S-F Magazine). This story builds on one of his prior stories, "Shimi" (Stain, 1965), in which he explores Friedrich Nietzsche's notion of the "eternal return" in a science-fictional manner. It also puts into practice his highly theoretical manifesto for science fiction, published in the same year in the same magazine, "Jutsu no shōsetsur-on" or "A theory of fiction as *Kunst*," in which he draws on Immanuel Kant's 1790 philosophical tour de force *Critique of Judgment* to provide a philosophical reading of Robert Heinlein's fiction. Aramaki's speculative fiction soon garnered critical acclaim. In 1972, his novella *Shirakabe no moji wa yūhi ni haeru* (The writing on the white wall shines in the setting sun) won the Seiun Award, the Japanese equivalent of the Hugo Award, decided by vote every summer at Japan's National Science Fiction Convention. The year 1972 also saw the publication of his first speculative metanovel, *Shiroki hi tabidateba fushi* (Setting out on a white day leads to immortality), which was selected as a runner-up for the Izumi Kyōka Award (established in 1973 to commemorate the centenary of the master of gothic fiction). This later novel expanded on his 1971 novella *Aru hareta hi no Wīn wa mori no naka ni tatazumu* (One fine day in Vienna lingering in the woods), structured around a profound meditation on the writings of the Marquis de Sade. In 1988, Aramaki published a sequel, *Sei Shutefan Jiin no kane no ne wa* (Listen to the bells of Saint Stephen's Cathedral), the second book in a projected and highly anticipated trilogy, whose final novel, tentatively titled "Mohaya uchu wa meikyu no kagami no youni" (Space Considered as a Mirror Maze), the author says will be completed and published by 2018.

Among his many critically acclaimed works, his 1978 novel *Shinseidai,* or *The Sacred Era: A Novel,* is widely acknowledged as his masterwork. The initial concept for *The Sacred Era* appeared in his short story "Shushi yo" (O seeds), originally published in the November 1970 issue of *Hayakawa's S-F Magazine*, in which Aramaki strives to emulate the art of Hieronymus Bosch in the form of speculative science fiction. In the late 1960s and early 1970s Aramaki frequently drew inspiration for his fiction from art, and from surrealist art in particular. His widely acclaimed 1968 short story "Yawarakai tokei," or "Soft Clocks," builds on the works of

Salvador Dalí, while his 1972 short story "Toropikaru," or "Tropical," delves into the art of René Magritte.[2] Together with such stories, *The Sacred Era* established Aramaki's reputation as the premier speculative fictionist in Japan. In his introduction to the original publication, Tsutsui Yasutaka pointed out that Aramaki was such a sophisticated writer and so far ahead of his time that his meticulously crafted fantastical visions, in conjunction with the profound metaphysical speculation at the heart of the novel, would surely puzzle more orthodox readers of science fiction in Japan.[3] The distinguished critic Nakajima Azusa also praised the novel highly, calling it Aramaki's "major work" and declaring, "There is no doubt that *The Sacred Era* has succeeded in completing an enormous and sublime fresco of a hellish pilgrimage full of idiosyncratic nightmares in which Japanese science fiction has never delved. This novel is a must-read book for anyone who would like to meditate on the essence of science fiction."[4]

Across its eight chapters, *The Sacred Era* takes the form of a pilgrimage within a parallel world ruled by a eurotheocracy styled as "The Millennium of Prosperity of the Holy Empire of Igitur." Its protagonist–pilgrim, simply called K, succeeds in passing the Sacred Service Examination and makes his way to the sacred planet of Bosch. Ever intent on troubling the distinction between inner space and outer space, Aramaki not only combines E. T. A. Hoffmann's theory of mannerism and quantum theory to unsettle the distinction between thought and act, but also populates his novel with fanciful gadgets that likewise challenge such distinctions: mechanical dolls reminiscent of Philip K. Dick's androids and Richard Calder's gynoids; memory books full of blank pages in which readers may store memories; and the Karnak propulsion system, which allows for ethereal navigation to other planets by means of affective and cognitive states.

In keeping with its interest in conundrums arising where religion meets history, and spirit matter, *The Sacred Era* pits a sacred prophet (the holy Mallarmean Igitur whose *Southern Scriptures* affords spiritual insight into the mysterious Planet Bosch) against a satanic heretic (Darko Dachilko). Recalling his days in a Catholic kindergarten in the 1930s, Aramaki has indicated that this novel encouraged him to challenge the Christian orthodoxy with which he had been familiar, displacing the doctrine of the Holy Trinity with that of the Quadrinity, which the novel presents as consisting of "Father, Son, Holy Ghost, and Igitur." The novel's epigraph, from the book of Job, invites us to consider the novel as a sort of new apocrypha in the form of speculative science fiction. Indeed, in the eighth and final chapter, Aramaki makes use of denounced scriptures to characterize a new cosmogony in which everything comes into being through "the Great God's nocturnal emission," while the end of the entire universe will begin upon "God's awakening." As literary critic Andō Reiji has recently pointed out, the novel's cosmogony is deeply influenced by the French symbolist poet Stéphane Mallarmé, who created the fictional young genius Igitur, whose tragic death does not fatalistically announce the end of life but rather the beginning of a new orientation.[5] This lineage may also be traced back to one of Mallarmé's influences, Edgar Allan Poe, whose prose poem *Eureka* (1848) redefines the universe as "a plot of God." Building on this lineage permitted Aramaki to overturn the received image of apocalypse within science fiction, that of the destruction of the planet, exemplified in the works of Arthur C. Clarke, such as *Childhood's End* (1953) and *2001: A Space Odyssey* (1968). In contrast, Aramaki offers a techno-surrealist vision in which the explosion of Planet Bosch affords dissemination and rebirth.

For the publication of the paperback edition in 1980, Aramaki contributed an afterword in which he broaches the personal psychological dimension of the novel, explaining that the father–son relationship between K and Darko Dachilko provided a way for him to work through his complex relationship to his father.[6] In fact, Aramaki's original first name was Kunio (K!), which he changed to Yoshio (akin to his father's first name, Yoshi) for his pen name. Similarly, in his autobiography, Aramaki recalls how he arrived at the idea for the novel's conclusion. His father passed away at Toranomon Hospital in Tokyo on March 19, 1977, while Aramaki was still writing the book, and his death inspired Aramaki to draw connections more explicitly between his father and the notorious heretic Darko Dachilko. This experience spurred him to radically rethink the meaning of the Planet Bosch and to highlight the significance of a Nietzschean eternal recurrence of the entire universe. He writes, "In completing *The Sacred Era* I felt certain that I could finally transcend my own father."[7] At the same time, *The Sacred Era* successfully overturned the Clarkean paradigm of apocalypse as world destruction by offering with Aramaki a unique new paradigm of speculative fictional apocrypha. In this respect, *The Sacred Era* also anticipates the cosmic family romance that would emerge as a global cultural trope with the *Star Wars* saga, beginning with the first film (chronologically) in 1977.

Aramaki's powerfully surrealist and idiosyncratically existentialist approach to speculative fiction also finds expression in two collections of short stories, *Kasutorobaruba* (Castrovalva) and *Goshikku* (Gothic). First published in 1983, *Kasutorobaruba* draws on the works of Dutch artist M. C. Escher. Published in 2001, *Goshikku* expands on his 1985 novella "Puraton dōri no deisuiyoku" (Mud bath on the rue Platon), which explores the Dadaist and surrealist work of Marcel Duchamp. Such writings have given Aramaki an unusual position within the world of Japanese science fiction. Where Komatsu Sakyō, who made his professional debut in 1962, is frequently acknowledged as the major voice of a first generation of Japanese science fiction writers and is thus compared to Clarke, Asimov, and Heinlein, Aramaki may well be considered the Japanese equivalent of Ballard, Dick, and Barrington Bayley. Aramaki's works thus invite us to envision a genealogy of speculative fiction in Japan ranging from Abe Kōbō, Tsutsui, and Aramaki, to Kawamata Chiaki, Yamao Yūko, and Tō Enjō (also written as Toh Enjoe).

The 1990s saw a dramatic shift in Aramaki's approach, marking a rupture with his previously unconventional and unabashedly metaphysical fiction. In 1990, Aramaki embarked on a series of virtual reality war novels, which he calls *kakū senki*. This series, calculated as hard-core entertainment, centers on the career of an actual naval commander of the World War II era, Admiral Yamamoto Isoroku, who is reincarnated in an alternate history. Although the first volume of the series, *Konpeki no kantai*

(Deep blue fleet), did not initially meet with great success, the series gradually came to attract a wider audience, riding the wave of interest in militarism following the first Gulf War. The series eventually proved so popular that Aramaki embarked on a related series called *Asahi no kantai* (The fleet of the rising sun). The two series together have sold some five million copies. This emerging subgenre of science fiction even caught the attention of the *New York Times*. In March 1995, Andrew Pollack ran an article titled "Japanese Refight the War, and Win, in Pulp Fiction," based on interviews with Aramaki and other writers of this subgenre based on alternative versions of Japanese military engagements during World War II.[8]

Readers may well be confused by the sharp contrast between Aramaki's speculative fiction of the 1970s and his virtual reality war novels from the 1990s. Yet the seeds of the later war fiction can be found among the short stories in the early collection *Ūchū nijūgoji* (25 o'clock space time), such as "Remuria no hi" (The day of Lemuria), which offers an alternative ancient history; "Aa, kōya" (Ah, wilderness), an anthropological meditation; "Mugen e no hōkai (Disintegrating into infinity), an adventure tale of a mutant hunter; and the title story, which recounts the fate of posthuman inhabitants of a reality studio–like Luna City, where the line between reality and virtual reality has vanished. These points of contact between his earlier and later works are interesting in that they not only demonstrate continuity between them but also open up a critical perspective within the later works, which are frequently dismissed as militarist apologia. Perhaps such works too will receive closer critical attention as Aramaki's contributions gain greater recognition in a range of literary and cultural fields. In 2012, Aramaki's first collection of poetry, *Gaikotsu hantō* (Skeleton peninsula, 2011), won the Hokkaido Shimbun Literary Award, and the Hokkaido Museum of Literature held a retrospective exhibition devoted to his works, *The World of Aramaki Yoshio: Toward a New Utopian City*.

If it is possible to speak of a countercurrent coming full circle, then that is precisely the unusual path Aramaki's work seems to have taken, arriving at last, like a pilgrim of time, not in a place but in a moment, a speculative moment, which lures us as readers to trace our own time of pilgrimage through his world beyond inner and outer spaces.

Notes

1. This essay appeared in English translation with a critical introduction; see Yamano Kōichi, Kazuko Behrens, Darko Suvin, and Tatsumi Takayuki, "Japanese SF: Its Originality and Possibility," *Science Fiction Studies* 21, no. 1 (1994): 67–80.

2. "Soft Clocks" has been frequently anthologized in English translation. See Yoshio Aramaki, "Soft Clocks," trans. Kazuko Behrens, ed. Lewis Shiner, *Interzone* 27 (1989); reprinted in *The Big Book of Science Fiction*, ed. Ann and Jeff VanderMeer (New York: Vintage, 2016), 544–56. For another work from this period, see Yoshio Aramaki, "Blue Sun," trans. Kazuko Behrens, *Strange Plasma* 4 (1991); reprinted in *Fiction International* 24 (1993): 36–60.

3. Tsutsui Yasutaka, "Kaisetsu" (introduction), *Shinseidai* (The Sacred Era) (Tokyo: Tokuma shoten, 1978), 237–42.

4. Nakajima Azusa, "Book Review," *Hayakawa's S-F Magazine,* September 1978, 211.

5. Andō Reiji, "Kaisetsu," *Shinseidai* (The Sacred Era) (Tokyo: Sairyūsha, 2015).

6. Yoshio Aramaki, "Kaisetsu," *Shinseidai* (The Sacred Era) (Tokyo: Tokuma shoten, 1980), 462–69.

7. Yoshio Aramaki, *Jinsei wa SF da* (My life as science fiction) (Sapporo: Sapporo Tokeidai Gallery, 2013), 42.

8. Andrew Pollack, "Japanese Refight the War, and Win, in Pulp Fiction," *New York Times,* March 3, 1995. Web source accessed August 26, 2016, at http://www.nytimes.com/1995/03/04/world/japanese-refight-the-war-and-win-in-pulp-fiction.html.

The Sacred Era

THE SACRED SERVICE
EXAMINATION

1

At last. I'm here!

K is famished as his train screeches to a halt. A few moments later, the train lurches forward again, creaking over the dusk-colored iron bridge as if being dragged like an oxcart. Not a single drop of water to be seen under the bridge, K notices. No different from any of the other dried-out riverbeds K had crossed along the way. The drought ravaging the lands of the Holy Empire has not spared the capital.

K presses his nose against the barred windows, looking out toward the rear of the train. Only a wall of darkness lurks behind him. But the blinding dawn lights up everything waiting before him on the other side of this iron bridge.

Like outstretched arms raised in praise of the glory of The Holy Igitur, gleaming white towers reach toward a sky painted with the light of the rising sun. Or perhaps this glorious view of the city before K is nothing more than a mirage, a hallucination of hunger? Just the latest dream to pass before him on his long journey?

This is no time to dream . . .

Only later will he come to terms with what these moments mean. Only later will he understand that crossing the bridge now behind him marked the beginning of a new day for K.

K is the first to stand up. He stretches his arm toward the luggage racks, reaching for the one bag he brought with him on this journey. Slinging the bag over his shoulder, he stumbles toward the deck between the train's cars, trying not to disturb the other passengers still slumbering in their seats. The train pushes its way past the high walls at the perimeter of the capital toward the dusty center of the city.

So much bigger than I'd imagined!

Breathing in the crisp dawn air calms K's nerves, and every breath he takes fills his lungs with pride.

The train rolls into the terminal, but K doesn't even wait for the train to come to a complete stop before he leaps off like a cat to land on the firm stone floor of the platforms. Walking forward with a determined stride, he knows this is no mere dream. His feet really are treading on the sacred ground of the capital city of Igitur.

The capital rises atop a massive plateau of exposed bedrock in the middle of a wasteland, with the terminal station standing at the foot of a high cliff at the edge of the city. A passage from the station's platforms carves its way through layers of ochre sandstone speckled with fossilized bones into the city proper. K enters this passage, ascending up a slope that leads to a stairway, until finally stepping into the Great Hall of the terminal. Carved columns of rock support high ceilings. Security personnel in their solemn uniforms stand guard around a series of barriers and gated fences. One of them approaches K.

"Where are your papers, young man?"

K retrieves the examination forms from his belt pouch and presents them to the security officer. That's all it takes for the stern-faced officer's demeanor to soften. Without hesitation, he stands aside to open a path for K.

"My apologies. Please proceed, sir."

K stands even prouder. As he proceeds down the hall, the officer resumes his thorough inspection of every passenger. Of course, his status as a candidate for the Sacred Service Examination confers all manner of special privileges. For the first time in his life, he rode the train all the way to the capital without hassle. Had he not received the passes along with the notification of his candidacy, he wouldn't even have been able to board in the first place.

K continues toward the exit of the Great Hall. He emerges on one side of a dust-strewn city plaza at the foot of a round sandstone hill. The towering structure at the opposite end must be City Hall, he thinks. And standing atop a protrusion on the hillside opposite must be the Papal Court, its spires glimmering in the light of the morning sun.

The Sacred Service Examination isn't scheduled to begin until tomorrow. Not having much money to his name, K will have to find shelter somewhere out on the street. But that is a problem for later. For now, he has the whole day ahead of him. His first thought is to head to the city library and prepare for tomorrow's examination. But K's growling stomach drowns out the thought. Instead, his feet lead him toward the crowds milling in the city center where a morning market has just opened. But it is still too early in the day, and the market stalls sell only a dubious selection of rice, grains, fruit, meat, and fish, along with large quantities of strange weeds that K has never seen before. No wonder everyone around him has parched skin, if these weeds represent a staple diet in the capital.

Hundreds of vagrants line the streets. From the many villages that dot the lands of the Holy Empire, refugees have been abandoning their dried-out farms only to find themselves on the streets of the capital begging for spare change or scraps of food. Even in K's hometown, most residents have either starved to death or fled, leaving behind a town torn apart by roving gangs. Scenes of poverty and starvation shouldn't come as a shock to K. But it shocks him anyway. If even the capital finds itself in such dire shape, he can only imagine how much worse off the surrounding towns must be.

None of the beggars approaches K. Barefoot and dressed only in dirty, brown rags, there is little to distinguish him from them. Not that he has the luxury of caring. Foremost in his mind is the incessant growling of his stomach. But he can barely afford any of the food in the market. Not that this fact stops him from looking at every stall that happens to catch his eye.

"Some chapa bread, please?" K says to an old man standing behind one of the stalls, the only merchant in the market who has any meat left on his bones. Even the other merchants are just as gaunt and starving as K.

K exchanges his last coin for a piece of flat bread. But he gets more than he bargained for. A sharp jolt of pain and a cracked tooth come for free with his bread. Biting into a small stone in the bread is all the proof he needs to conclude that mud has been mixed into dough. Still, K keeps on eating. Rancid bread without much nutrition won't be good for his digestion. But for now, all he needs is something to calm his growling stomach.

K soon realizes that wandering the city only worsens his hunger. Noticing the throngs of bodies lying along the side of the road, moving as little as possible, K decides to follow their example. Surely that is how to make it through the day. He remembers seeing a massive banyan tree spreading a lush canopy of verdant leaves despite the severe drought near the intersection of a boulevard he passed earlier.

I guess that's where I should go . . .

Others have the same idea. Vagrants gather under the shadow of the banyan tree. K joins this mass of filthy human bodies searching for a spot to sit. Each of them returns K's gaze with exhausted eyes, some with eyes so hollow you can no longer tell whether they are still alive or already dead.

As K steps over sleeping bodies to make his way toward the tree, he spots a small area with just about enough space for him. The eyes of a beggar woman seated there catch his gaze. With a slight nod, she picks up her baby to make room for K.

"Thank you," K says as he sits down.

The woman says nothing, as if even the simple act of forming words in her mouth is already too much for her.

With so little space to go around, their bodies come close to touching, but the woman doesn't seem to care. Without a word to K, she exposes her breast to feed her baby. K does all he can to avert his eyes. His gaze wanders, eventually resting on her unexpectedly beautiful face. A cool breeze flutters the clumps of disheveled hair stuck to her dirt-caked cheeks. She looks too innocent to be a mother, barely out of adolescence herself.

K flinches at the sight of the naked baby girl. She gazes up at K with a smile, so he forces himself to smile back. Seeing this sad tableau, the poor, naked baby suckling at the bosom of her dejected mother, fills K with discomfort. A wave of guilt sweeps over him as he comes face-to-face with the stark realities of life.

Stop staring!

As penance, K recites the name of The Holy Igitur to himself ten times, focusing on the dried-out and dead-silent cobblestone street nearby, emptied by those hiding from the midday heat. Vehicles pass by every so often, but only a few pedestrians are to be seen.

It doesn't take much time for K to grow weary watching the empty streets. The pride that had propelled him through the streets that morning had vanished, and not even thoughts of tomorrow's examination can rouse him from his exhaustion now.

How did I make it this far? Tomorrow's exam is going to be a disaster. But there's nothing I can do about that now. At least I was able to ride on a train for the first time in my life. At least I was able to see this city.

K's thoughts wander.

2

K grew up in an isolated village hundreds of miles away from Igitur. Traveling to the closest train station takes two days on foot across a landscape scattered with rocks and desert sands and little else. At one time, the land had hosted an abundance of farms. But today, little more than an endless parched desert remains. Only the presence of a saltwater well in the area allows the village to limp along. This had been K's home. After completing his primary schooling, he joined the seminary to learn the teachings of The Holy Igitur once he reached the age of ten, as required by law in the Holy Empire.

K's time in the seminary was like an oasis, filled with wonder. His teacher, a cleric, taught K to read and write. But more than that, he paid special attention to K for some reason, giving him access to his library and letting K read whatever texts he found there. Perhaps he thought K would become his eventual successor, or perhaps he intended to use him as his personal assistant to help with housework and other mundane tasks. After all, K did receive better marks than any of the other boys in the village.

K's teacher was named Hypocras, and he enjoyed a notoriety that spread beyond the seminary and K's village to other nearby towns due to his many eccentricities and enigmatic activities. He was tall and muscular and had such a mysterious, commanding presence that when he bared his eyes, his expressions would appear so frightening that babies often burst into tears. Yet despite his oddness and impassivity, he commanded respect from everyone in the village. Or to be more precise, he commanded their awe.

From even a very young age, K had heard all sorts of rumors about Hypocras. He never understood why Hypocras seemed to take a liking to him. While Hypocras was known to mete out whippings on his students, not once was K subjected to these punishments. And over time K began to develop a fondness and appreciation for Hypocras. Soon after they met, K moved out from the shed he had built for himself at the other side of town and began living in the groundskeeper's room in the temple.

Carrying water, cleaning the grounds, and other household tasks—these were K's duties in the temple in exchange for meals twice a day. Compared to the long days of farm work and animal husbandry that K was used to on the family farm, his tasks in the temple were far less onerous. Coupled with the improvement of his living conditions, there was little for K to complain about. At times, he even considered his life one of relative privilege.

But make no mistake. Compared to the truly wealthy boys in town, this was not, by any means, a life of leisure. Any spare time quickly went toward his studies of the various texts inside the temple's library. For years, K went about his life like this. Little by little, he gained the knowledge expected of him by his teacher to the point that he could begin to teach classes in his place.

Even then, there still should be no way for me to make it this far. Candidates for the Sacred Service Exam come from the top theological institutes! This must be some kind of mistake!

Almost a hundred people applied to take the Sacred Examination in K's district. Among them, only K was accepted as a candidate.

Noon in the capital city. Temperatures climb to over a hundred degrees. At least it's a dry heat, still somewhat bearable under a shade. K can't even begin to imagine what life here must be like in the midst of a humid summer. Across the Holy Empire, several million people will die from the heat this year. Nothing to be done about it now but to lie down in the dust and wait for the inevitable.

The planet is changing. The past several centuries have witnessed a radical transformation in the climate. Much of the land, once abundant in trees and farmlands, has turned into dried-out wastelands. At the height of the Holy Empire of Igitur's Millennium of Prosperity, a staggering six billion people resided within its borders and among its territories. But today, the population of the planet has been decimated a thousandfold. What caused these changes in climate? There are many theories, but the most plausible among them points to the extraction of hydrogen energy from the oceans as the root cause. This led to a two-hundred-meter drop in sea levels, with significant consequences for the planet's climate and ecosystem. Now, all that remain from this energy boom-and-bust are the scattered ruins of water decomposition facilities. K used to explore these ruins as a child, finding only rusted pipes and the broken carcasses of old machinery still half-buried in the desert sands.

K falls asleep and dreams of food, as usual. After what seems like only a few brief moments, the renewed pangs of hunger wake him. The piece of bread he ate that morning has long been digested. His fingers dig up the roots of the dried brown weeds around him. He brings them into his mouth, not caring about the toxins they carry and what they might do to him. Many lose their minds chewing too much of these weeds. But despite the dangers, they really can't help themselves. What else is there for those who need to take their minds off the hunger they suffer?

Torpor grows on top of K's hunger, his body stiffening as he watches the crowd swirl around him. The many people lying immobile on the ground near him may very well be dead, for all he knows. But despite their skeletal bodies and swollen stomachs, somehow they live on.

A miserable sight, indeed. But one must remember the Temperance Proclamation from the year 420 of the Igituran Era. Pope Algol IV spoke of the virtue of restricting one's consumption and the sin of gluttony in a homily shared with the citizens of the Holy Empire: *If my people have to starve, then I shall starve with them. If my people have to die, then I shall have to die as well. But before we pass on, I call on all of us to follow the sacred teachings of the great prophet The Holy Igitur and separate the Holy Spirit from our soiled bodies.* To serve as an example to all, the pope fasted. The palace sent out the fasting regimen via the Ion broadcasting system: a daily diet of no more than two glasses of water and a minimal cut of meat, a tiny bit of bread, and some vegetables mixed together in a small dish.

Famine had already ravaged every corner of the Holy Empire when K first came into this world. Things were certainly bad in the Southern Hemisphere. But the more populous Northern Hemisphere was far worse off. None of the old states survived the famine there. The few still living in the north turned to barbarism, with some even resorting to cannibalism to survive.

We must struggle against hunger in this world.

K closes his eyes.

Hunger is the fate of all living things.

Why do the pope's words remain etched in K's memory? It must be because one of the questions in the qualifying exams he took half a year ago asked him to articulate his views on the Temperance Proclamation. K's answer then was little more than a statement of his heartfelt opinion. He confessed to the smallness of his mind, to the weakness of his willpower. Yes, that's right—The Holy Igitur teaches us all that humans are born into this world when the spirit enters the body. So all it takes to live without food is to separate the starving body from the spirit that is beyond hunger. This is how The Holy Igitur himself fasted continuously for 777 days, if you believe the *Southern Scriptures.*

K has been taught to feel shame at his own lack of will. Even the tiniest bit of hunger makes him feel wretched. Those vagrants, collapsed on the ground, waiting for death without a word of complaint—they deserve far greater respect than K.

How long have they waited like that? A month? Two months? They will be dead soon. But that will signal nothing more than the death of the flesh. Their spirits will be guided by The Holy Igitur to the Fertile Gardens of Heaven.

K's mind clouds over. The enthralling scent of milk brings back his hunger pangs. Next to him, the young beggar woman is breast-feeding her child again. Her breasts are the only part of her body that still retains color and health. Once her baby is satiated, the woman looks straight at K with her pale blue eyes.

"Do you wish to suckle my breast too?" she asks him.

"Mmm," K almost says, before immediately catching himself. "Oh, no, sorry. I didn't mean—"

K lowers his gaze to hide his flushed face. He can hear the thumping of his heart inside his chest.

Had she caught him staring at her body? K has never seen a naked woman's body in the flesh. But he imagines it. He fantasizes about it. K chants the name of The Holy Igitur under his breath. He must repent for his crimes. He must wash away his sins.

The city's odd odors, the smell of animals in heat, mixes with the sweat trickling down K's brow, washing over his body.

3

The next morning finally dawns. Now it is time for K to head to City Hall to take the Sacred Service Examination. But the past day has wiped away much of the confidence he possessed when he first arrived in Igitur. Far more people than he had expected—

over a thousand candidates from all over the realms of the Holy Empire—gather at City Hall. The sheer numbers of applicants milling about turn the air inside City Hall stale as the guards take their time with inspecting every detail of every single candidate's paperwork. One by one, names and fingerprints are taken and matched to records in the database.

Finally, K enters a cavernous lecture hall with a domed ceiling so high that to gaze up at it feels like peering into heaven itself. Painted on the surface of the ceiling is a fresco depicting the life of The Holy Igitur. Sunlight streams through the windows from an inner courtyard where a row of arches marks a path leading toward the grand lecture hall. A seat with K's name on it awaits him in the center of the hall.

Unable to sit still, K looks around the room. Everyone has an air of confidence. The candidates come from all ages and all walks of life, but as far as he can tell, no one else in the room is as young as he. Next to K sits a man as old as his grandfather. Did he wander into the wrong hall? Eavesdropping on his conversation with another candidate quickly makes it clear to K that, like many of the other candidates, this is not the first time he is taking the Sacred Service Examination. These veterans of the examination compare notes with one another, discussing the questions they encountered in their previous attempts to pass the exam in the hope of anticipating what awaits them this time around.

Formal examinations for Sacred Service are held only once every four years, and many of the candidates here must have spent much of their adult lives preparing for this exam. Among them are professors of state schools and private educational institutes, all of whom are clad in their impressive academic gowns. The young men seated in the front row look like students from the Holy Igitur University, the most prestigious school here in the capital. They wear their confident faces like badges and converse among themselves in the refined language of the educated, using jargon far beyond K's comprehension. Is it any surprise that K finds all this thoroughly overwhelming?

This can't be right. I shouldn't even be here at all! There's no way I could have qualified for this exam.

Oddly this thought calms K's nerves.

The dark iron doors at the front of the hall swing open, and all talk is immediately silenced. The examiners in their clerical uniforms enter the hall, an assistant behind each one of them carrying a stack of examination booklets in their hands. They form a line on the stage and bow in unison. Once the candidates return the bow, they begin passing out the exams.

K holds his copy, its thick blue cover reflecting the sunlight streaming in from the courtyard. His heart races, and beads of sweat form inside the clenched fists he hides under the desk. Silence reigns as they pass out all of the exam booklets. Until the sharp ringing sound of a bell breaks the silence. It is the city's bell tower signaling the start of the examination.

K lifts his pencil from the desk. With one deep breath, he opens the booklet's blue cover.

> Question I: Produce an affirmative critique of the Trinitarian theories of the heretic Darko Dachilko, which contradict the Quadritarian theories of The Holy Igitur.
>
> Question II: Discuss the resurrection of Jesus Christ from the Twilight Civilization in terms of the teachings of Book 56 of the Southern Scriptures.
>
> Question III: Discuss how the origins of the Sacred Era explain the construction and destruction of the world.

A wave of gasps sweeps across the hall. Evidently, this year's questions go far beyond what the candidates in the room are expecting to see.

"Silence!" shout examiners on the stage to quiet the commotion.

K does not say a word. Instead, he picks up his pencil and begins writing.

The first-day examination proceeds until the evening throughout a day of suffocating heat. Few candidates remain in the hall when K completes his answers and hands his booklet to the examiners. Every joint in every part of his body is sore and aching from sitting continuously all day. At least he still stands. Some applicants had to be carried out on stretchers after passing out during the exam, which surely would have happened to K, with all his hunger and anxiety, if it had not been for what had happened under the banyan tree that morning.

K's face turns red as he remembers. In that moment of darkness before sunrise, the beggar woman offered the poor famished K her milk. Still half-asleep and lost in the middle of some dream, K inched his body closer to her and began suckling on her soft breast, drinking the milk warmed inside her body.

"Do you like that?"

Her words were gentle, motherly.

"Yes," K whispered.

"Then drink as much as you want."

For the first time in his life, K drank mother's milk. He had never known his real mother. Tears rolled down his cheeks as his mind searched for a past that did not exist.

My hands . . . caressing this woman's skin! I've passed into sin! The commandments forbid me!

As much as a part of K might have wished to put a stop to his sinful acts, he could not muster the willpower to release his mouth from the soft flesh of the woman's breast.

The woman's vague smile greets K when he returns to the banyan tree after the first day of the examination.

"Things go well at the exam?"

K nods without saying a word. He places himself on the spot next to the woman and turns his eyes toward the already darkened streets beyond.

"I'll have more milk for you tomorrow morning."

K wraps his arms around his knees, offering only another silent nod in response.

Such a strange power in this milk! One sip was all it took to calm my stomach all day.

K goes over the questions from the day's exam once more. It seems like these particular questions have never before appeared in any of the previous years' exams. It was certainly odd that almost a third of the candidates stood from their seats and quickly left the hall as soon as it began. He's positive that it was the candidates who had taken the Sacred Examination before who left early too.

K will never forget the quivering voices of the other candidates as they received the exam booklets.

"Why is there a question about that heretic Darko Dachilko?"

"Is this a trick question? Is it?"

Right from the very first question, the name of the most enigmatic man from the whole history of the Holy Empire of Igitur appeared before them. To make things worse, the question's instruction "to produce an affirmative critique" makes no sense whatsoever. After all, to take the question at face value and affirm Darko Dachilko's theories means no less than declaring oneself a heretic.

Predictably, K at first had no idea what to write in his exam booklet. All he could do was take his usual stance of naive sincerity and simply state his honest opinions without embellishment. The truth is that the only reason he even has any opinion on this rather challenging question is due to the oddness of his own teacher back home. Hypocras kept a wide range of research materials on the writings of the heretic Darko Dachilko in his personal archive, despite the fact that, at least as far as K knows, these documents have long been subject to strict bans on their publication and reproduction.

The second question surely presented a challenge to the other candidates too. After all, Book 56 of the *Southern Scriptures*— the so-called "Book of the Seed"—makes use of a densely allegorical style known as the Sacred Euclidean language. There's a reason it is known as the most perplexing of all the sections of the *Southern Scriptures.* As for the third question, well, K can't really be sure he even understood what the question was all about. He thought that it might be connected to the millenarian theories of the heretic Darko Dachilko. Darko Dachilko lived during the third century of the Igituran Era. Even at the height of the glory of the Holy Empire of Igitur, the heretic was already prophesizing the eventual destruction of the world. It was precisely these prophetic pronouncements that led to his trial for heresy during the First Papal Conference in the year 313 of the Igituran Era.

The night turns even more arid than the previous one. K tosses and turns through his dreams. Like the Möbius Strip Theories that The Holy Igitur wrote of in the *Southern Scriptures,* the world of K's dreams perplexes him. Follow one side of the strip and you end up on the opposite side without realizing it. Somewhere there lurks the devil. Or is it that heretic Darko Dachilko? Or is it his own teacher?

Rumors flew far and wide that Hypocras would often vanish for weeks at a time. K knows for a fact that there is some truth to these rumors. When he first moved into the groundskeeper's room in the temple, he sometimes noticed his master locking himself inside the room at the top of the tower. Without the barred doors opening even once, he would vanish from within the locked room, leaving no trace of himself whatsoever.

4

In total, the Sacred Service Examination is a seven-day affair. Little by little, the numbers of the candidates dwindle, dropping like flies in the tense heat of the examination room. Each day, the examiners publish the names of those who passed the previous day, while the names of those who did not pass are omitted from the list. Somewhat perplexed, K finds his name on the list day after day.

Question for day three of the exam:

> *The exalted character of Loulan architecture is visible in its exploration of the limits of the ideas surrounding the expansion of space to engender a polynomial psycho-geography. Grossen's spatial theories and Gerber's general theory of polynomial structuralism have long been widely recognized as the foundations of Igituran theories of architecture. The discovery of phenomenological manifestations of Escher's "impossible objects" facilitated the further*

development of Loulan architecture. Further to this, the so-called characteristics of Loulan interior design were facilitated by the further development of optical techniques such as photochemical phenomena, light dissolution, and light-separating curtains. As such, the unification of physics, psychology, and optics was achieved in the name of The Holy Igitur. With this in mind . . .

This question pertaining to the Loulan Space City, some five hundred light-years from Earth, gives K a severe headache.

K's nerves begin to calm by the third day of testing. Every now and then, he manages to find the time to rest his writing hand atop his answer sheet. The heat and stillness let up, and a seductive breeze blows through the arches from the adjacent courtyard, dancing over his skin to the beautiful tinkling music of the massive crystal chandelier hanging from the ceiling.

Established by Pope Algol I in the year 323 of the Igituran Era, the origins of the Sacred Service Examination system can be traced back to an amendment to the "Law of Five Galaxies and Sacred Knowledge" first legislated in the year 223 during the Third Papal Congress. Set up as a system for the selection and licensure for prospective researchers in the fields of Sacred Inquiry, including such areas of study as Genetic Theology, Sacred Psychology, Sacred Evolution, Exobiology, and Infinite Engineering, the exam confers on those who pass the privilege of doing any research in any of the Holy Disciplines.

What prompted the establishment of this system was precisely the heresy trial of the heretic Darko Dachilko. So heated were the debates surrounding the trial that the very foundations of all of Igituran society came into question. Even though Darko Dachilko had quite a number of disciples, he received a sentence of death in the year 313. This all happened long before K was born, but the stories have endured.

On the last day of the examination, K and a few others are all that remain. To K, this is nothing less than a miracle.

I did my best. Not much more I can do beyond that.

Though he feels his own fate is no longer in his hands, a sense of accomplishment fills K. All he can do now is wait for the announcement of the results in a week's time.

By the time the city bells ring to signal the end of the Sacred Examination, only a fraction of the original number of candidates remains. Gathering together all the remaining candidates in a small side room, the chief examiner extends to them an invitation to a humble dinner party. But there is nothing humble about it in K's eyes. So much meat prepared on various small plates for the candidates to partake of. And if that isn't enough, the Papal Court provides several bottles of wine just for the occasion as well.

The chief examiner congratulates and compliments everyone for their completion of seven straight days of examination. As a reward for their hard work, the candidates from out of town all receive a booklet of blue tickets. As K picks up his booklet, the staff explain to him that he is entitled to free meals in any of the public cafeterias within the city upon the presentation of these blue tickets.

The candidates go their separate ways. K returns to his old spot underneath the banyan tree. So many stars—the Southern Cross, Circinus, Triangulum Australe, Centaurus—glimmer in the cloudless sky that night. K recalls the stories of Earth's manned missions to these constellations. The glory of Igitur expanding a thousand light-years into space. Somehow, these stories always put K at ease as he gazes up toward the stars. The night deepens. The vagrants on the street slumber without making a sound. That night, K has his first wet dream in a long time.

The intense light of the sun glows above the city. A sudden overnight squall has washed the streets of their usual sand and dust, though the dry white sands will soon blow over the city again. The cool breeze is a momentary reprieve. Soon, heat will once again blanket the city. K watches over the city from a terraced house on a hill. He still remembers how he once thought the city so radiant from behind the windows of the train when he first arrived. But once he stepped onto its streets, it revealed its true face, wrinkled and dirty.

In the days since the end of the weeklong Sacred Service Examination, K's life has been transformed thanks to the book of meal tickets. The privileges they provide him are worth far more than gold in this city.

At first, K skips a few meals, trading his meal tickets for used sandals and clothes in the black market. Now, no one could ever mistake him for just another miserable vagrant about town. Despite these changes, he still calls the spot under the banyan tree his home, where he continues to have intimate conversations with that beggar woman who shared the spot.

The dawn has yet to rouse the city from its sleep when K awakes on the first day since the end of the exams. The wailing of a baby wakes him. She had slipped from her sleeping mother's arm and fallen onto the ground.

Was the woman still lost in her sleep? No, one close look is all it takes to figure out that she's ill. Kneeling beside her dirt-stained body, K places his palm on her forehead. She's burning up.

K peels off his shirt and carries it in his hands toward the water fountain in the middle of the park. Soaking the shirt with water, he makes his way back to where he had left the woman, placing the dripping shirt over her head.

As soon as the morning market opens, K runs off to exchange another meal ticket for some medicinal herbs. He also procures some goat's milk to feed the woman's baby in the meantime. Having exchanged his allocation of rations, he of course will have to fast for the rest of the day.

To K's relief, the herbs turn out to be quite effective. It must be the first time she's ever taken them. It takes no time at all for her to begin her recovery. Before long, she feels well enough to tell K her story. With weak whispers, she talks into the night about marauding gangs, her family murdered, her long journey to the city with her baby. The woman's name is Eva.

////

K dozes off and on as he waits for time to pass him by.

No matter whether they are old or young, rich or poor, the women in the city walk the streets, wrap their gaunt bodies in black cloth, and hide their faces from the sun's radiant heat with black veils. The law controls even fashion, restricting the residents to wearing only black. Exempt from these laws are the youngest children. Such fussy rules and regulations can never stop them from doing what they please with their naked bodies as they play around the water fountain.

The robes K acquired from the black market follow the usual style of men's clothing, which shares much with the flowing robes of the priests. Simple tunics, pulled over the head and secured around the waist with a piece of rope. While all the men have shaved heads, this does not mean that they are Sacred Service officers. They simply follow what is prescribed by law. Real Sacred Service officers can be distinguished by the ropes of different colors they wear around the waist. Some bit of gray coloration is even permitted to them, but only for those in the higher ranks of the order. Even at a glance, you will not ever mistake an officer of the order for a member of the rest of the population.

As the sun continues its slow march toward the western half of the sky, throngs of men begin to gather around the terraced house. The time for the afternoon nap that will last until about four o'clock approaches. Next to the terraced house stands a large wooden sign that reads "Men's World" with the solemn seal of the papal authority affixed below the words. That's as clear a sign as any of the prohibition on women from taking even one step inside this place. It's just one example of the legal segregation of men and women evident everywhere in the capital.

A black horse carriage loaded with passengers scampers across the street. One after another, a series of rickshaws all painted black follows behind it. Girls for the Sacred Service officers—every one of them dressed in her standard black uniform—ride in these rickshaws. All of the capital is painted over in black and white. No colors other than these to be seen anywhere in this city.

Only the bleached ochre slopes of the cliff sides, the blue skies above, and the lush green of the banyan tree's leaves provide any exceptions.

The recent rain showers having washed off the dust, the leaves of the banyan tree look especially verdant. K finds comfort in gazing at their deep glow of green. Such a large tree is quite unusual even back in K's hometown. Is there another tree like it anywhere across the lands of the Holy Empire? All that's left to be found anywhere are vast expanses of barren plains and deserts. Exposed rock surfaces and endless stretches of sand and dust are all that remain of the mountains and hills and farmlands that once dotted the landscape.

The voice of a passing merchant interrupts K's thoughts. The man stands before a small cart, pouring drinks into cups from an attached hand pump. Black syrupy liquid trickles out of the spout. K picks up a cup from atop the cart and places an order for what turns out to be a rather coquettish and fashionable drink that dampens the appetite for a few moments.

K turns his attention to a small group of men sipping some drinks as they intently watch a game of Stellar Chess. The match is just about to enter the endgame sequence. One of the young men playing sets a trap by sacrificing his Sol piece.

Such a curious strategy . . .

K finds the move impressive. To an untrained eye, the gambit will not make any sense whatsoever. But K can see that it's all a clever setup for a finishing move. He lets out a small gasp.

Certain that he is about to win the match, the other player— a slightly overweight man with the bearing of a merchant—moves his Moon piece into the third dimension. To his chagrin, a beaming smile forms on his younger opponent's tanned face. His Comet slips through the orbit of the Moon to cut off the path back to Earth.

The merchant groans. The game is over.

"One more round?"

The young man gives his opponent a piercing look.

"Nah," the older man says.

The overweight merchant stands up and shakes his head. He passes a bean-sized silver ball to the other player.

The young player slips the silver ball into his sleeve.

"The placement of your Home Planet could have been better," he says. "Maybe you'll have better luck on the next match."

The overweight man mumbles something to himself as he

walks away. He is probably going to get another drink. With a wide grin on his face, the young player turns his attention toward K.

"How about you, kid? Fancy a game? The bet can be anything you want. And, yeah. If you have tickets, that'll do too."

"No, thank you. I'm a total beginner at this."

"Oh yeah?"

The young man doesn't try to push K into a game any further. No way for K to stand any chance against him. It's quite obvious that he's quite a pro. Only the best players would even think of making such wild plays. Evidently, even the capital has its share of smart men with excellent educations wasting away their days on gambling and games of chance.

The young man offers K a hash-laced cigarette.

"Thanks," K says.

The man pulls out a small lens from his pocket. With it, he lights the cigarette using the sun's rays with a surprising finesse.

K accepts the lit cigarette. He takes one long drag, then asks the man a question:

"When your Sol was taken back there, what if your opponent moved his Comet back one dimension? With Pluto in dimension zero bearing down on Jupiter, how would things have turned out in that match?"

"I would have lost," he says, smiling.

"But you took the chance anyway?"

His smile widened.

"Of course," he says. "I must say, if you figured out what I was plotting, you must be pretty good yourself. No way you're a beginner. Which school do you attend? Pythagoras? Or maybe—"

K shakes his head.

"No, I'm not from around here, actually," says K. "I mean, I can't afford to go to private school. I just like to watch. That's all."

The young man doesn't hide the surprise on his face.

"Really, now," he says. "You sound like an amazing guy, you know that? Now I really want to play you sometime. No bets, of course!"

From their conversation, K learns that the young man used to be a student at Pythagoras until his delinquency finally got him expelled. Pythagoras is quite famous for two things: the skill of their Stellar Chess team and their ridiculously high tuition fees, which help to pay for some of the best teachers in the Holy Empire. Their student body is drawn mostly from members of the holy order or from wealthy families. Is it any surprise that their players were known for putting more weight on the elegance of their matches than simple win-loss records?

"Yeah, well," the young man says. "Those fancy matches they liked to promote just weren't for me, if you know what I'm saying. I mean, what's the point of playing if you don't play to win, right?"

K does not offer an answer. The man looks like he wants to continue their conversation, but K isn't having any of it.

Once again, K's eyes wander as fatigue begins to set in. His thoughts turn to the young beggar woman, her breasts and her nourishing milk. He continues to return every day to share with her some of the food he has acquired with his meal tickets.

Most of the time, K simply leaves her a portion of the food without making much of a fuss. Before she can say anything, he rushes off somewhere else. K himself has no explanation for what he is doing. Perhaps he's too conscious of the watchful eyes of everyone around him when he offers the food to the woman? Or is it because, in the end, even if she's just a beggar with little more than rags to wear, there's no denying the fact that she's still a young and fertile woman? Undoubtedly, this is one of the reasons. But the truth is that he cannot really make much sense of this confusing fluttering of his heart. The urge to cry wells up within K every time he recalls the touch of her breast on his face. Bittersweet emotions overflow from within him. There's simply no controlling this impulse. K has no idea what is happening to him.

With no memory of his parents, all K has known is loneliness, living and struggling on his own. Is this what he's looking for? A family? Is this the reason he moved into the groundskeeper's quarters in the temple? He must have not realized it at the time, but his old master, Hypocras, became a surrogate father to him. This time around though, it's a surrogate mother he's found in Eva.

CLARA HALL

1

The day has come. The bells of City Hall's carillon tower reverberate through the city, waking everyone all across the capital. Today is the day they announce the results of the Sacred Service Examination.

K rises from underneath the shade of the banyan tree. His feet follow the crowds to the plaza in front of City Hall. They gather before the bulletin board and search for their names on the posted lists.

Someone taps K's shoulder from behind.

"So I take it you're also a candidate?"

K turns around to find himself face-to-face with the young Stellar Chess player from the terraced house two days ago.

"Yeah, I am. You too?"

"Right you are. My second attempt, in fact. How about you?"

"This is my first try, actually."

"Really now?" His eyes beam. He's maybe five or six years older than K.

"Let's see how we did then," the young man says. He runs his fingers through his hair as his eyes search the names on the bulletin board.

"Well, well, well," the young man murmurs.

"What?" K says.

"Oh. It seems I managed to pass the exam. That's all." His face betrays no trace of any joy or excitement.

"Really? You passed?" K's eyes lock on him, drawn to his impassive face like a moth to a bright light.

"Sure did. Top row, fifth column. You see the name 'Hoffman' there? Sure sounds like my name to me. I guess I somehow managed to get a score good enough to be accepted into the Sacred Genetics Department. Just enough." There's no change at all in Hoffman's placid demeanor as he explains it all to K.

"Congratulations!" K says. Surely this Hoffman is no mere side street Stellar Chess hustler. His speech patterns, his gestures, his demeanor—he has to be a graduate from a top theological school, or his father must be a high official in the Papal Court.

"So, what department did you apply for?" Hoffman asks K.

"I don't know. I don't really know much about departments and disciplines," K says. "So I left it blank."

"Oh?" Hoffman says. "If that's the case, my guess is that they'll place you in 'Planet Bosch Research' or something like that. If your name doesn't show up in that section, it would probably be best to give up. I did hear a rumor that only two people were accepted into the Planet Bosch Research Center this year."

Hoffman stands on his toes, trying to catch a glimpse of the other end of the bulletin board from behind the crowds milling about before it.

"This won't work. I can't see anything from here. Let's head over to the front."

Hoffman signals to K to follow him forward. The two force their way through the crowd until they finally reach the very front of the pack.

"So, what was your name again?"

K is just about to tell Hoffman his name when he catches a glimpse of it printed on the board from the corner of his eye. He can't believe what he's seeing. But there is no denying it. His name is one of just two listed under the row marked "Planet Bosch Research."

"I found it!" K's exclamation startles a few onlookers.

"Your name is on the list?" Hoffman checks for himself.

"Right there."

"My friend, you are officially amazing," Hoffman says, smiling. "It's no small feat to pass the Sacred Exam at your age, and on your first try, no less." Hoffman slaps K on his back, nearly knocking him over. But K barely notices. All he feels at that moment are his stiff shoulders finally relaxing.

"Just what is this whole Planet Bosch Research thing all about anyway?" K asks Hoffman.

"You've never heard of it before?" Hoffman says. "I guess I shouldn't be surprised. All I know is that they only just recently added it as an official field of sacred study. But enough of this for now! Let's ditch this crowd and find somewhere to celebrate! I know the perfect place!"

"Shouldn't we head over to registration first?" K asks. "That's what it says right here—accepted candidates are to register with their respective departments."

Hoffman waves off K's concerns.

"Oh don't worry about that," he says as a knowing smile forms on his lips. "They're on their lunch break right now. Registration won't even start until four o'clock."

K follows Hoffman to an area behind the City Hall complex. They approach a high sandstone cliff, the same cliff K saw from the terminal station when he first arrived, where several small tunnels have been carved into the face. Hoffman leads K toward one of them, pushing open its door. It takes K's eyes some time to adjust from the glaring light of the sun outside to the shadowy space behind the door. He is well inside the place before he realizes that the inside of the tunnel has been fashioned into a small bar.

Hoffman greets the man at the counter in his usual jovial manner. He brings K all the way into the back, where curtains conceal a small cavern with a wooden table in the center encircled by a long bench carved right out of the sandstone walls. The pair plant themselves on one of the fur-covered seats.

"The best wine in the house!" Hoffman sticks his head through the curtains to bark his order to the man behind the counter.

They wait.

"It's nice and cool in here," K says as his eyes take in the inside of the bar.

Hoffman only grunts nonchalantly in response.

The bartender finally serves them a black bottle of wine. In a single practiced motion, he slides the glasses on the fingers of his left hand, gives them a quick wipe of his apron, and then sets them on the table. Without missing a beat, Hoffman picks up the bottle and begins to pour. After a quick sip, he turns to the bartender.

"That's nice. Quite nice."

Hoffman beckons the bartender closer, whispering something in the man's ear. A broad grin forms on the man's face. He points a finger toward K as he whispers something back at Hoffman.

"Oh it's all good," Hoffman says to him. "Believe it or not, my friend here passed the exam too."

The bartender furrows his brows in disbelief, but it doesn't stop him from giving them another grin.

"Well then!" he says before dashing back to his spot behind the bar.

Before K can drink more than half a glass of wine, a beautiful young woman enters the bar and makes a beeline to him. Suddenly, this beautiful stranger is standing right in front of him, and K can only stare.

"Say hello to Serena, K," Hoffman says. "She's cute, right?"

He turns to Serena.

"Come and sit between us, Serena."

K watches, his mouth hanging open, as Serena flashes them both just the hint of a smile. The delicate folds of her dress slide against her legs as she ever so slowly makes her way around the table.

"Hoffman, is this really a good idea?" K asks. He can hear his own heart racing. He can't stop himself from noticing Serena's cleavage framed by her low-cut dress.

"Oh don't be silly, K. Today is our special day. Don't just sit there, Serena! Pour the poor boy a drink!"

"As you wish," she says. "Here, now. Have something to drink, K."

Serena's face beams as she refills K's glass with wine. Her body's sultry fragrance overwhelms K's already racing heart. Resistance is futile.

Has it really just been only an hour? K could have sworn that he has been in the bar for far longer, wrestling with the first true test of a young monk's asceticism. But Hoffman seems completely unconcerned with notions of propriety, ignoring the commandments without any hint of shame. He draws Serena's body close to him, slipping his hand under her dress, to which she does not object. She allows Hoffman to do whatever he wants. K catches a glimpse of Serena's legs—the first time he's seen a woman's bare legs up close—he gasps at the sight of the muscles all taut, the dark brown skin glistening with sweat.

Pushed to the very edge of breaking, K's body is drenched in sweat. Only when he finally steps out of the bar can he breathe again. Not a word passes between him and Hoffman during their walk back to City Hall, where they go their separate ways to complete their respective registration procedures.

"Since we'll probably run into each other again at some point," Hoffman says with his hand extended, "why don't we play a match of Stellar Chess the next time we meet?"

K shakes Hoffman's hand. But he has no response to his invitation. All he can do is bow without saying another word.

What is taking so long? No one can say why K's department has taken so long to call them in for registration. K remains in the waiting room, even as all the other examinees from other departments finish up, sitting around not knowing just whom or what he is waiting for. Just one other examinee—an elderly man with a bad back and salt-and-pepper hair—waits with him. At first, neither of them says a word to one another. But with the passing of time, even as their periodic fidgeting and joint cracking break their mutual silence, the air between them becomes so unbearable that they have no choice but to exchange pleasantries.

"Hi there. My name is Abir," the old man says. "This is seriously taking much too long. I wonder what's keeping them?"

"No idea," K says.

So much older is Abir that a random passerby might mistake them for father and son. The old man tells K that he works as a professor of fine arts at some provincial university, speaking at some length about his research on the classical art of the Twilight Era.

"So, to tell you the truth, I'm not really sure why they've assigned me to the Planet Bosch Research Center. Actually, the authorities here sent me specifically a formal request to take the exam for this division. So I did. Still, I couldn't tell you what my field of study and research on Planet Bosch have to do with each other."

The old man lowers his voice. Whispering, he tells K about how the inclusion of "Planet Bosch Research" among the Holy Disciplines was something quite out of the ordinary. Not a single new field has been added to the traditional list of Holy Disciplines of Sacred Inquiry since the time they were first declared by none other than Pope Algol I. Until now.

"How about you? What sordid circumstances brought you here?" The old man gives K an inquisitive look.

"Nothing special, really. It's not like I have an education in any particular field."

"Oh?"

"The thing is . . ."

"The thing is?"

The old man waits for K's answer with probing eyes. Is he in complete disbelief that a young man of K's age could have passed this year's exam? Does he think there's some special reason K is here with him?

"The thing is, I'm only here because I got an official notice from the Papal Court too. The local officers in my area came all the way down to my village. They told me it was my solemn duty to take the exam."

"Right . . ." Does he know something more than he is letting on?

"Do you know what exactly this so-called field of Planet Bosch Research is all about? I've been asking around, and I can't seem to get a straight answer from anyone."

"Neither have I. By special executive order of the Papal Court, all research material on Planet Bosch is classified."

"Classified?" K's confusion is painted on his face. "What does that mean?"

"It means that the release to the public of the content of this research is prohibited by law. All I can tell you is what I already know: some twenty years ago, a new planet was discovered. Then as soon as the Papal Court learned of this discovery, they immediately ordered that this research be classified top secret."

"Okay." K lowers his voice. Now, even K's suspicions have been aroused as well.

Just what is going on here? Did I really pass the exam? Or was that not a reflection of my true abilities? Or is there some kind of secret plan behind all this?

Perfectly timed to suspend K's doubts from growing any further, the door right in front of him swings open, and the old man is summoned by name.

2

Not long after, Hoffman's wine starts to take its effect on K. Unable to fight the overwhelming drowsiness taking hold of him, he falls into a deep slumber. How long does he sleep? Who knows? All K remembers is the servant—the same one who called in Abir—shaking him awake, breaking him out of his stupor.

The servant in black robes instructs K to follow him. K does as he is told. But his mind is still half-asleep, still dreaming elsewhere.

K dreamed that he was crouching with his knees in his hands in the middle of a mosaic-patterned floor. Still vivid in his mind is the feeling of standing on a faraway beach surrounded by strange plants he had never seen before. But other than details of these plants, their spherical leaves, there is little else from the dream that he can remember.

No, there was something else. A woman. Who is she? Verdant leaves covered her from head to toe, as if she were some kind of child of the forest.

K follows the servant down a long hallway, through a large gallery lined with rows of columns, then another long passageway. At the end of the tunnel, they find an elevator designed to look like a large birdcage. The elevator lets them off at the top floor, leading to another long walk through another long hallway.

A copper-colored door stands before them.

"We are here," the servant says, his finger pointing toward the door.

The servant does not wait for K's response. Before K can say a word, he turns around and retraces his steps back through the long hallway, leaving behind only the distinct soft thuds of his footsteps.

With some trepidation, K pushes open the door. The room is so small and cluttered that there is barely any place to stand. Wooden boxes filled with piles and piles of books and papers cover every inch of the floor. Behind a desk tucked into the far corner of the room sits a man wrapped in gray clerical garb poring over documents.

"Please take a seat," he says as soon as he notices K's timid entrance into the room.

There's something almost familiar about his imposing demeanor. His old mentor, Hypocras? With a nervous glance, K follows the man's instructions. No other words pass between them in what stretches into a long, uncomfortable silence. The man carries on with what he is doing, fingers flipping the pages of his documents back and forth, cold disinterest visible on his face. K stiffens in his seat. His eyes catch a brief glimpse of the cover page of the papers—it's his personal file.

Finally, the man is done. He turns his piercing look toward K.

"I understand that you don't know anything about your

parents?" His voice chills the air between them. "No brothers or sisters?"

"That's right, sir." K averts his eyes.

"No communicable diseases? That is correct?"

"That is correct."

"So you're in good health then." The man's stare softens. "Good!"

His eyes look over K's body from head to toe, as if studying some unfamiliar species of animal.

"I can't say you're a picture of a strapping young man though. But that shouldn't be a problem. Your frail body is just more evidence that you've been living in accord with the commandments of the Papal Court."

Is he being sarcastic? K can't be sure. Regardless, he doesn't give off the impression of someone who has showed much diligence in his work as an officer of the Sacred Service.

All K can do is wait for the next question.

"Well, that's all the time I have for you," he manages to mutter while stifling a yawn behind gritted teeth. "Let's get this over and done with."

That's it? After all that waiting?

"Uh, may I go now?" K asks with some hesitation.

"Oh, yes, of course" is the man's hurried response. "Here are your registration papers. Fill out these sections here and here. Once completed, please hand them over to your department on your first day. See, they're all already signed for you."

K pores over the papers. The procedures outlined seem straightforward enough. Printed on the back of one sheet are the instructions for registering at each department. On another page is a note instructing all successful candidates to proceed to the monastery for training prior to their designated assignments.

"Understood," K says, relieved.

"Good. This here is your Sacred Service identification." He hands K a badge. "As you may already know, you are entitled to access any public facility upon display of this badge. Clara Hall, for example, is one such place, but there are many other places. Please keep your badge somewhere safe."

"Can I also use this at public cafeterias?" This is the one thing that matters the most to K.

The man burst into laughter.

"Don't be silly! Of course you can. Eat at the staff cafeteria of the Papal Court, if you wish."

The man's expression changes. Is there something he is forgetting to tell K?

"Incidentally, did you know that you're the youngest man ever to pass the Sacred Service Exam? I'm told your age was a matter of some deliberation at the meeting of the final selection committee. In the end, there were no objections to your selection. Your marks were simply too good. There was one thing though . . ."

K looks at the man's face. His eyes fix right on K.

"How shall I put this? You see, members of the Sacred Service are entitled to, shall we say, certain privileges. There was some concern among the members of the selection committee that such things might not be appropriate for someone of your age. This is, after all, the first time someone so young has passed the exam."

What exactly is he blabbering about? K has no clue. He certainly makes it sound like a matter of some significance.

"How do I explain this?"

Of course, K has no basis to even begin to offer a response.

"How should I know? I mean, this is the first I'm hearing of any such privileges."

"Is that so? Well, don't worry about it then."

What was that look he gave K? Something between surprise and admiration, perhaps.

"I'm sure you'll figure out these privileges soon enough," the man continues. "All in good time. Although it might be better if you didn't. At least for now. Any other questions?"

"I hope this isn't impertinent, but are you an officer of the Sacred Service too?" K blurts out.

"I am indeed," the man says, standing up from his seat.

"Well, the thing is, I'm wondering if you know about this Planet Bosch?"

Just what was K getting himself into? It is imperative that he find out.

"Planet Bosch? That's where you'll be going. Actually, I'm supposed to get new orders to travel there myself, too. So, you never know, we may very well meet again over there."

The man's vague response provides no clarification for K.

"Just what sort of planet is this Planet Bosch, anyway? I've never heard of it before."

A faint smile forms on the man's face.

"It's a joyous place. You might even call it Heaven. Or the promised land, maybe."

"The promised land? Meaning what, exactly?"

"You'll just have to see for yourself."

The man brushes aside K's questions as he shuts the cabinet doors on the bookcases and locks them up.

"All right," he says. "That is all for today."

Together, the two exit the building. When they reach the rows upon rows of columns that line the path toward the main gates of City Hall, the man looks up toward the blue skies above.

"Earth is just far too hot now. Hell is already here," he mutters to himself. "Just another few years before our so-called Millennium of Prosperity all burns into a cinder. Hotter and hotter it goes. Nothing left to look forward to but a planet blanketed in hot desert sands. Total extinction. That's humanity's destiny. All right, take care then!"

With this cryptic premonition, the man walks down the stairs out of City Hall, vanishing into the throngs of people still milling about in the city. No matter how many times K repeats his words in his mind, he does not come any closer to making any sense of them. All he can do is just stand there in front of the columns at the gates of City Hall.

That is when K remembers his badge. A closer examination of the badge reveals a heavy silver medallion engraved with glyphs and the image of The Holy Igitur. Attached to the medallion is a chain he can use to hang the badge from his neck. K tries it on right then and there. His pride at passing the exam once again flows all through his body. K stands tall. A glint of light from the setting sun sparkles off the medallion as he struts down the stairs.

3

K rejoins the usual crowds on the city streets. His next destination is the Papal Court, located atop an isolated crag standing on the eastern side of the capital. The only way to reach it is to ride a cable car that bars all but those with Sacred Service authorization from boarding. But such restrictions no longer matter to K. There can be no questioning the power and privilege conferred by the silver medallion on his chest.

The cable car squeals as its steel frame lifts above the ground to make its way skyward. K is in especially good spirits now. Nose pushed against the window, he watches the ground beneath him fall away. Curtains of dusk shroud the capital, forming a dark backdrop for the dazzling display of the city's flickers of light.

He has no words for the sense of freedom he now feels.

Is this what it feels to come of age, to become a man?

Yet, lingering in some hidden part of the back of his mind is still some trace of disbelief.

How could this have all happened? There must be some mistake!

Perhaps it's only fair that such thoughts still preoccupy K. Thousands gathered, but only a few dozen bested the challenges of the Sacred Service Exam. It will take some time for K to understand.

Solemn-looking sentries stand guard at the terminus of the cable car atop the rocky crag. K steps onto this sacred ground, displaying his medallion as he asks one of the sentries for directions to the cafeteria.

"Show me your papers!" comes the sentry's response.

Does the sentry not expect to encounter such a callow young man?

K produces his registration documents. He fails to conceal his pride upon presenting them to the sentry.

"Thank you very much, sir." The man's tenor sees an immediate transformation. "Please accept my apologies."

The sentry offers to show K the way.

The Papal Court complex is far less ostentatious than what K had once conjured up in his mind a long time ago. Only the solemn, pale-white marble structure of the papal residence in the center of the complex turns out to be as impressive as he had imagined. Looking skyward from the cobblestone courtyard, K's eyes linger over white towers, which remind him of the shape of a woman's bosom. Fully uniformed sentries of the Sacred Service stand guard before the staircase leading up to the entrance to the structure. K speaks with one of the guards after again flashing his medallion.

"Which room is the pope's personal chambers?" he asks.

With a grave look, the guard points upwards at one corner of the building.

"It's on the top floor of the tower, third window counting from the corner."

The guard nods after K thanks him.

As soon as K looks up, that window swings open, revealing a man in gray robes behind it.

"Who is that?" K asks the guard. "Our new pope?"

"Yes, I think." The guard says, even as clouds of doubt and concern hang over his look.

"You think?"

"I can't say for sure. It's not like there's been any official word about who His Eminence will be. But who else could be up there?"

"Oh yes, of course."

Pope Job Kerim II passed away more than five years ago. So it's certainly strange that no successor has been named as of yet. Is there no one qualified to succeed him? That can't be the only reason for such an unprecedented event. At no time in history since the glorious founding of the Holy Empire of Igitur has there been any such delay in the papal succession.

"I'm sure there are all sorts of rumors, but tell me, do you know the real reason why they still haven't named a successor?"

Another one of K's ill-advised questions. Even before all of K's words escape his lips, the sentry's attitude turns portentous. His eyes dart up. It doesn't look like there's anyone listening in on them from the windows of the tower above this time around, but you can never be sure who might just overhear an ill-advised conversation.

"You really should be careful about what you say around here." His trembling words are all he leaves K before hurrying away from him.

The warning startles K.

Just what is going on here?

K returns his eyes to the window above. Right on cue, beams of light from every lamp in the tower shoot out the windows.

"Oh!" K exclaims.

The flash of illumination reveals the face of the man in the tower. With such haste does he dart back inside the tower that he leaves K very little time to confirm his suspicions. But that single moment is all the time K needs to recognize him. There is no doubt in K's mind at all. There is no mistaking his uncanny resemblance to someone K once knew.

That's impossible! How could it be?

K cannot deny what he saw. It was none other than K's old teacher Hypocras himself. He was the man at the window of the papal chamber. But explanations will have to come later. For now, K has other concerns.

Already famished even before arriving at the Papal Court, once again K turns to his more immediate problem: his growing pangs of hunger. The sentry at the gate told K to cut across the courtyard and enter one of the buildings in the back, then go down a stairway leading to the basement. K does just that. Once inside, locating the cafeteria of the Papal Court simply becomes a matter of following the crowd of clerics to a fan-shaped chamber large enough to hold some three hundred people.

K joins the queue. It does not take long for his turn to come. When he arrives at the front of the queue, he finds out that he is free to pick and choose whatever he wants from the selection of foodstuffs on display. He piles them up on his tray, taking far more than he can finish all by himself.

A voice comes from behind K's back.

"Excuse me, chef, what's this over here?"

"That's flying fish from Yilan," answers the chef, who is also dressed in clerical garb.

"Well, that's different." The man shrugs.

The chef pries open the refrigerator door and takes a whole fish from inside it. He holds it out to the man with his bare hands.

"This is what the fish looks like," he says.

Heat from the chef's hands somehow revives the fish. It twitches and jerks around. Almost transparent in color, it appears to be close to the size of a salmon. But when its wings outstretch themselves, it must look twice as big.

"I think I'll pass. Just a yeast burger for me."

The chef does not say anything more. He simply hands the man a plate of more familiar food.

K makes his way to an empty table in the corner of the room. The man is still in a heated conversation with the chef when K sits down.

K does not notice when the man approaches his table in search of an empty seat.

"Is this seat taken?" he asks.

"Please, go ahead."

Seeing that both his hands are occupied with trays of food, K pulls out a chair for him.

"Looks like the chef managed to convince me to try the dish."

Hardly any resemblance remains between the flying fish the chef showed earlier and the dish that has ended up on the man's plate.

The man takes a bite of some of the white flesh as soon as he peels it off the fish with a fork. He uses the utensil with the precision of a surgeon. Little by little, he takes apart the fish, breaking it down to distinct little bits and pieces.

"This is really good," he says. "I believe that this here is the lung of the flying fish. Interestingly enough, it's a completely distinct evolutionary development from the respiratory system of land-dwelling creatures. Quite an achievement in the adaptation of function."

"Are you a specialist in . . . ?" K begins.

"General Xenobiological Evolution."

The man cleans off his plate of flying fish. After wiping off the grease from his lips, he turns toward the chef.

"The chef tells me he's planning to add deep-fried worms to the menu," he says. "What do you think about that?"

K does not know what to say. Not that it matters, since the man continues to speak before K can attempt a response.

"If you ask me, I don't think it is a bad idea."

"Why is that?" K asks.

And so began his pontificating spiel.

"Why? It should be obvious to all by now. Don't all of us citizens of the Holy Empire see the food crisis unfolding before our eyes? The only thing that can save us now is a revolution in food cultivation! Let me tell you something. Had humanity never discovered agriculture, the world's population would have never grown beyond a mere three million people. And yet by the year 1960 of the Christian Era, over three billion people walked this Earth. What an amazing feat of progress, you'd say! But was it? Here's the dirty little secret: technologies that increase Earth's population carrying capacity can only continue a vicious cycle."

As he speaks, the man picks at a large strawberry in his bowl with a fork.

"Now, tell me, suppose that through technological development since that time, we find ways of feeding a population two and a half times this size—think of improvements in animal breeding, new chemical fertilizers, the extermination of pests, or the cultivation of the oceans, forests, even deserts and barren lands—I would surmise that people at the time would conclude that such developments provide more than a sufficient margin for further growth."

Finally, the man pauses to catch his breath.

"But think about it. Take a population increase of 1.8 percent every year. What would be the result? Compounded?"

"Double in forty years?" K hazards a guess.

"Precisely. By the time humanity migrated into space upon reaching a population of one trillion, only two hundred years had passed. Extrapolating from this, we will completely saturate an area of space with a radius of two billion light-years within only eight hundred years."

"Sorry, but isn't all this in the *Southern Scriptures*? Chapter 103, verse 63, I believe."

"Oh, is that so?" the man's voice is sour with sarcasm. "Well, here we are today. Despite the optimistic projections back in the day, where have we ended up? We've exhausted every last bit of our resources. We've dried out the oceans. Our population is now a tenth of what it was, but more and more people eat less and less. There seems to be no end to all the suffering."

"This is true," K says.

"But what if it's possible for us to cultivate worms for food? Don't you think that we should at least try to mitigate even just a little bit of this suffering? The chef over there was telling me that silkworms are a promising prospect. Did you know that they once bred and cultivated silkworms in the East long ago? We could relearn their techniques."

The man will not stop speaking. K gives him a long look. Somewhat overweight and dressed in the usual long-sleeved clerical robes, it is obvious that his gut hangs out because he hasn't been living in accordance with the commandments. The sin of gluttony consumes this man.

"Of course, all this can't really amount to much more than a temporary reprieve. After all, the rate of worm reproduction has nothing on the amount of food you can get out of grains."

"So, are you telling me that you don't believe in the papal edicts, sir?" K asks.

"No, not at all," The man says, shaking his head. "That's not what I mean."

A vague awkwardness—a cloud of doubt—hangs between them.

"I can follow your logic," K says. "About using worms for food, I mean. But still, I feel that—"

"Why not? It's not like there's never been a custom of eating insects in history. People have eaten locusts or locust eggs in various places before."

"I know that," K says with a shrug. "But my point is that no matter how logical your reasoning might be, I still think it will soon be all over for humanity."

"Oh? Please, do go on." The man stares at K like he's studying an unknown specimen. "You're still quite young, yes?"

"Yes, sir. I just passed the Sacred Service Exam, actually."

"Well, good for you. You must be the youngest to ever do so."

K tries to stifle a smile.

"That's what I've been told. Anyway, I believe in the doctrine of a millennial prosperity. So, it really doesn't matter what we do, since the world will come to an end in several years or so, no matter what."

"Right . . . well, I can see where you're coming from. But do keep in mind that this is only one way of thinking. There's no way to know if any of these prophecies really are accurate. Maybe the end of the world won't happen after all."

"Of course," K says, deciding that it is pointless to argue with this man. "Interestingly enough, several questions about this subject appeared in this year's Sacred Exam. In particular, there was the third question on the first day. That was the day when the most people simply gave up in the middle of the exam and walked away from their seats."

"Really? What was the question?"

His face openly betrays his surprise. This must be the first time he's hearing any of this. This is why K takes his time to explain in some detail.

The man sets down his knife and fork. He draws his face closer to K.

"That is very interesting," he says. "So, what were your answers?"

"I just went by the teachings in the *Southern Scriptures*. It says that the creation of the world is a figment of God's dream, so God's awakening from this slumber will bring about the world's destruction."

"Yes, you're right," he says. "There was something about that in several verses of the *Southern Scriptures*."

"It's in there. Chapter 73, titled 'the God's Dream.'"

K's smile made his delight at recalling the reference quite apparent.

"Correct me if I'm wrong here, but isn't that one of the more densely allegorical sections?"

"Yes, it is. According to the scriptural notes, the section is supposed to be symbolic of the glory of God's creation of all things under the sky. But that's not the case at all—it's actually a literal account. Well, at least, that's what my master taught me."

"Hm, that's a somewhat unorthodox take on it. So, tell me, who is your master, anyway? I promise I won't tell another soul."

Only now does K notice that all trace of the man's optimism and energy has been wiped away from his face, replaced by a vague melancholic expression.

"His name is Hypocras. He was a cleric assigned to my village. I guess you could say he was a rather strange fellow, but then again, I followed his teachings when I wrote out my answers, so I guess his interpretations were correct, seeing as how I passed the exam with those answers."

"So, let me get this straight, this guy Hypocras claims that this 'world' is nothing more than the dream of the creator, is that right?"

"That's right," K says, his mouth full from the food his hands ply into it.

"This is serious."

"Is it?" K has never really given much thought to the subject.

"Utter madness, I say," the man says, shaking his head anew. "You're telling me that you actually passed writing such answers in your exam?"

"It's the truth. That's what I wrote, and I passed the first day of testing. Since you have to provide a correct answer to every single question or you are barred from proceeding to the next day's exam, my answer had to be correct."

"Yes, that is how the rules work," came the man's half-hearted response.

His eyes glaze over. Is there something he's just realizing now?

That is when K stops speaking for a while. For the moment, his attention goes to the task of cleaning off his plate. Despite what he said earlier, if a plate of worms were placed in front of him now, he would still eat every single bite of it. In the end, hunger surpasses any preconceived notions. It really doesn't matter to him. If only the man hadn't been wasting so much of the food on his plate, then maybe K would not have bothered to challenge his assertions.

It isn't particularly fancy, but for K, the food in the papal cafeteria is plentiful sustenance. Nothing for him to complain about. This time around, he can look forward to emptying his bowels of proper food. Plenty of real food will lead to plenty of real shit. This thought brings joy to K's mind.

"Are you going to eat that? If not, do you mind if I have it?" K asks the man, finger pointed toward his plate.

"Sure, if you want it. But what are you going to do with it?"

"Wrap it up and take it home with me."

The man gives K a look of disgust. But he does not say anything as K wraps up the leftovers in a dirty old washcloth. His plan is to bring the food to the woman by the tree as a token of his appreciation for the milk that she shared with him.

K has found his very own personal heaven in this cafeteria. He must be pleased with himself. With nothing but his own grit and perseverance, he has obtained the privilege of joining the Papal Court. Of course, he should also offer a word of thanks to his old master for making it all happen.

Something's not right.

After gulping down his glass of water, K brusquely wipes his mouth with the back of his hand. Now that he is satiated, his thoughts can finally return to what he saw in the papal chambers earlier.

"Do you mind if I ask you something?" K says to the man.

This whole time the man has been watching K, mouth agape in amazement at his incredible appetite. Other than the two of them, few still remain in the cafeteria. Little by little, the crowd thins, until no one else is standing around waiting for an empty seat.

"What do you have in mind?"

"Do you know why there hasn't been any announcement of a new pope? The thing is, I actually saw someone standing in the window of the papal chamber earlier."

The man lets out an audible gasp of surprise.

It's an effort for the man to keep his voice low: "You saw it? You saw the ghost?"

It is K's turn to be surprised: "Ghost? What do you mean?"

"The man you saw in the papal chamber—he's a man who does not exist."

K gives him a long stare.

"What? No way," he says. "You're not pulling my leg, are you?"

"It's the truth. Listen, I've been hearing rumors about it for years now. Everyone knows about it. The man you saw no longer exists in this world."

"What do you mean?"

"Someone who's been dead for a very long time now is inside that room."

The story sends a chill down K's spine. According to the man, the papal chamber that the sentries pointed out to K has actually been sealed off from any access. No one should be able to get into or out of the room. Nevertheless, this ghost keeps showing up every so often. At first, the Papal Court believed that undocumented passageways that somehow no one knew anything about let someone sneak into the chambers. They actually went as far as taking apart the walls during their investigation. But there was no evidence whatsoever of any such passageways.

"What sort of being is capable of such feats as entering and exiting a sealed-off room without leaving a trace?"

"If not merely a figment of the imagination, then it must really be a ghost," K says in disbelief. "So who is this ghost?"

"Darko Dachilko."

"You mean, the heretic?" K let slip an exclamation.

"That's right. What you saw is the ghost of a man who died seven hundred years ago. Or I should say, as the experts on the phenomenon suggest, that it's a kind of extradimensional mirage."

"An extradimensional mirage?"

Hearing such technical jargon unfamiliar to his ears flummoxes K.

The man shows the slightest hint of a smile.

"It's an idea not many are familiar with, so I'm not surprised you haven't heard of it before, but put simply, it's a concept employed within the field of Sacred Ontology."

This is how, by happenstance, K ends up listening to a long lecture about the fundamentals of what is widely recognized as the most prestigious field of research among all the Holy Disciplines of Sacred Inquiry. Although it is only to be expected that little of what he hears makes much sense to him, since the subject is intimately wedded to the foremost thing on his mind at the time—namely, Planet Bosch—he soldiers on. And so he lets the man carry on with his long lecture.

"So, in other words, what all these outstanding issues raise is the question of the true essence of the *Southern Scriptures.* What impetus prompted The Holy Igitur to author the dense text of the *Southern Scriptures*? This becomes a particularly thorny problem to navigate for anyone attempting to do an analysis of the famous 'Book of the Seed.'"

The man addresses his imagined audience with narrowed eyes looking to the distance.

K leans close. He urges the man to continue.

"Please, do tell me more. Earlier you talked about the creation of this Planet Bosch. Who created it? And for what purpose? Are you saying it wasn't the same God who created our universe?"

"Ah, yes. Now, this is really just a hypothesis at this point. One of many hypotheses among the researchers who have been studying this in secret on the instructions of the Papal Court, for that matter."

Blink, and you may just miss the almost imperceptible moment of hesitation before the man continues speaking with such fury and passion that one might wonder if he weren't possessed.

"You are aware that the classic theory of evolution—Darwinism—was radically revised some time ago, yes? Well, let me explain. Moving away from the old understanding of evolution as a process directed by environmental and natural conditions to one that is put into motion by a supernatural power gives us a far more thorough understanding of how it all works. Sure, some people raised the criticism that this was little more than a regression to medieval theology. But I don't agree. It's not so much an *overturning* as it is an *overcoming* of Darwin. You're familiar with the Galvanon trans-theory? Anton's transcognition methods? What touched off these discoveries was humanity trekking some five hundred light-years into space, far beyond this sphere of six thousand kilometers in radius that we call the planet Earth. There, they made contact with the so-called Invisible City of Samarkand."

"I see. Isn't it supposedly a mirage-like city of unimaginable beauty?"

The man takes one breath. His voice turns softer when he speaks again.

"Exactly. They say it appears from time to time inside the Taklamakan Space Desert. The city materializes into empty space from out of another dimension beyond our reach, as if it were being mass-produced from a single template. Think of it this way: Samarkand is capable of reproducing itself—it's a self-replicating city. The stories of this 'Invisible City'—stories that seem to have been passed on from one generation to the next among the crews of interstellar trading vessels—are almost reminiscent of pilgrimage allegories or bardic songs. My interest in them lies in their mode of transcription and replication, which are akin to those of living organisms. My own field of molecular biology has long taken an interest in the concept of templates. It's what unmasked the secret to carcinogenesis, which is connected to mechanisms of DNA–RNA transcription, that is, to mutations in the DNA template strand. I think that these same mechanisms hold the key to unlocking the secret of Darko Dachilko or the legend of Planet Bosch."

"I'm not sure I get it," K says. "Are you saying that Darwinian natural selection has been debunked?"

"No, no, that's not it at all. Please don't misunderstand. It's not that it's been debunked at all. Let me put it this way. Within specific local contexts, natural selection describes evolutionary phenomena quite well. The field of Sacred Evolution, however, goes beyond these contexts. Its interest is the epistemology of the relationship of this world with other worlds, in other words, the evolutionary elucidation of a multidimensional universe. Think of it like a philosophical investigation into the template of our phenomenological universe. Samarkand's momentary manifestations in space suggest that it is the materialization of a mirage. You might even say that it's a four-dimensional projection from a wholly different dimension of the universe. Likewise, our galaxy, and even Planet Bosch, might just work the same way."

"I guess that makes sense," K whispers, still deep in contemplation. "Does Planet Bosch have a template then? Could it be—"

K freezes in place as a frightening thought overcomes him.

"—the Earth itself?"

"Possibly."

Now the man falls silent. Why is that? Is it because these questions go to the very heart of the *Southern Scriptures*? Or is it because the man is not telling K everything he knows.

4

It is late, but K still finds his way back to his old spot under the banyan tree. But she is gone. He looks everywhere, but he cannot find the beggar woman anywhere.

"But I have all this food for her," K mutters. "What a waste . . ."

Another woman, unfamiliar to K, now sits in the spot. Yet oddly, this woman carries in her arms the same baby that K recognizes from before. K offers her the leftovers he brought with him, asking her just what exactly is going on here.

This is what the woman tells K: "She gave me some money. Wanted to switch places with me for some reason. So I let her have my baby for a few days. Looked like she had lots of money. Probably from an important family too. Couldn't say where she's from though."

Nothing to do now but stand here dumbfounded.

All K can do the next day is wait under the banyan tree. Somehow, he thinks—he is convinced—that the beggar woman will make another appearance there. But no such return comes to pass before the dusk begins to set in.

K finally makes a decision. Might as well move on from here. There's that place he was told about at his interview. Clara Hall, was it? Might as well check that place out.

And so K ends up back at the public plaza, where he stops a patrol officer making his rounds. But when he asks him about the location of Clara Hall, all the officer gives K in response is a quizzical look. Did he get a good look at K's face under the glow of the street lamps? Did his youth give him pause? Why else would he raise his truncheon at him?

"Wait! Wait!" K screams.

"What do you want, you punk? You trying to take the piss out of me, boy?"

"This is a misunderstanding! Please, take a look at this!" K presents to him the silver medallion. The officer's face stiffens.

"You steal it?"

"No, officer. It's mine."

"You better not be lying to me. Stealing such a thing is a capital crime."

"I know that. But I'm telling you, this medallion is mine."

K is completely calm in his insistence. The officer gives his face a long, hard stare.

"Tell me, boy, what's your name?"

K tells him his name. This is all it takes for the officer's attitude to take a sharp turn.

"So, you're that kid? The youngest ever to pass the exam? Please do accept my sincerest apologies. If you wish, it would be my pleasure to personally show you the way to Clara Hall."

It appears that K is in luck, as the officer has heard about the exam results from the prior day.

"Follow me, sir," he says as they make their way past the small gaggle that has formed around them, curious about the commotion. So this is the power of this silver medallion. This is K's power.

Clara Hall turns out to be a rather nondescript building hidden on a side street off the main thoroughfare. On their arrival, the officer stands at attention, then bows to K once, before finally leaving the scene. For an instant, it looks like K might waver. But the moment passes. K proceeds to step through the gates.

Perfectly manicured shrubbery lines both sides of the path past the gates. In contrast to the unadorned exteriors, the interiors display an elegant refinement. As K walks down the pathway, a rickshaw passes right next to him, suddenly skidding to a halt just a few steps from him.

The man inside calls out to K.

"Hey, you there! You're not supposed to be in here!"

Not this again. K presents his silver medallion.

"Well, what do we have here," the old man says, eyes widening as a smile forms on his lips. "So you're the one. Youngest ever to pass the Sacred Exam, eh."

"Yes," K says to the man in the rickshaw.

"So is this your first time here?"

K nods.

"Well, you should follow me, then," the old man says.

"Thank you, sir. There's one thing I should tell you though. I don't really have much money on me right now."

"Money?" The man starts to giggle.

"Um. Did I say something wrong?" There really is no hiding K's confusion.

"You know nothing, do you? Well, you and me both. I was just like you when I came here for the first time. Let me show you around."

"Thank you," K says with just the hint of a stutter.

Clara Hall is an exclusive social club for Sacred Service officers, K finds. And it doesn't take long for K to finally learn what exactly these so-called privileges of holding a silver medallion are all about. The man from the rickshaw—an expert in the field of Sacred Astrometrics who goes by the name of Erasmus—tells him all about it.

Erasmus and K find their way to the cafeteria of Clara Hall, where once again K faces a wide selection of fine foods, none of which he's ever laid eyes on before, none of which have names he's ever heard before.

"Please don't hesitate to go for seconds, young man," Erasmus tells him. "I told you—money does not matter here."

But K declines to do so. To eat any more than he already has done entails violating the papal edicts on one's diet. Such an act cannot but become a stain on his conscience. So they finish their meal with a yogurt dessert. The professor eats only half of it before rolling up a cigar, which he then dangles on his lips.

"How was your meal? Satisfied?"

"Yes. I'm quite stuffed, actually."

Amused by K's words, Erasmus chuckles like a cooing pigeon.

"Shall we head over to the library, then? There are quite a few books there that I think you'll find interesting. Or you can have something to drink there. Or play cards or Stellar Chess. And of course, the other kinds of games too, if you know what I mean."

The professor gives K a knowing look.

The two arrive at an unusually quiet library. A black-tinged red carpet is spread out over the floor. Meticulously arranged around the room are elegant antique furniture and fixtures, each piece looking like it was taken right out of a museum. While the lighting in the room is on the dim side, each seat is also equipped with its own light to accommodate the preferences of every reader.

"The bookshelves are over there," Erasmus tells K.

K walks over to the other side of the room. Books line every inch of the wall. A stack of magazines sits in one corner. His eyes are drawn to the color-printed pages, the first time he's ever seen such a thing. But K does not recognize the archaic language of the words printed in them.

These must be old materials from the Twilight Era. Preserved in their pages must be pictures of unfamiliar landscapes, stories of unfamiliar cultures. Overcome by his curiosity, K picks up a magazine and flips through its pages.

The photograph of a woman from the Twilight Era takes K's breath away. Her body is exposed. Only her slim midriff and the swell of her breasts remain covered. K's eyes dart around the room. No one appears to be watching. Still, his fingers tremble as they leaf through the pages, as each image becomes increasingly more explicit. One picture stands out. The woman wears not a lick of clothing. She is as naked as a newborn. His eyes fix on the space between her legs, on the dark patch of pubic hair exposed there.

////

K returns from the reading room overflowing with the shame of his sinful ways. He finds Erasmus, who invites him to sit next to him as he casually lounges in a chair with a pipe in his hand.

"Find any interesting books?" His voice is a gentle whisper.

"Ah, yes, I suppose so," K says, stammering and stumbling over his words.

"Well, the archive does contain quite a few stimulating materials from the Twilight Era. There's nothing to it though. You'll get used to it in time."

Even this simple offhanded remark makes K wonder if Erasmus can read his mind.

Not knowing how to respond, K simply remains silent. But the silence does not last. All of a sudden, Erasmus asks him a question.

"So, K, copulation—how about it?"

"Huh?" It's not a word K is accustomed to hearing. Still, it conjures an image of crossbreeding flowers in his mind, which gives him a good idea of what the word means.

"Have you or haven't you?"

"Of course not."

"Would you like to give it a try?"

K finds himself at a loss. Erasmus's casual composure thoroughly bewilders him.

"If it is your desire, it is quite possible to facilitate this experience for you in this club."

"No, Professor, it is not my desire. Not at the moment," K says, his voice trembling with the unsettling of his soul.

"Another time, perhaps. See that door over there? There's a staircase leading upstairs to the anteroom behind it. The females are waiting for you there. Simply select your preference among them."

K can offer only a piercing blank stare in response.

"These females, they are very well versed in the techniques of the rituals. If you let them do their work, there's no need for you to say a word at all."

K keeps his disapproval unspoken. Erasmus must see through

his silence though. Not that he lets his own amusement show in his eyes. Such an amicable expression, such a steady composure is possible only in a man who knows his way around the world.

"These females are Sacred Courtesans. They are the chosen few tasked with taking care of our pleasures. If you seek them out, they will welcome your company. Regardless, you are still a virgin, still quite young. Once you've had a chance to acquaint yourself with this place, it will be good for you to go pay them a visit."

Later that night, K accepts Erasmus's invitation to play a match of Stellar Chess with him. K wins the first three straight games they play. Only when K agrees to a handicap does it become a real intellectual challenge. Onlookers flock around them, no doubt impressed by K's impressive talent.

In this game, differences in age or social rank lose all meaning. The only thing that matters is your skill at the game.

Now, it is their final match, and K makes a show of his inspired flashes of brilliance. He jumps his Moon into the sacred fifth dimension, dislodging his opponent's Jupiter and its cluster of orbiting blue satellites. When Jupiter collides with Saturn, their impact creates a small opening to the Sun. Seeing this opening, K immediately sends in his comet on a suicide run to break through and set up a direct attack on Earth.

Erasmus has no choice but to concede now. Recognizing his untenable position, he surrenders his pieces with a bow in acknowledgment of K's victory.

"The positioning of your Home Planet could have been better," K whispers.

5

Right after their match, the conversation in the group unexpectedly turns to the subject of Planet Bosch. While K and Erasmus review their last match, a simple joke from one of the spectators prompts a discussion that leads to K finally learning some of the secrets of Planet Bosch.

"Looks like we'll need to revise the rules of Stellar Chess, what with the discovery of Planet Bosch," the spectator says.

"Indeed," Erasmus replies. "Once upon a time, the planet was apparently linked to our solar system, until some unknown force moved it to its present position some one thousand light-years away in the Aldebaran system."

"Do you happen to know when this migration took place, Professor Erasmus?" asks another one of the spectators.

"Yes, I do. If my understanding of the new data that my division just recently discovered is correct, we can surmise that the migration of Planet Bosch must have occurred around fifteen hundred years ago."

A loud gasp ripples like a wave over the group gathered inside the library.

"If that's true, then there can be no doubting the truth of the prophecy of The Holy Igitur!" says one of the gray-robed Sacred Service officers. "Look it up—there's a verse in chapter 56 of the 'Book of the Seed.'"

"This is amazing! It is the proof of the existence of the Sacred Era from The Holy Igitur's teachings that we've been searching for!"

"Right. It means that sacred beings did exist in our solar system at one time," came the interjection of another man, a scholar of the ontology of sacred beings. "What we have here is powerful physical evidence that proves the existence of God."

Evidently, Planet Bosch has a mass about half that of Earth's moon.

"In fact, all indications suggest that Planet Bosch was once a subsidiary satellite in Earth's system a long time ago," Erasmus says. "In other words, it was a satellite of the moon. Now, research into Planet Bosch is still in its infancy at the moment, so our understanding of all its mysteries is nowhere near complete. But what we can conclusively say is this: from the artifacts we've excavated, it is clear that the sacred planet was very much connected to Earth somehow at one time, long ago."

"So, does the planet have any inhabitants?" another man inquired.

"Oh, yes. Naked nymphs live there. Lots of them."
More gasps disturb the air in the room.

Something about the story of the sacred planet of Bosch seems oddly familiar to K, something about it feels connected to a memory that he's had for a long time. Bosch. K has heard that name somewhere before. Bosch.

Bosch. Bosch. That's it! Hieronymus Bosch! It's a man's name! Bosch was a painter from the Twilight Era. K still remembers the first time that wondrous painting of Bosch's caught his eye. It was in the personal chambers of his master Hypocras. Was it mere accident that he stumbled upon that four-hundred-year-old book of collected paintings splayed open on his master's desk? K can only wonder. At the time, K was not aware of the longstanding ban on the publication and circulation of the book. Only later did his master mention something about the launching of an inquisition concerning the proper interpretation of Bosch's painting, *The Garden of Earthly Delights*. That went all the way back to the year 567 of the Igituran Era.

A planet named Bosch and a painting by a man named Bosch. Are they linked somehow?

K's memory of the painting remains as vivid as the day he first saw it. A pond sits in the center of everything, around which scores of naked bodies frolic. Men and women dance around strawberries and pomegranates the size of people. A woman with a blueberry for a head lies flat on her belly as a man chats her up. A man and a woman with grotesque pig snouts whisper secrets to one another while they push their faces into flowers shaped like bells. And don't forget the winged beings dancing in the sky.

The solution to the riddle dawns on K while he listens in on the discussion in the library. This has to be the key. This mysterious planet, this Planet Bosch, is precisely what the painting is all about.

K waits for things to settle down in the library before he approaches Erasmus.

"Professor Erasmus? Do you know where I should go to learn

more about this Planet Bosch? You see, I've actually been assigned to the Planet Bosch Research Center."

Erasmus laughs.

"Well, that certainly explains things," he says.

Erasmus brings K back to the stacks on the other side. He scans the shelves until he locates a slim volume among the rows and rows of books. He hands the book to K.

"Here, you should read this."

K examines the book in his hands. Its title reads *A Brief Account of the Discovery of Planet Bosch.* A whispered word of thanks later, K makes himself comfortable on one of the lounging chairs. His fingers peel open the cover of the book.

The book dedicates its first few pages to the customary biographical notes about the author and the prescribed acknowledgment of the papal curia. K skips these and jumps right to the beginning of the book proper.

> *Under the leadership of a succession of popes, peace and prosperity reign all across the lands of our Holy Empire of Igitur. Like the small circular ripples that race across the surface of a lake following the strike of a small pebble, many events, phenomena, and discoveries mark the continuing spread of Igitur's Millennium of Prosperity to all the corners of the empire's one-thousand-light-year span. The devotion of our pope deserves the admiration of all citizens. His leadership has led to the discovery of Planet Bosch as we approach the closing of the final century of the millennium in this year 975. This most recent discovery elevates the glory of our pope, showing us a sign that more good fortune will come our way.*

As K continues to read, his eyes periodically glaze over at some of the more stylized language employed in the book. But it does not take too much effort to work through some of the trickier passages, which is why, for the most part, K manages to grasp the gist of the author's account.

One thing is odd though. If the discovery of Planet Bosch was supposed to have been an occasion for celebration, a sign of promising days to come, why then has this led to keeping every piece of knowledge, every piece of information about it under lock and key today?

Did their study of Planet Bosch uncover something, some new discovery that could not be shared with the public? That would have been terribly inconvenient for the leaders of the Holy Empire.

He isn't quite able to put it into words, but something bothers K about all this secrecy. The preface of the book reveals that a strange sort of shadowy curse seems to shroud the sacred planet, with several of the researchers linked to the study of the planet all meeting inexplicable and untimely deaths. It doesn't help that earlier Erasmus mentioned to K that the author of this book himself met a tragic end, stumbling out of a window of his own home without any explanation.

"Be warned," Erasmus told him. "Reading this book might just bestow the same curse upon you. But don't let me stop you from reading if that's really what you insist on doing."

Erasmus's face did not betray anything. Whether he was making a joke or completely serious about the matter, K could not say. But what is certain is that Erasmus himself has never read it, even though its author was once his own colleague.

K does not finish reading the book from beginning to end until well into the night. He pored through its pages, vacillating between a sense of curiosity and a feeling of trepidation with each new page he turned, even as he learned a great deal about the mysteries of Planet Bosch. He did not know beforehand that the existence of the sacred planet was already known several centuries prior to its official date of discovery, with the Papal Court going so far as to record its existence in its official Astronomical Almanac. But because no one understood the planet's significance, no one paid much attention to it for a long time. The opening act of the history of Planet Bosch—its supposed discovery by the astronomer Surim during the reign of Pope Job Kerim II in the year 975 of the Igituran Era—is really just its rediscovery. Prior to this point in time, the planet had been known by two other designations: Aldebaran 5954 and Planet Katavolos.

The detailed account of the history of the planet in the book gives K much to ponder. He takes his time to make sense of it all in his own mind.

The history of the verdant planet begins with its inclusion for the first time in the Sigmen Astronomical Almanac, the catalog of the territories of the Holy Empire of Igitur, in the wake of the discovery of the Field Theory of Hyperspace Navigation in the year 288 of the Igituran Era. Oddly enough, the book does not disclose the planet's location. Perhaps this omission is a consequence of the standing publication ban on information about Planet Bosch? What it does reveal though is the distance of Aldebaran 5954 from Earth. It is nine hundred light-years away in the southern celestial hemisphere, thus placing it within the one-thousand-light-year territorial frontier of the Holy Empire, in accordance with the terms of the Treaty of Two Worlds signed in the year 182 following the two-hundred-year North-South War during the reign of The Holy Igitur.

However, observations of the planet did not begin until the turn of the fifth century. In part, this is because the planet's very existence could not be ascertained for quite some time. It turns out that the orbit of Aldebaran 5954 does not follow any of the known patterns of orbital movements. Only with the construction of the Loulan Sector Observatory in the year 469 by the Astronomy Division of the Papal Court could research on the planet properly advance. At the heart of this research on the planet was the question of how to explain its strange orbital movements. One hypothesis suggested that an almost imperceptible "string" attached the planet to its central star. It took nine years—until the year 478—for any evidence of such a "string" to materialize.

Since that time though, the planet has attracted only a minimal interest. It is, after all, just another planet among the countless others recorded in the Astronomical Almanac, warranting only a few lines of description. One important discovery did come about in the year 611, when an astronomer from the Yilan Observatory at the edge of the Loulan Sector transmitted a report advancing the theory that the planet appeared to be organic in composition; that is, that the planet was nothing less than a mass of vegetation floating in space. What prompted this idea was the astronomer's long struggle to explain the excessive quantities of chlorophyll he detected on the planet. Sadly, not many recognized the epochal nature of this discovery at the time, a consequence of the brutal civil war engulfing much of the Holy Empire since the year 567. Had it not been for this one interstellar trading vessel wandering off course and wrecking in the Aldebaran system some four hundred years later, that might have been the end of any further research on Planet Bosch. It took the development of large spacecraft that could regularly travel all the way to the very edges of the Holy Empire's sphere of influence in the year 900 to make this event possible.

6

Only one member of the crew—a man named Tinguette—survived the wreck. On his return to Earth following his rescue, he brought back with him astounding new discoveries about Aldebaran 5954.

Tinguette was the man who gave the planet its second name—Planet Katavolos. He was apparently quite the starry-eyed utopian dreamer, a psychological profile not uncommon among those who travel into the deepest reaches of space. Although his official role on the wrecked ship was chief medical officer, as is often the case with the crews of spacefaring vessels, he also had to be knowledgeable in several areas beyond his own field of specialization.

Tinguette took the name "Katavolos" from the name of William Katavolos, an architect and industrial designer from the Twilight Era civilization. Apparently, he saw a striking congruence between the planet's features and the organic architecture that Katavolos discussed in his work, a fact that so astounded him by its sheer improbability that it practically restored his faith. Indeed, even though he produced only one report of his time on the planet, the sheer number of citations from the work of this architect Katavolos in this one report is remarkable. For example, he references this passage from Katavolos's manifesto titled "Organics":

Now this becomes very possible using blow-molded methods of plastics with a double wall, which could be filled with chemicals of various densities, which could allow the outside surface to be structurally ribbed in a beautiful pattern, which would allow the inner shell to flex and to receive the body, a chair which could easily again bring coolness or heat through chemical action, vibration and flex, a chair which could incorporate electronic devices for sounds, and also for creating correct ionic fields. A chair which would be an affirmation of all that has gone before and that which is now necessary. This we can do without mechanics, organically, in much the same manner as similar actions such as respiration, peristalsis, and pulse rhythms occur in many natural forms.

Another passage:

Carrying the principle further from furniture into containers for food, for liquids, we find that again the double wall, structurally ribbed on the outside, smooth on the inside, could eliminate the need for refrigeration by chemically cooling the product within, or when activated or opened such a container might then chemically cook the soup, provide the disposable bowl itself from which to drink, and thereby make the stove, the sinks for cleaning, the areas for storage unnecessary, as we know them.

Thus Tinguette explained what compelled him to name the planet "Katavolos":

Having spent three years of my life on this giant mass of vegetation, it was only inevitable that I would call it such. The moment I stepped into one of the organic vesicles on the surface of the planet for the first time, I could not deny the fact that Katavolos's vision of organic architecture from the twentieth century now materialized before me. What else could this green chamber of vegetation be if not the imagination of Katavolos made manifest? This cannot be chalked up to mere cosmic coincidence. No, if anything, this made me believe even more in God's plan.

Even as Tinguette had become the talk of the town, elsewhere an obscure astronomer by the name of Surim was coming up with his own perspective on Planet Bosch. The Papal Court had sent him to the same Yilan Observatory that had originally discovered the "string" attached to Planet Bosch. Now, an assignment to an observatory in some far-flung star system often involves days upon days of babysitting a giant electronic telescope, an experience that's not all that different from exile to some far-flung penal colony. Only the ticking off of days in the calendar breaks the monotony of it all. Not having much of a reputation as an astronomer, he did what many before him did to pass the time, devoting himself to the serious study of the *Southern Scriptures*. This is how he stumbled upon a discovery of an intriguing detail in one of The Holy Igitur's prophesies.

Because The Holy Igitur is said to be the reincarnation of the author of the "Book of Job," the *Southern Scriptures* incorporates many passages from the older text. Surim found one such passage in the chapter called "The Laws of Heaven."

> *Can you bind the cluster of the Pleiades,*
> *Or loose the belt of Orion?*
> *Can you bring out Mazzaroth in its season?*
> *Or can you guide the Great Bear with its cubs?*
> *Do you know the ordinances of the heavens?*
> *Can you set their dominion over the earth?*
>
> —Job 38:31–33.

Surim focused on the opening verses: "Can you bind the cluster of the Pleiades / Or loose the belt of Orion?" Most theologians concur in their allegorical interpretation of these verses as illustrations of the extent of God's power over the heavens. But lacking in any formal theological training, Surim took the meaning of these verses quite literally. Noting that Aldebaran follows Pleiades in the night sky, he saw an intriguing correspondence between the "string" that guided the movements of Katavolos in the Aldebaran system with the image of binding Pleiades. So taken was he by this idea that he even wrote his own commentary on the infamous "Book of the Seed" in the *Southern Scriptures*.

A little-known edict once issued by Pope Algol IV imposed a standing requirement to report the findings of any scholarly work done on the *Southern Scriptures*. Few actually still remembered this order, despite the fact that it was never officially rescinded. Surim was not, however, one of those who had forgotten. He wrote up a report summarizing his findings and sent it over to the Papal Court. Normally, such a report would have simply languished in a pile of other reports and documents. This time, though, it attracted the attention of the pope's private secretary, who singled out this piece of correspondence from the farthest reaches of the empire.

Famous for his journalistic eye for detail and a finely honed sense for public relations, this man realized the power of a report from the frontiers of the empire should it be incorporated into the pope's memorial speech for the birthday celebrations of The Holy Igitur. That is how the report of an obscure astronomer somehow managed to make its way into the hands of the pope himself. There is no way to tell how the young and progressive Pope Job Kerim II reacted to this report, but telling enough is the fact that in that year of 975, "Planet Bosch Research" was elevated to the list of officially sanctioned Holy Disciplines.

7

K returns the book to its proper place on the bookshelves. Looking around, he finds no one else remaining in the lounge. Only the dim illumination of K's lamp cuts through the dull silence and dark shadows of the room.

K reclines on a sofa. What now? Maybe head back to the old spot under the banyan tree? Or maybe—

This is the moment it happens. A pair of girls—each one a dead ringer for the other—pass through the lounge to find K all by himself.

"Oh!" says one of the girls.

"May I ask what you are still doing here?" asks the other.

Both girls are close to K's age and endowed with an elegant beauty that so dazzles him they might as well have been a blinding light by the way K averts his eyes.

"Are you talking to me?"

"Of course we are. Do you see anyone else here? But first things first. Who are you, exactly?"

Her words bear a glint of an edge.

Too overwhelming are their half-exposed bodies. K displays the silver medallion hanging from his neck as he desperately searches for a place to plant his gaze.

"I just passed the exam."

"Oh, so you are the famous one! The youngest ever to pass the Sacred Service Exam!"

One girl studies K's face. In turn, the other girl—her sister? her colleague?—turns to her.

"Remember? Everyone was talking about him earlier. This is him in the flesh," she says.

K straightens up.

"I guess I'm not supposed to be here. I better get going then."

"What? Leaving already? But you're always welcome to stay over if that's what you so desire. That is why we are here, after all."

"Really? Sorry about all this. I guess I got carried away reading this book from the library and lost track of—"

The girls do not wait for K to finish his apology before taking his hands in theirs.

"Come now, please follow me," one of them whispers to him. Her voice is at once gentle and commanding.

Wrapping their hands around his wrists, the two girls snatch K away from the lounge. They lead him to a spiral staircase in the center of a round chamber. Ascending to the second floor, they emerge in a red-carpeted hallway where rows upon rows of doors line both walls. The girls push K into the dark room behind one of these doors. But this darkness does not last long. A lamp lights up as soon as they step inside, setting the room ablaze in a vibrant green glow.

K gasps in awe. Mirrors cover every inch of the walls and the ceiling of the room, giving the room an almost magical quality. A large four-poster bed draped in curtains sits at the center of the room. Everything in the room—the walls, the curtains, and the bed itself—is painted in a vibrant emerald green that glimmers in the light reflecting on the mirrors all around them.

"This is amazing," K says. "Is this your room?"

"That's right. Now don't just stand there. Come over here and take off your clothes."

"Oh, no. That's all right. I'll sleep with my clothes on. That's what I always do."

The girls laugh.

"You know nothing," they say in unison.

One of the twin girls surprises K when she starts peeling off K's soiled black robes without a word of warning.

"No, I shouldn't."

But K's protests and attempts to free himself from her hands fall on deaf ears.

"No, stay," the other girl whispers as she leans in close before pressing her lips on K's.

K loses his balance as one of the girls pushes him down onto the bed. His breaths quicken. The other girl's glistening lips continue to press against his lips. Her perfumed hair gently flutters over his face. He breaks into a cold sweat.

Holy Igitur!

But K's silent scream cannot overcome his intoxication at the soft sensuous bodies pressing against him. The girl does not stop undressing K. At first, he makes a point of kicking his legs in resistance. But even K has to admit that this is just perfunctory, just a matter of simply going through the motions. He drowns in the girls' all-too-sweet fragrance as he lets this pair of seductive fiends completely undress him.

"You really do know nothing, do you, Mister Prodigy," they say to the now fully exposed K. "Look at how he glares at us. Do you not like us?"

K grabs hold of the sheets and scrambles to cover himself.

"No, that's not it at all." K's voice comes out as barely a whisper. "But . . . the commandments . . . my sins will be punished by The Holy Igitur."

The girls giggle like a pair of songbirds humming in unison.

"Is that all? No need to worry about that, officer of the Sacred Service . . ."

This must be it. This must be that special privilege granted only to those who pass the Sacred Service Exam. Finally, it all makes sense to K. Now, he understands what they were talking about. Now, he understands what Erasmus was telling him.

"Now it's our turn."

With these words, the girls undo the shoulder straps of their dresses. Their dresses drop to their feet in two neat circular piles. They too are exposed now. Only their skimpy underwear remains on their bodies. But that does not last long. Those garments are quickly peeled off too, leaving K with the sight of two bodies naked as newborns, just like those pictures he had glimpsed earlier in that ancient Twilight Era magazine.

"You can call us Freesia," they say in unison.

"Is that your name? Which one of you?"

"No. We are both Freesia."

"This is confusing," K says. "Same name. Same face. How am I supposed to tell you two apart?"

Like perfect mirror images, they are exact reflections of one another.

"No need to concern yourself with that—we are chimera."

"Are you telling me that you're incubates? Clones?"

"That is correct."

The girls plant themselves on the edge of each side of the bed. They swing their legs around to face K. From both sides they crawl toward him, wrapping their arms around his body.

"Let us make love to you now."

K lays eyes on their crotches. Not quite what he once imagined. Until today, all he knew of women's bodies came from pictures in medical textbooks. He remembers this one book that his master, Hypocras, kept on his bookshelf, a sizable hardcover volume under lock and key. One time, while his master was away, he sneaked out with the book to catch a peek.

Such a strange thing it is. It looks like a clam.

When the girls notice K's eyes intently fixed on their crotches, they again speak with a single hollow voice.

"You are a very strange boy indeed!"

K turns his flushed face away.

"Go on now."

The girls take hold of each of K's hands in unison, inviting him to touch their crotches. He can no longer resist their spell over him. All he can do now is grimace. His fingers feel their wetness. What is all this going through his mind now? A heady mix of an aroused curiosity, a sense of guilt at his sinful acts, and above all else, a nebulous haze beyond any words, beyond any comprehension. Responding to his touch, the girls close their eyes in pleasure. K looks up toward the ceiling. Reflecting back at him on the massive mirror above them is the scene of their three bodies intertwining in some sort of strange sacred ritual.

8

The next morning, the piercing voice of an owl in a cage startles K awake.

"Good morning! Good morning!" it shrieks.

The Freesias are nowhere to be seen. Someone must have thrown open the curtains and the windows to the veranda, letting in the light of the sun as it rises above the hill where City Hall stands watch. K breathes in the fresh morning air.

"I saw it all! I saw it all! You were all enjoying yourselves!"

It is the shrill voice of the owl again.

Stupid bird!

Disgusted, K glares at the strange talking bird. It flaps its wings around its cage as it prattles on about the events of the previous night in surprising detail. This flusters K at first. All he can do is stare back at the bird with his mouth agape. Once he gathers his wits about him, he promptly gives it a tongue lashing.

"Shut up! Or I'll strangle you to death!" he yells.

Clever bird. It lowers its head, making a show of its drooping face.

Such a strange owl. It must be some kind of magical bird.

"Look at the mirrors! Look at the mirrors!"

Was the damned thing shrieking again? K glances at the mirrors. What he sees makes him gasp. Every single mirror is replaying the events of last night. Every obscene act atop the bed is replayed from every angle.

Is K still dreaming? No, this is no dream.
Do these mirrors have memories?

K heads downstairs, returning to the lounge. There, he finds Erasmus alongside the other guests from last night. It looks like they all spent the night here at Clara Hall as well.

When Erasmus sees K come in, he flashes him a knowing smile.

"Good morning, K."

"Yes, good morning, Professor," K says in return. "Do you mind if I sit with you for a while? I have a few questions I want to ask you."

"Please, be my guest," says Erasmus as he adjusts the glasses on his face.

"Thank you."

With a nod of acknowledgment, K plants himself on the leather seat next to Erasmus. And then, without missing a beat, he explodes, flinging question after question at him.

"—Do you know what I'm saying? Why? Why should I not think that this place is a house of sin? Just what exactly is going on here? No, not just here! With everything! Nothing makes any sense!"

Erasmus maintains a polite silence, nodding along as K goes on and on with his long-winded diatribe. When K finishes, his expression takes a serious turn.

"I'm not surprised that this place confounds you. But K, my boy, what you're talking about, that's all intimately intertwined with the deepest mysteries of our universe. Don't try too hard to untangle it all by yourself. If you keep obsessively picking at the knots, you may very well end up destroying our universe."

"What?" K gives Erasmus a long, wide-eyed stare. All he's doing is trying to make sense of the nature of the Freesia clones, that damned talking owl, and the mirrors with memories. "What exactly do you mean by that, Professor Erasmus?"

"Well, well. It sounds like I just put my foot in my mouth," Erasmus says. "Best you forget about this 'destruction of the universe' business I just mentioned."

"Now that you mention it, there was a question in the exam about this whole 'destruction of the world' business. Is all this connected, somehow?"

"Ah yes, that question. The third question on the first day, if I recall correctly."

"Yes. Everyone in the examination hall kept nattering on and on about it. They were saying something about how unprecedented that question was."

"Not surprised at all. I served on the committee that put together the exam this year. Even we couldn't figure out what the intention behind that question might be."

"Meaning?"

"The questions on the first day of the exam—all three of them—were written up and communicated to us by none other than the central council of the Papal Court itself."

Erasmus explains that this was an unprecedented change in the procedure.

"In fact, there were all sorts of grumblings within the committee itself, so we made a formal inquiry to the Papal Court. But when we received no guidance from them, we had little choice but to present the questions as they were."

"So I take it the committee didn't evaluate the first day's questions either?"

"Exactly. For the first day, the central council of the Papal Court did all the evaluations themselves. So, even if you were to ask me now, I couldn't tell you the correct answers to those questions."

Hearing all this sends a strange tingle up K's spine.

"Thinking about it some more, I'm sure the central council had something specific in mind," Erasmus says. "Take me, for example. I work in the field of Sacred Astrometrics. There's a way to make sense of it from the perspective of my field. Consider the issue of who brought about our Millennium of Prosperity. Who will bring about its end? The data in my field point to only one possible answer to these questions."

I don't get it. He knows something here. But there's something he's not telling me.

Erasmus continues:

"The foundation of my field is the view that our world was brought about through God's 'dream.' There's a reason it's *Sacred* Astrometrics, after all. But there's another view. What if it were not God but the Devil who is doing the dreaming, and our universe is the manifestation of this dream."

K's confusion only deepens.

"What?" he says. "So, are you saying the Papal Court is trying to identify adherents of such a perspective?"

"Possibly. The thing is, not many know about this yet, but something seems to be going on within the inner circle of the Papal Court. Not much from inside there ever leaks out, so the best anyone can do is speculate. But of course, there's always talk among the officers of the Sacred Service. I mean, why else would a new pope not be promoted yet? It's been five years since the death of Job Kerim II. But that's just one piece of evidence of the strange machinations taking place."

"Yeah. About that, I was there at the Papal Court the other day, so I heard some of the stories. I even saw the ghost. Darko Dachilko's ghost. Wait a second, Professor, the previous pope— didn't he pass away right after Planet Bosch Research was added to the list of Holy Disciplines?"

"That's correct. Wait, did you just say that you saw the ghost?"

"I did. Through the window leading into the pope's private quarters. Anyway, the book on Planet Bosch you showed me yesterday noted the date of when Planet Bosch Research was appended to the list of Holy Disciplines. It just crossed my mind that maybe these two events are linked together somehow."

Erasmus nods repeatedly.

"I think you're on to something," he says. "Job Kerim II's death did indeed happen right after. Since then, the seat has been empty. By the way, were you aware that there's another man brought in to do Planet Bosch research?"

"Yes, his name is Abir. He teaches at a regional university. Specializes in the visual arts of the Twilight Era."

"I see," Erasmus leans toward K. "You know, the first time around, they assigned quite a few candidates to the center. But then, every single one of them vanished off the face of Earth. No one can locate anyone from that group."

"What? Did they all travel to Planet Bosch?"

"Could be. But there's another theory. I don't mean to scare you, but there's a rumor going around that every single one of them was killed by that ghost."

"What? Professor Erasmus! Please don't try to scare me with these strange jokes."

There is no hiding the pallor on K's face.

THE QUADRINITY

1

Warm effervescent water overflows off the edges of a bathtub made from hewn rusty-red stones, so polished that its smooth surface has become almost reflective. A pitcher plant sits inside a flowerpot next to the tub. Its sweet dew entices a nearby fly into its snare. Slowly, the fly slides down the plant's dew-slicked trunk.

Other potted plants—ferns, hemp, and palms—surround the pitcher plant, forming a makeshift curtain concealing the bathing woman inside the bathtub. The woman picks a flower from one of the black orchids, drawing it to her delicate nose. Eyes closed, she imbibes its bold and seductive fragrance in one deep breath, only to then let the orchid flower slip between her long fingers, scattering its petals onto the surface of the warm water. The petals float toward the sides of the bathtub, where they linger for a moment before finally washing over the edge one by one.

Another day in the Holy Empire, another afternoon of dozing off.

What is it that the woman yearns for as she slips her fingers down to the swell of her breasts, ever so gently caressing them? Does her body still tingle with every vivid recollection of the days she spent beneath that banyan tree? Does a bittersweet memory of the young man suckling at her breast remain etched on her very body?

I wish I could see him, let him suckle my breasts once more.

Ah, a mother's longing for her child! The chance to see her son, once wrenched away from her arms by the twisting weave of space and time, gave her much solace. But that brief time with him is now over.

She stretches her slender neck to steal a glance of the inside of the pitcher plant next to her. The fallen fly has already dissolved.

Just like me.

All that's left for her now is to languish in her pool of ennui, to daydream once again.

All this should have been nothing more than occurrences happening on another world, on the other side of the universe. Yet why does she find this other world inhabited by her son to be more real to her? Is it because this world without her son is little more than a threshold, a place of passage?

Now waking from her dream, the woman rises from her bath. "Amalia! Amalia!"

The woman calls out for her hidden handmaiden with a voice endowed with an enchanting luster and a solemn dignity.

"Yes, Lady Piponoclara."

There is an almost mechanical quality to the handmaiden's response.

"I'm coming out," the woman says. "Dry me off."

The woman lifts her legs over the edge of the bathtub, exposing her slender body as she steps out. Betraying no hint of embarrassment, she stands before her handmaiden with her legs slightly parted as her handmaiden dries her off from her legs up with a white towel. All the while, she gazes at a full-length 3-D mirror, studying her own body with unabashed eyes.

The woman walks off the tiled floor, making her way to the dressing room. Still with Amalia's assistance, she slips on a set of black underwear, then drapes a matching black gown over it all. Her gown flutters with the delicacy of a butterfly as she walks through the lounge on her way to the garden.

High walls on every side envelop the inner courtyard garden. Arranged on the ground are alternating black and white tiles that form a pathway leading toward a pond with a fountain in the center of the garden. Black water lilies blossom in the pond, all under the cool shade of the lush green leaves of the subtropical trees, with black fruits hanging from their branches. Hibiscus flowers, their unusual black petals in full bloom, surround the pond.

"Amalia!"

After calling to her handmaiden once more, the woman removes the gown and underwear she had just put on earlier.

Her handmaiden gives the same response as before.

"Yes, Lady Piponoclara."

The woman stretches out atop a low bed while her handmaiden kneels beside her. The handmaiden drags a small cart close to her, then pulls out one of its drawers. Bottles upon bottles of perfumed oils fill the drawer. She takes out one of them and begins to massage oil onto the woman's back.

Someone inside the bedroom can easily spy on both women. The bedroom lies beyond a door in the lounge, cracked open just enough to see the large mirror installed on one wall. When viewed from just the right angle, its surface reflects the scene from the garden. Installed on the wall opposite the mirror is an artificial waterfall that serves in place of an air-conditioning unit. The falling water powers a set of multicolored gears, which propel a four-bladed fan attached to the ceiling of the room. It also activates the playback of breezy melodic music. While it is difficult to ascertain the workings of the contraption, one thing is certain. The texture of the music it plays is exquisite.

But there is no one here to spy on them. All appearances suggest that only these two women reside in this version of Clara Hall, existing on this side of the universe. Moreover, the handmaiden Amalia exhibits a distinct stiltedness to her movements. Indeed, a closer inspection reveals her secret in an instant— Amalia appears to be a mechanical doll of some sort.

The heat of the sun sears the arms of the date palms beyond this Clara Hall. The outer walls of the hall are painted in a solid white, dazzling under the light of the sun. This Clara Hall stands in the same northern suburbs of the capital city of Igitur, with the same rows upon rows of elegant homes that mark it as an affluent residential neighborhood.

Smaller rolling hills dot the landscape beyond the high plateau of the capital, seemingly expanding all the way out to the hinterlands under the boundless vista of the cloudless blue sky. But below the horizon, patches of the dark-brown color of devastation blot the terrain as far as the eye can see. With the incessant haze rising from the scorched earth, the whole area looks as if it were shimmering.

Like a navel marking the center of the belly, a solitary crag juts out of the ground. High walls surround the summit, enveloping within them a round white tower known by the name of the Holy Igitur Monastery, so beautiful as it shimmers in the haze that it looks almost unreal. All too easy to mistake its gleaming for nothing more than a mirage.

2

K marches toward this white tower under the blazing heat of the sun. His feet tread on a wasteland so searing hot it might as well have been an empty frying pan left forgotten on the stove. It is a torturous heat far beyond what he could have ever imagined.

The rocky trail K walks is the only road out of the capital. It leads straight to the crag where the Holy Igitur Monastery stands. Turn your head one way and you come face-to-face with the walls surrounding the capital looming above you. A faint line of white sand cuts across the ground just outside the base of the city walls, the only remnant of what used to be a beach. Now, sun-blackened vegetation covers much of what was once a white sandy shore. Could this land have once been the sea floor? The vestiges of the centuries-old ruins of salt extraction plants certainly suggest as much.

Not a single tree as far as the eye can see.

Even the wind steals away your breath.

"So hot . . ."

His waterskin has long been emptied. K curses at the sky.

The white-hot rays of the sun above his head burn brighter, as if ready to burst into an explosion.

What's the point of cursing at the sky now?

Halfway to his destination now—or at least that's what the sign left by the road like a grave marker informs him.

This is what K wants. This torture is what K seeks.

This morning, an official at City Hall tried to steer K from this path he had chosen.

"Don't do it. It would be insane to try to make your way to the monastery at this hour. Temperatures will go up so high that you could boil an egg under the sun. Follow the others, and go by horse in the evening, when it's cooler."

This is what he told K when he returned the registration paperwork with his signature affixed. "The assembly isn't scheduled to begin until later tonight. There's really no need to rush off now," the official added.

"Fine, I'll just head over there on foot after the sun goes down," K said.

The officer shook his head.

"That's even more dangerous!"

"Why?"

"There are snakes all over the place along the way. Poisonous snakes. You'll never survive a bite from one of them."

But in the end, K went off despite these warnings. Of course, there was the fact that he had no money to purchase a horse. But more than that, in his heart, what K truly sought was punishment. Feelings of shame at his actions from the previous night welled up from the bottom of his heart. That orgy that unfolded between him and the Freesias left indelible memories on K's body.

No longer does K's sweat flow. His mouth too has dried out. At this rate, his body will soon be drained of all its fluids until it turns into a pile of shriveled-up, sun-dried flesh in this utterly dry heat.

K stops to look for shade. He's in luck—a large boulder had rolled up from somewhere to a spot a few steps just off the road. The sun is still high up in the sky, so it barely casts any shadow. But that's still far better than staying exposed to the direct sunlight. K steps off the road and squeezes his body into this tiny bit of shade.

Heeding the warnings, K first checks for any venomous snakes lurking underneath the rock. Not seeing any, he lies down on the ground, repurposing his waterskin into a pillow. Being in the shadow of the rock should at least let him hold out for a bit longer.

He is supposed to be heading toward the monastery. But this intense heat has given K a slight headache. All he can do now is to behold it from a distance. So vivid is it in the searing heat of the air that it looks almost unreal. The haze refracts the air around it, giving it a somewhat deformed appearance. As he stares at the glistening white tower, a vague vertigo begins to overcome him. Such a strange, indescribable sensation. Still conscious but with a blurred sense of time and space. His surroundings lose all sense of solidity, as if he has somehow crossed the threshold of this reality itself.

For K, the hazy sight of the white tower of the Holy Igitur Monastery standing atop the darkened crag passes from mere mirage to something else, to something like a structure seeping in from another dimension. At first, it is only the tower. But soon after, this curious vision takes hold of everything before his eyes. He is overcome by the sensation of some kind of invisible wave from another dimension steadily advancing toward his body, and a ripple of fear washes over him. But once this extradimensional wave sweeps over him, this fear turns into relief.

K refuses to let go of this feeling of rapture. Gently, he closes his eyes. Somehow, in his mind's eye, the swell of the bosom of the beggar woman and the white tower of the Holy Igitur Monastery become one.

Sunset approaches by the time K notices anything amiss. He falls into a deep slumber while still in a state of rapture. The cool luscious sensation on his skin turns into the touch of Eva's arm in his dreams. They are sitting by the water and talking.

But something startles K awake. A huge yellow-and-black-banded snake coils itself around his feet. K's blood curdles. One false move is all it will take to be bitten. His hands grope his surroundings for a stick or a rock—anything he can use as a weapon. But no such luck. The snake must have noticed him waking. It raises its head.

Looks like this is the end.

The snake starts to uncoil itself before his eyes.

That is when it happens. Without warning—without any warning at all—a deformed black hand materializes out of thin air, grabbing the snake by its neck. The snake's mouth snaps open in a high-pitched shriek. Its scales glint as it squirms violently in the air. It tries to coil itself around the misshapen hand. But its efforts are futile. The six-fingered hand is already cut off, dripping blood from the wrist. Nothing for the snake to grab hold of.

The hand and the snake struggle with each other. Suddenly, they shoot upwards into the air. All K can do is watch the scene before him in a daze.

They dart up so high into the sky that K loses sight of them for an instant. But not long after, the snake plummets back to earth as its scales glint in the setting sun. Its head strikes against the rock face on landing. It dies instantly.

All this time, K remains flat on his back. Only after the whole ordeal ends does he regain his senses. Did he just see a miracle? What other explanation could there be for what K has just witnessed?

"K, is that you? Are you all right? How'd you end up here?"

K turns his eyes toward the voice. He sees a man on horseback lit up from behind by the setting sun. With the sun behind his back, the man first appears to K like a saint outlined by a scintillating halo of light. But it soon becomes clear that he is the Stellar Chess player Hoffman.

Behind Hoffman stands a column of more men, all marching toward the monastery on horseback, all casting long shadows behind them.

As K ponders whether to tell him about the miracle that he

witnessed, Hoffman offers him a ride, an offer that K promptly accepts.

"The officer at City Hall told me that you took off on foot, so I got concerned," Hoffman says as he extends his hand to K. "You are one crazy devil, you know that? I figured you might have collapsed along the way, so I hurried out to find you."

K leans his head on Hoffman's rather large back.

"Sorry for all the trouble, but I didn't have any money to buy a horse."

Not a prayer of a chance that K will tell Hoffman his real reasons, that he will tell Hoffman about losing his virginity at Clara Hall. That is for K alone to know.

"Oh, don't be silly," Hoffman says with the hint of a chuckle. "I could have easily lent you some. Oh, by the way, Serena asked me to say hi to you for her. She seems to have taken a liking to you."

Serena. The woman at that wine bar. Hoffman makes no attempt to hide the fact that he spent the night with her.

"So what happened to you out here?"

"Nothing special, really."

"Sure . . ."

Did Hoffman swallow his story?

"You know, when I was your age, I had already bedded quite a few women."

Hoffman regales K with the stories of all the women he has slept with. Make no mistake, he has not been living his life in accordance with the commandments of the Papal Court. Is it disgust that K feels toward him? Or admiration?

The setting of the sun in this desert wasteland mounts a sublime display for them. The massive fireball of the sun slowly descends behind the horizon. Shrouded in a deep-red glow, the monastery and the rocky crag it stands on extend a shadow all the way to the ends of the still blue-tinged eastern horizon. On the western horizon, the sky is set ablaze like a forest fire. Little by little, the colors deepen, from orange to crimson, until the darkness blankets it all.

Hoffman spurs on his horse to speed off on the road toward the Holy Igitur Monastery.

Total darkness has fallen by the time they arrive at their destination.

Upon their arrival at the foot of the crag, a large old man wearing a black hood over his head emerges from the stables that stand underneath the rocky canopy of the crag. The horse's bridle passes from Hoffman to the old man.

"So, good man, how do we get up there, exactly?"

Hoffman hands over a few coins to the old man. But the old stable hand must be mute, as his only response is to gesture toward a precipice on one corner of the crag.

Hoffman nods.

"This way," he says to K.

Approaching the cliff face under the cover of darkness, all they find is a single rope dangling from above them.

Hoffman gives the rope a tug. That must be the signal, for as soon as he does so, a lift cage descends from the top. Only one person can ride at a time, so Hoffman goes on first. After another tug of the rope, the cage hoists up, creaking its way to the summit.

Now, it is K's turn. K flinches when he steps into the total darkness. Unable to see anything, it is not the ascent to such a great height that perturbs him. No, his fear comes from being left all alone in the darkness. Is it because of his encounter with that strange, ghostly hand earlier? Is it because he wonders whether that blood-spattered hand will again appear before him in this darkness?

3

And so it begins. K and all the other students embark on a life of meditation sequestered from the outside world. Some thirty-odd students have gathered at the Holy Igitur Monastery. Not all who have completed the Sacred Service Examination are here though. Those already inducted into the clergy are exempt from this pre-scribed six-month period of training. The Law of Five Galaxies and Sacred Knowledge permits only properly licensed clerics to practice research on any of the Holy Disciplines. Obtaining such a license in accordance with papal edicts is the objective of this period of theological training for K and the others.

K's life at the monastery begins the day after his arrival. As much as it involves a strictly regimented routine, little of it involves any kind of academic work at all. After all, everyone here already counts among the intellectual elite of the Holy Empire of Igitur, so any further academic training would only be superfluous. Certainly, with the likes of Abir, who already teaches at a regional university, not to mention all the others who have also successfully completed the Sacred Service Exam, there is some basis for this thinking.

Still, K finds it all immensely disappointing. Whether you call it a lofty intellectual ambition or a strong sense of passion for research, the desire to learn is what K came here to satisfy, not long hours of meditation and repetitive prayers alongside all these older men. It isn't supposed to be such an excruciatingly dull affair.

But K's luck has not run out just yet. Because they are the only two assigned to the Planet Bosch Research Center, he ends up sharing a room with Abir. So, he takes advantage of his good fortune by asking the old art professor if he would be willing to tutor him.

At first, the old professor is taken aback.

"You passed the exam just the same as I did. What could I possibly teach you that you don't already know?"

But once Abir realizes the earnest nature of K's request, he accedes to his wishes.

The first thing Abir teaches K is the ancient language of The North. As the center of Twilight Era civilization was located in the Northern Hemisphere in days long ago, learning the language is essential, an invaluable piece of foundational knowledge that K will need. K demonstrates exceptional powers of memory in these lessons, making quick progress that renders Abir speechless.

Alongside these language lessons, Abir also provides instruction in his particular area of specialization, the art of the Twilight Era. K always hangs on to every word Abir says, to the point that anyone watching the two during these times might think that they're related, that they're an old man with his grandson. Abir speaks with an air of casualness, making his lectures seem more like bedtime stories. And there are plenty of stories to tell.

Only one thing causes Abir to go tight lipped on his student, and oddly, it is precisely the most important matter at hand, namely, Planet Bosch. Sheer dread overcomes Abir every time K brings up the subject, repeatedly making Abir lose his usual calm composure.

Hoffman, however, has a thoroughly different experience of life in the monastery. He quickly becomes the ringleader of the younger students, with his room becoming the place to hang out. There, students vent their frustrations at the monotony of their lives at the monastery, which always begins at sunrise and ends at sunset, but without a single clock to tell time precisely. At some point, his room is christened "Hoffman's Bar," a name that comes about from his access to contraband prohibited within the premises, specifically narcotics and alcohol. K later learns that Hoffman has bribed the man taking care of their horses at the base of the crag to procure and deliver the goods to him in secret.

When one time Hoffman asks K to receive the delivery at the gates, he teaches him the signal. First, tug on the rope of the lift three times. Then pause. Then another two tugs. The same signal will come back from below. Only then should he hoist the lift to the top to retrieve the contraband.

Late one night, past the scheduled lights-out, howling laughter gushes out of Hoffman's room. The next day, he is promptly summoned into the rector's office. All he receives is a warning though. Surely, the staff at the monastery are perfectly aware of Hoffman's violations of the regulations. Still, he does not receive any further punishments.

"Perks of having a big shot at the Papal Court for a dad," Hoffman explains.

Clearly, the staff overlook what they consider minor violations of the regulations, if only to be able to manage all these young and vigorous students day after day. Hoffman himself must recognize this, making sure to never cross any lines that would actually get them disciplined.

Being the youngest student there, K too sometimes visits Hoffman's Bar. But whenever he does so, he lingers in the corners without saying a word to anyone. All anyone talks about are girls, with Hoffman repeatedly regaling everyone with lively stories of his many sexual conquests. The wealth of Hoffman's experience always astounds K. Of course, listening to these stories always brings a tinge of regret, as he wonders if this will lead to the gradual corruption of his soul, perhaps even turning him into a man like the heretic Darko Dachilko.

For troubled souls, the appropriate place to seek penitence is the central chapel in the white tower, where they meditate all afternoon every single day. According to Abir, the design of the chapel is based on the Byzantine architecture of the Twilight Era, which emphasizes the idea of a revival of the microcosmos. At the time it was built eight hundred years ago during the reign of Pope Micros I, this was the fashionable choice of style.

Abir tells K that architecture is often a reflection of the intellectual climate of a given time.

"The reign of Micros I is known as a time when humanity longed to advance into space. The two-hundred-year war between the Northern and Southern Hemispheres had just ended in the year 182 of the Sacred Era, drawing the boundary between the two worlds. It's important to remember that the origins of this conflict can be traced back to a dispute about who had the right to lead an advance into outer space. The war erupted out of the two hemispheres' scramble to acquire colonial territories in outer space."

"I see," K says. "So, I know that by treaty, the Holy Empire's domain goes as far as one thousand light-years. But is this also the reason why missionaries only travel to stars in the Southern Hemisphere?"

"That's correct, K. This dream of advancing into space is also an important context for the promulgation of the Law of Five Galaxies and Sacred Knowledge in the year 223."

And so began a time when the idea of a "Millennium of Prosperity" spread across the entirety of the Holy Empire, first articulated by a small group of scholars, before being promulgated as official doctrine.

Abir's face takes on a grave look.

"I do believe that this was a glorious period in the history of the Holy Empire. But our Millennium of Prosperity will soon end in five years. Lately, I can't stop thinking about how little we have left in this world."

Abir's words are certainly melodramatic. Or so K thinks.

The discovery of the Field Theory of Hyperspace Navigation came about less than a century after the death of Micros I. Finally, the Holy Empire's dream of advancing into space could be realized. The glory of the Holy Empire could now spread far and wide across star systems several hundred light-years away. What made this possible was the development of the Karnak propulsion system, a revolutionary engine design that opened the possibility of ethereal navigation, thus providing the means for the first wave of massive space colonization vessels to travel vast distances at much faster speeds.

Among his cohort of students, K may very well possess the most knowledge of this history of the Holy Empire. This is why he finds every bit of Abir's lectures so fascinating. And now here they are, at a time when the yearning for outer space and for space interweaves with mythology, going so far as to serve as the inspiration for the architecture of the chapel within the monastery's white tower.

The domed ceiling of the chapel makes these connections visibly apparent. While the specific workings of the mechanism elude K, through the clever use of some kind of optical illusion, the normal deep-blue glow of the domed ceiling can be made to display the night sky, showing the constellations that constitute all the interstellar territories of the Holy Empire of Igitur in the southern half of the sky. As they move, they provide onlookers with an elegant theater of the stars.

Seating himself in the silent chapel and casting his gaze upon the scattered glittering of stars in the heavens always purifies K's spirit. There was no way around it. Seeing all these stars lets you grasp the smallness of your own existence, allowing your material body to fade away until you become a being of pure consciousness. It opens the eyes to the utter truth of astral projection as laid out in the *Southern Scriptures,* when the soul splits off from its physical body.

4

Three months into their isolated lives in that crag in the middle of nowhere, a series of uncanny occurrences, a series of ghostly encounters, create ripples of unease over the monotony of the students' daily lives. The first to appear is that ghostly hand K has already seen. Then a torso. And a leg. No one recalls who first reported seeing these ghosts. However, it does not take long for one, then another, until ten, then fifteen people all claim to have seen the ghost, giving these sightings an air of credibility. Yet not a single one of them panics or starts a commotion. These are the intellectual elites of the Holy Empire, after all. Such responses are not acceptable. No, they instead attempt to formulate a theory to explain these ghostly appearances.

When they gather to debate a range of opinions about the identity of the ghost, the most cogent and persuasive explanation that emerges comes from a young man named Mullin. K gathers that quite a few people consider this Mullin a genius. Not only did he score the top marks among those who passed the Sacred Examination, he also studies the field of Divine Incarnation. Rumor has it that he possesses the talent and caliber to eventually be elected pope in the future.

Mullin believes that these five ghostly limbs, including the floating hand that K first encountered, are none other than manifestations of Darko Dachilko.

Not a single person in the empire still needs to be told the story of the heretic Darko Dachilko. While his trial for the crime of heresy happened almost seven centuries ago in the year 313 of the Sacred Era, even now few can forget this momentous historical event. Of all the events, discoveries, and developments that have taken place during the Millennium of Prosperity of the Holy Empire of Igitur, none is more shocking than this execution.

Having just risen from the ashes of a two-hundred-year civil war, the Holy Empire was on the cusp of beginning anew an unprecedented era of glory. The world of theology was in full bloom, generating various theological debates and discussions. Of these debates, one that split the members of the Papal Court was the question of the divine incarnation of The Holy Igitur, a debate revolving around the question of whether The Holy Igitur was indeed a divine incarnation or merely a prophet.

Darko Dachilko vigorously participated in these debates, taking on all manner of thorny theological issues. Mirroring an old controversy concerning the doctrine of Trinitarianism during the Twilight Era from days of long ago, in the end these debates eventually resolved in the enshrinement of a doctrine of Quadritarianism consisting of God, the Holy Spirit, Christ, and Igitur. However, Darko Dachilko rejected the idea of The Holy Igitur's otherworldly divinity, insisting instead that he was a material being, an embodiment of the concept of the *Übermensch*. This led to his expulsion from the Papal Court and his forbiddance from further theological practice.

Thus branded an apostate, Darko Dachilko ended up leaving his post. This, however, did not stop those who admired his genius from continuing to follow his teachings. They remained in great numbers, transforming the man's teachings into a countervailing theology in opposition to the Papal Court and its orthodox theology. So influential did he become that his disciples even regarded him as the second coming of Christ, in effect elevating him to the status of a divine incarnation. Because his influence refused to wane, the Papal Court increasingly regarded him as an alarming challenge to their authority. They had no other recourse but to put him on trial for the crime of heresy.

A slight smile forms on Mullin's elegant face.

"Just between all of us here, there were those who believed that Darko Dachilko was a time traveler of some kind," he whispers. "We can talk about this now, but back then even the mere mention of time travel could bring down the powers of the inquisition upon you. It seems to me that not even the Papal Court could categorically deny that he was a time traveler, hence the brutal crackdown."

Mullin then reveals a secret long held by the Papal Court.

"Not many people know this, but it was actually none other than Darko Dachilko himself who first developed the Field Theory of Hyperspace Navigation."

Shock is the only reaction K can muster at hearing this fact. It all makes sense though. Every single textbook in the Holy Empire teaches that no one knows who discovered this theory of hyperspace. But if it were indeed the case that the famous heretic made this discovery, then maybe there is some truth to the idea that Darko Dachilko is capable of traveling through time. As Mullin tells it, Darko Dachilko possessed a truly keen mind capable of authoring scores upon scores of books during his lifetime. Of course the Papal Court suppressed his work in the wake of his trial, so it's almost impossible to get hold of them now. Some volumes, however, still remain in the archives of the Papal Court.

Mullin continues.

"Actually, one time, I snuck a peek at one of his books in the library. When I read his essay "On Hedonistic Nature," what immediately struck me was just how different it was from the official accounts known to the general public. I was quite surprised, to be honest."

It was precisely this work, "On Hedonistic Nature," that brought Darko Dachilko to the attention of the inquisition, eventually leading to his trial and execution.

"Accusations of moral obscenity have always been a weapon of last resort for those who seek to destroy their intellectual opponents," someone blurts out.

Hoffman, who is also present at their meeting, says something in turn.

"Precisely! There's no way they can convince me that he was just some corrupt hedonist!"

"Hoffman? What are you saying?" K whispers to him.

"Hey, man, don't get me wrong," Hoffman says. "All I'm saying is that I think issues of morals often stand in the way of getting to the truth."

"If you say so."

Hoffman's explanation makes some sense. Still, it's far too reckless to be openly making such statements. Rumor has it that even now those who follow Darko Dachilko's heresies are among them, forming secret societies organized around his ideas. Could Hoffman be a member of one such secret society? That is the question in K's inquisitive mind.

5

According to the proper interpretation that K once learned, the "Book of the Seed" from the *Southern Scriptures* strictly prohibits sex acts for the sole purpose of carnal pleasure. A papal proclamation declared that the sole purpose of sex is conception, which must be duly regulated. This proclamation simply followed the path of righteousness shown to all by The Holy Igitur himself, who committed himself to a life of celibacy by never marrying. Naturally, the alignment of this principle with interest in controlling the planet's explosive population growth only served to increase its support among doctrinal scholars. Of course, marriage can legitimate the love between a man and a woman. Even then, such a love must be entirely spiritual in character, permitting only a kiss as an expression of affection.

However, Darko Dachilko advanced ideas in his "On Hedonistic Nature" that run counter to the interpretations of the "Book of the Seed." He espoused the cause of contraceptive freedom, contending that sex had a dual function: reproduction and carnal pleasure. For example, according to the court documents that Mullin happened to glance over, before his execution he sent a woman a letter—scandalous at the time as sending letters to those of the opposite sex other than one's spouse was considered immoral—writing the following:

> *The pleasure of sex is one natural attribute of the human body and should thus not be disdained. Insofar as conception resulting from sexual intercourse is considered the proof of the human body's natural providence, then the pleasure of sex must also be understood as a sensation that itself belongs to nature. I find no merit in the insistence of many of the Papal Court's doctrinal scholars that contraception is contrary to natural providence.*

*No, contraception is a sacred act that we undertake in the name
of God's mercy. Inasmuch as this world is a hell of starvation, why
would God prefer to see those made in his image and spirit be
born in this material world?*

Much of this letter is no longer extant, and what parts of it that still
remain have been subject to all manner of redactions. But even
these remaining fragments shed light on the key facets of his doctrine. As Mullin explains, there's a clear logic to Darko Dachilko's
thinking. However, an important point of contention was his char-
acterization of the Holy Empire as a hellish world. There was no
way the Papal Court could ever abide by such an assertion, thus
compelling them to treat his argument as a heretical doctrine.

"We all know the rest of the story—Darko Dachilko was pro-
nounced guilty at the papal inquisition and sentenced to life imprisonment," Mullin says. "Now where do you all think this prison
was located?"

Mullin pauses to survey the room.

"Right here at the Holy Igitur Monastery," he finally says.

There is no concealing their gasps of surprise. None could
deny the truth of Mullin's words though. The ruins of a brick tower lurk in the northeast corner of the crag. There, the remnants of
a prison still linger.

"Do you mean that place?"

"That's correct," Mullin says. "Now, all this happened seven
hundred years ago, so the details are quite murky, but the torture
he endured there was apparently quite brutal."

The story goes that Darko Dachilko was locked alone in a
pitch-black cell, isolated from the rest of world for years upon
years. Some believe that the real aim of the Papal Court was to
simply let him die of natural causes. Yet somehow he kept living
on. Despite the fact that all he received for food was a glass of
water and a thin slice of bread daily, he did not lose any weight.
Despite the fact that he did not see any sunlight this whole time,
the healthy glow of his face and body made it seem like he had
been free to bathe in the sunlight anytime he wanted.

Finally, on July 14 in the year 313 of the Sacred Era, the court dragged out Darko Dachilko, chained and manacled, with an iron muzzle over his face. They brought him to the plaza in front of the prison, where countless sentries kept a close watch on his every move. Having vividly displayed his seeming immortality, Darko Dachilko left the leaders of the Papal Court no choice but to concoct a scheme at the very start of the Papal Conference. They called into session a special trial, concluding with the sentencing of Darko Dachilko to death.

The executioner's block they used to behead him that day still survives within the monastery.

"You know that half-buried rock at the center of the plaza? That's the one. They say that when the massive axe fell on his neck, a geyser of blood sprayed everywhere while his head flew straight into the air over everyone else."

Mullin's next words hush everyone gathered in the lounge that night, until all become silent as a grave. He finally tells them the still unsolved mystery at the heart of his historical account. Darko Dachilko's head vanished into thin air on the day of his execution.

"That's what I heard too," one of his listeners whispers. "My father told me the story. He said that his headless corpse did not die, even after all that."

"I heard that too!"

Another two or three more confirm that Mullin isn't just making up a story.

K too recalls hearing similar stories. In his younger days back in his hometown, neighbors would regularly frighten unruly children with stories about Darko Dachilko's ghost, who might just visit them to suck out all their blood if they didn't behave.

Mullin has just one more thing to add.

"You should all know that everyone present at the execution found it all very eerie, not the least among them the chief executioner. Quite perturbed by the turn of events, he ordered the headless corpse be dismembered. But within a year's time, every single one of those gathered at the execution met mysterious deaths."

"Is that true?" someone asked. "Not a single one survived?"

"Yes. Everyone died."

"How?"

"Their bodies were found mummified the next day. Not a single drop of blood remained in their bodies. Some sharp object tore through their throats and dug out the carotid artery as if it had been surgically incised. Abandoned next to the corpses was a bloodstained straw."

An eerie tale indeed.

"We were right! The ghost we've been seeing has to be Darko Dachilko," someone said. "All of our stories add up—the hand and all the other body parts make a complete set."

"Except none of us has seen Darko Dachilko's head yet," Hoffman interjected. "Whatever happened to the head after it disappeared into the air, anyway?"

"That's where the story ends, Hoffman."

"So, are you saying that no one alive today knows what Darko Dachilko's face looks like? I mean, it's not like there are any statues of him or anything like that around anymore."

Mullin gives Hoffman a questioning stare.

"Sounds about right. Your point?"

Hoffman shrugs.

"No, no point at all, really. Just curious about what he might have looked like."

He tries to force a chuckle. But all can see his face go pale.

"If you say so," Mullin says.

Someone else begins speaking with Mullin, so he turns his attention to the other man.

The night grows late. The dim light of the room's lamp shudders slightly.

"Uh, Hoffman?" K whispers. "You've been acting a little strange. Is something wrong?"

Something is different about Hoffman. He's not his usual unflappable self. Deep in thought, he does not hear K speaking to him. His fists, resting atop his knees, tremble.

"Hoffman?" K repeats.

"Hoffman?"

It takes a few more tries before Hoffman finally answers.

"What is it, K?"

Mullin must have overheard them. He fixes his eyes on K.

"You haven't said a word tonight, K," he says. "If you have something to add to our discussion, then speak up."

"Ah, well." Suddenly put on the spot, K finds himself at a loss for words.

"Come on, don't be shy."

Finally, K speaks.

"To tell you the truth, a ghostly hand saved my life on the way here to the monastery." K recounts the story of his encounter with the snake under the shadow of the boulder in the middle of the desert. "Right before it all happened, I experienced this odd sensation of being in some kind of warp in space. I thought it was my imagination at that time, but come to think of it, I wonder if it doesn't have something to do with the appearance of the hand out of thin air. What do you think, Mullin? Could this be a phenomenon linked to warped space?"

"Can you elaborate?" Mullin urges K.

K continues.

"Suppose that Darko Dachilko had in fact figured out the structural secrets of hyperspace. Wouldn't that make it a simple matter for him to link together the world of the year 313 with our present time? I mean, they do say that Darko Dachilko was some kind of time traveler. That's why he wouldn't die, even when they kept him locked up in prison. What if he had the ability to escape prison at will by using his knowledge of the structure of hyperspace?"

"That makes sense. If you're right, then that would also explain why he had a healthy glow all that time."

Mullin's answer pleases K. It's not every day that the de facto chairman of their gathering agrees with his contribution.

"One other thing—I have to wonder, I don't know, but there's a part of me that thinks that these strange occurrences are somehow connected to the disappearance of that Hieronymus Bosch painting, the one called *The Garden of Earthly Delights*."

"Wait, didn't they burn that painting?" an older man says.

At first, the rest of the group nod in agreement, but Mullin shushes them.

"No, K is right. The painting may have been stolen," he says. "Do you know much about Bosch?"

"Not really," K answers. "I'm no expert. But my roommate, Abir, once mentioned that theory to me."

"Oh, him," Mullin says. "He's an art professor, right?"

He gives everyone in the room a quick glance. Not finding Abir present, he returns his attention to K.

"So, what did he tell you?"

"He said that all this was written about in the book *The Enigmatic Heretics* by Bervera or some such. Of course, the book is banned, so most people don't know anything about it. Apparently, the Papal Library keeps a copy of it though."

"And Abir has seen it?"

"Yes, that's what he told me."

"Okay. I wasn't aware such a book existed." Mullin tilts his head back. "So how do you think these two events are connected?"

"As I recall, there was a Second Papal Conference held to discuss the proper interpretation of *The Garden of Earthly Delights*. I don't want to get in trouble here, but . . ."

"You have nothing to worry about, K. We're already discussing the heretic Darko Dachilko, so no one here is free from guilt at this point. So, quit with the hedging, and just tell us, will you?"

"Okay, if you say so. What I heard is that *The Garden of Earthly Delights* was stolen by the disciples of Darko Dachilko after he died. So the painting that was destroyed in the year 567 was a forgery. The original is still somewhere out there."

"I see. But wasn't that painting displayed in the Papal Court's special gallery? Only the most highly regarded works were kept there, so I imagine the security was rather tight. Stealing it would have been a real challenge."

"Sure. I mean, all this could just be idle speculation. But what if it's more than just that? There really is no way to know. I mean, all this happened more than four hundred years ago. But even at the time, rumors were already in the air. One dark night, a junior cleric was doing his rounds in the building when just as he was approaching the painting, a bloody hand suddenly materialized from out of the wall and grabbed hold of the painting, only to disappear into the wall again. The cleric who witnessed it all fainted right there. But once he recovered, he found the painting right back where it should have been."

"Now that's an interesting story," Mullin says as a smile forms on the edges of his lips. "So you're saying that the Bosch painting was replaced?"

"I think so. Well, Abir thinks so, anyway. This is really his theory."

"Got it. Abir's theory. Sounds like he knows quite a bit."

"He sure does. I mean, the Papal Court summoned him specifically to take this year's exam. I guess they think Abir has specialized knowledge that will be crucial to solving the mystery of Planet Bosch. That's what I would think, at least."

With those words, the bells of the monastery chime. That's the signal for the scheduled lights-out. Leisure time at the lounge now ends. One by one, the students arise from their seats.

Will Darko Dachilko's ghost make an appearance tonight? I wonder . . .

If it's going to show up, now would be the right time.

Everyone in the room makes a show of their unperturbed composure. But now that they all know the stories, they must be filled with fear buried deep in their hearts. It's no surprise that not a single one of them makes a move to return to their rooms all alone.

6

The passageway is long and dark. With a new moon that night, only the stars cast a pale light over the inner courtyard. A single underground passage serves as the only route between them and their dormitories. All the students maintain a stony silence. Now that they know the truth, their fear of the ghost becomes more palpable. Events from seven hundred years ago chip away at the walls of time to drill directly into the present, with Darko Dachilko freely crossing these barriers back and forth.

How does a man whose body has been dismembered into five separate limbs continue to live? This matter became a point of contention within the Papal Court. Scholars have offered various explanations, each one with its own merits. Many of the specific points of discussion escape K's understanding, as these theories are premised on a grasp of the fundamental structures of the space–time continuum. Nevertheless, he does understand this much: Darko Dachilko's flesh has transcended into a hyperspatial plane. His mode of being is no longer anything like their own. Each one of Darko Dachilko's limbs that K and the others had encountered exists as some kind of temporal mirage. Even though they do not exist in *this world*, they exist nonetheless, albeit in a different plane, in a different state of being within this world. These are matters of debate under the purview of the discipline of Universal Phenomenology, which ranks among the highest of the Holy Disciplines. Current thinking on this subject posits the existence of four modes of being in the world, with Darko Dachilko existing in the fourth mode.

K catches up with Hoffman at the top of the stairs leading into the underground passage.

"Hoffman," K calls out. "You seemed quite startled back there. Is everything all right?"

Hoffman does not utter a single word.

"What was up with that exchange with Mullin about Darko Dachilko's face?"

Finally, Hoffman responds with a heavy voice.

"K, maybe you should stop by my room later."

Just as I thought. Something is going on here.

No one encounters the ghost that night. Once they make it back to the dormitory, Hoffman invites K into his room, immediately locking the door behind them. After checking the other bedroom to confirm that his roommate is deep in a snoring sleep, he closes its door and offers K a chair.

With a knowing look to K, Hoffman takes out a bottle of tequila from under the table. K declines Hoffman's invitation, so he takes a swig of the strong drink right from the bottle without saying a word. The drink seems to calm Hoffman's nerves a bit. After taking one deep breath, he finally speaks but still with hushed tones.

Just as K suspected, Hoffman is a member of one of the secret heretical societies that follow the teachings of Darko Dachilko.

"Please, K, don't let any of this leave the room," he pleads.

Hoffman's secret society is known as "The Flower of Life." Their symbol is a cross with a rounded circle on top, a symbol for eternal life once known as an ankh. It originates from a civilization that emerged in northern Africa during the Twilight Era, whose ruins have since been excavated.

"I'm not studied enough to know all that much just yet," Hoffman says. "But from what I know, this symbol represented the renewal of all living things. The goddess of resurrection known as Isis and the god of fertility, Osiris, were quite popular among the people at one point during the Twilight Era, with cults forming around their worship."

Hoffman continues.

"Our group's doctrinal interpretation of Darko Dachilko's esoteric teachings draws inspiration from the worship of Isis and Osiris."

According to Hoffman, echoes of the stories about Darko Dachilko's miraculous survival in spite of his decapitation and dismemberment are everywhere in the histories and myths of the Twilight Era. All of these stories are new to K, so it's not surprising that he is so easily drawn into Hoffman's tale. As Hoffman tells it, Darko Dachilko must have somehow learned the secret of the mystical mechanism of resurrection, just as the likes of Christ, Isis, and Osiris before him did back in the Twilight Era.

K speaks with Hoffman in his room for quite some time. By the time he returns to his own room, the long night is already breaking into dawn. He immediately falls into bed. But so worked up is his mind that he finds himself unable to fall asleep, instead continuing to ruminate over the various stories Hoffman told him.

That must be why Hoffman was so spooked back at the lounge. There's only one explanation. Hoffman knows what Darko Dachilko's face looks like. He told K about a portrait he glimpsed once at a secret gathering of the members of the Flower of Life he attended. What if not all of Darko Dachilko's images were seized and burnt in the wake of his execution? What if his remaining disciples hid a few of them somewhere? One such portrait must have been what Hoffman saw that time.

7

K drifts into sleep for just an instant before his eyes snap open again. He had forgotten to shut the blinds before going to bed, and his face is immersed in the light of the morning sun as it rises. He gets up. He checks on Abir but finds his bed empty. Thinking that he was on his routine morning stroll, K decides to go search for him. There's something about the relationship between the Planet Bosch and Darko Dachilko that troubles him. Maybe Abir knows the answer to his dilemma.

K knows where to find him. Every morning, Abir strolls over to the northern end of the rocky crag. That's where K goes, making his way around the chapel, then cutting across the rubble-strewn courtyard behind it. This is the highest point of the rocky crag. Standing right at the edge of the cliffside gives one a view of the entire desert wasteland beyond. The sun has just about fully risen over the horizon, looming large as its white-hot glow gradually warms up what was once cooler night air.

K stands atop the bare exposed rock, searching his surroundings for Abir. But the man is nowhere to be found. Somewhat discouraged, he gives up his search, retracing his steps back to the dormitory.

So what does K wish to speak with Abir about? It concerns the question of why Darko Dachilko's ghost needed to steal the painting *The Garden of Earthly Delights* in the first place. While he doesn't really expect Abir to give him a straight answer, it's worth asking anyway if he's to get to the bottom of all this.

He has to know something. So why is he keeping it to himself? What is so important that it all has to be kept secret? I need to find out what's going on.

When it is almost time for the routine morning prayers, K heads over to the chapel. Oddly, Abir is nowhere to be seen there either. Nor does he show his face at breakfast. Something isn't right here.

Where in God's name could he be?

Other students soon note his absence as well.

"Hey, K, isn't Abir your roommate? Do you know where he's gone?"

"I've been looking for him all morning myself."

"Was he in your room last night?"

"He was. But he was gone by the time I woke up. He usually goes out for a morning stroll. But when I went over to the northern ridge, he wasn't there either. This is really strange."

A commotion erupts outside as they are all conversing. All at once, the students stand up when they hear the mad screeching of a younger cleric from the courtyard.

"Let's go!"

Hoffman leads the way as all the others follow behind him.

That is how they find out that Abir stumbled over the cliff side and fell to his death. It appears that a guard at the base of the cliff found the scene and sent word up to the top.

A witness to the events identifies himself to those who gather at the crag upon hearing the news.

"At the break of dawn this morning, I saw someone running around in circles while screaming with all his breath."

"Now that I think of it, it looked like there was something chasing after him."

He is not the only witness. One by one, others come forward. All of them attest to seeing the same thing.

Once the clerics haul Abir's body up to the top of the crag, Mullin steps forward before anyone else can do so, as if to act as the representative of the students. He leads the prayer. Everyone else joins in, even as K remains standing at the back of the crowd, unable to hold back his tears.

Abir's body appears to have fallen straight to the bottom of the cliff. Because he landed on sandy ground, it does not show much in the way of scars or bruises. They lay down his body in the inner courtyard. Something curious strikes Mullin. He takes his time to study the body, before finally turning back toward the crowd as he points a finger at Abir's neck.

"Everyone, take a look at this."

Painted in dark coagulated blood on Abir's neck are the distinct marks of bruising, of someone's fingers pressing on his skin.

"Someone murdered Abir. Someone strangled him by the neck. Someone with a six-fingered hand."

Mullin's voice trembles ever so slightly.

Not a single one of the students—no, not a single one of all the people in the monastery—possesses such a hand with six fingers. It does not take even a split second for everyone to lose all doubt about the identity of the perpetrator.

No mere mortal could have done this. The sentry at the base of the cliff confirms that no one boarded the lift last night. The cage remains undisturbed, right where it should be. That means the murderer cannot be someone sneaking in from the outside. Besides, it is impossible to make it to the top on your own. Of course, this does not rule out a coconspirator on the inside secretly hoisting the killer up to the top of the crag. But hauling up the lift requires the strength of at least four people. Unless there's a massive conspiracy within the ranks, in the end the most fantastic answer may be the most reasonable.

Only the ghost of Darko Dachilko could have done this. It does not matter that the official report to the Papal Court will indicate that Abir's fall was an accident due to his own negligence. No one present has any doubt that it was the ghost who murdered Abir.

No more sightings of the ghost are reported after this incident. Once again, life for the trainees at the Holy Igitur Monastery returns to its old tranquility. But things are not so simple for K. This means so much more, providing real evidence of a close link between Abir's presence and the appearances of Darko Dachilko's ghost. Make no mistake, the old professor was killed because he knew the secret of Planet Bosch, thwarting K's own desire to unravel the mystery of the planet.

It is Hoffman who provides K a detailed explanation of the six fingers on the ghost's hand. He tells him that records clearly document that Darko Dachilko's hands had six fingers on them. He's even seen a mold of his hands several times during the secret gatherings of the Flower of Life. As one might surmise from the marks left on Abir's neck, his hands were fairly sizable, with the thumb and little finger in their normal position, even as the index, middle, and ring fingers all skewed toward the little finger; the so-called sixth finger was slotted in between the thumb and other fingers.

"'The Finger of Life,' we called it," Hoffman says. "Sometimes though, it's also known as 'the Shining Finger.' You can probably guess why from its name. It's said that Darko Dachilko sometimes radiates light from this fingertip."

Whispered stories of Darko Dachilko's strange glowing finger have spread all across the Holy Empire. Some stories say he can cure fatal illnesses, sometimes even bring the dead back to life, with a single touch of his finger. Other stories tell of times when he holds aloft his finger pointing to the sky to call forth rain or thunder. Even more stories talk about his power to turn lead into gold.

"It's this finger that lets him perform all his miracles. Now, this is my own take on it, but I believe that Darko Dachilko has the power to harness all the energy of the universe into his own body, using his finger as a conduit."

"Do you think that Darko Dachilko is some kind of god?" K asks.

"Well, yes, I suppose you could say that. Or at the very least, he's some kind of divine incarnation. But that guard . . . no, it couldn't be. That's impossible!"

Hoffman's face turns sullen.

I'm sure of it. There's something else Hoffman isn't telling me, a secret he's keeping to himself.

The once sunny and bright Hoffman has disappeared since the night of the incident, replaced by a man with clouds always hanging over him.

No matter how much K needles Hoffman to tell him more, all he offers are vague remarks. It's not that he's being tight lipped for no good reason. No, it's because of his concern for K.

"For your own sake, K, don't get yourself entangled in these mysteries. It will be better for your health."

8

Before long comes a little bit of rain, watering the parched land of the Holy Empire of Igitur, if only for a brief moment. The desert surrounding the crag sees an overnight transformation as sprouts of grass peek out from the dried-out cracks. But everyone knows that this gentle green grass is but a fleeting mirage. Soon, the searing heat will sweep through every inch of the Holy Empire once more. The long, endless summer begins anew.

Now another sweltering day is here, as sweltering as the day they first arrived at the monastery. But today is no ordinary day. Today, K and all other students complete their clerical training. They hold a ceremony, with the rarely seen rector of the monastery offering words of congratulations as he hands a certificate to each student. It is their last day all together. Soon, everyone will scatter all over the lands of the Holy Empire to take up their respective assignments.

His next destination already confirmed, Hoffman bids K his farewells as he packs his belongings in his room.

"I'm heading off. It was great to spend the six months here with you. Next time we meet, it will be another round of Stellar Chess."

"Yes, it was great to have you here. Take care of yourself, Hoffman."

K assists Hoffman in hauling his luggage to the lift.

From the edge of the cliff, they watch as all the others who have just departed cut across the desert below. Just as the day they arrived six months ago, once again they travel on horseback, returning to the capital.

"See you around, K!"

Finally, it's Hoffman's turn at the lift. Hoffman shakes K's hand. Once he steps on, the lift descends. Just like that, he is gone.

Now, only a few students still remain at the monastery. It does not take much longer for the last students to also descend the lift, until only K remains still standing atop the crag, now all alone. Only K's assignment is still yet to be confirmed.

He asks the cleric in charge about it. But he only shakes his head. No one seems to have any explanation for this turn of events. Every passing hour deepens K's nagging unease.

"Just what is going on here?"

Soon, the sun begins its plunge to the west, until the night fully blankets everything in darkness. The dormitory has long been shuttered. That afternoon, junior clerics went into the rooms to put away all the beds and fixtures.

"Just what is going on here?" Again and again, K repeats these same words. He fixes his eyes on the gray cloister while leaning back against a wall in the arcade. All he can do now is wait for someone to come get him.

The darkened arcades envelop three sides of the cloistered courtyard in silence. The open side leads to the base of the cliff, with the lift's winch apparatus installed on one corner of the cut-stone courtyard. Beyond the eaves of the rows of arches, all he can see is the bell tower. Beyond it is nothing but the deep darkness where stars twinkle. The whole edifice looks fossilized under the cover of this darkness.

Pangs of hunger hit K.

What is happening?

Tired of simply waiting, K decides to wander about the complex. He checks the cafeteria that abuts against the arcades. Inside all is silent as a grave, white cloth covering every table and chair. Things are no different in the kitchen. Not a single soul in sight anywhere.

Where did everyone vanish off to?

Has K been abandoned here? Nothing but silence and darkness surrounding him now. He returns to the arcade, finding the same spot he sat at before still undisturbed. Looking up, his gaze is met by a night sky strewn with stars. Some distance away, the Large Magellanic Cloud watches over him while the great arms of the Milky Way slice across the small square patch of the sky visible from under the cloister. K finds the light of the stars oddly enthralling. Whether it's because of the stars' enchantments or simply his hunger, he slowly starts feeling faint, almost as if he were intoxicated.

How much time passes before he comes to his senses? The

sound of approaching footsteps walking along the arcade must have brought him back. A figure emerges into the dim light of the stars from the utter darkness of one corner of the cloister. He makes a round of the arcades, before making his way in K's direction.

K fixes his eyes upon the approaching figure. He does not wear the usual robes of the clerics of the monastery. The man stops right in front of K.

With a deep, husky voice, he addresses K.

"The director wishes to speak with you," he says.

The overlapping shadows of the arcade's pillars conceal the identity of the man. Only when he gives a slight bow and steps off to the side where the stars offer just enough illumination does he reveal who he is. K is taken aback.

It's the sentry stationed at the base of the crag.

What's he doing up here?

Feelings of suspicion—then fear—well up inside K.

"This way, sir."

Isn't he supposed to be mute? How is he able to speak now?

K lets him lead the way to a narrow passage whose existence no one seems to have noticed until now. Somehow, it has been kept secret, hidden within the thick stone walls of the monastery.

The man leads K into a candlelit room whose every inch is shrouded in black. Walls, ceiling, and floor. The table in the center of the room and tablecloth atop it. Even the dishes and utensils arranged on the table. All of them have the same black sheen.

The sentry calmly takes the head seat of the table even as K keeps his watchful eyes on him.

"Shall we begin?"

To K's astonishment, the man's face transforms right before his eyes. The dim candlelight makes it difficult to get a clear view of his face. His master, Hypocras? The rector of the Holy Igitur Monastery? In that instant, they may as well have been one and the same in K's eyes.

Another guest joins them, a woman, who is of course also dressed from head to toe in solid black. But her face! Her face too looks familiar! When the woman gives K a gentle look, he loses all doubt. She has the face of the beggar woman, Eva.

"Let me introduce you," the man says. "She is a dear old friend of mine."

"Yes, we've known each other for a long, long time," the woman says as she flashes K a tender smile. "My name is Piponoclara."

Her voice tinkles like chimes in the wind.

Time passes as a darkened dream, as K slips into a rift between dimensions. Does time even still mean anything here? Where is here?

K's strange evening continues with a banquet beyond description. His hosts insist that he partake of the black wine served in a black glittering glass. But enchantments infuse the wine's inebriating effects, lulling K into a deep, pitch-black intoxication. Before his very eyes, all the foods atop the table turn black: bowls of black grapes, black berries, black figs.

None other than Darko Dachilko himself. Doubtless, this is the man at the head of the table before K. Now, for the first time, he can finally fathom the sheer terror of this man that Hoffman expressed.

Has all this been a mere dream? Does the Holy Igitur Monastery actually exist in the middle of this desert wasteland? Or is its existence nothing more than a mere illusion, nothing more than a mirage that has warped the flow of time to traverse here from seven hundred years ago, from another dimension altogether? Nothing makes sense to K. All he can do is continue drinking the black wine this six-fingered man keeps pouring for him. At the very least, maybe it will dull these unfathomable feelings of fear.

The woman in black stands, circles around the table, and approaches K's side. She takes his hand in hers while holding aloft a black candle in her other hand.

"Follow me," she urges.

K stutters.

"Where are you taking me?"

"This world is an illusion. Shall we go see an even greater illusion?"

Her answer is cryptic. But K no longer has any power to

resist her charms. Still dreaming, he follows the footsteps of the woman, who leads him through the black walls, which turn out to be layers upon layers of darkness. The black flame of the black candle casts a dark glow on the darkness. Finally, at the end of this labyrinth with more darkness beyond the darkness, more time beyond the time, the woman stops in her tracks. Bright white light gleams in this room. A black bed awaits them.

Time swirls into a vortex at once instant and eternal. K drowns in this dark ocean of sheer sensual pleasure.

"Where will I go?" K asks.

"To a place far, far away." She pants as K suckles the milk from her breasts. "Oh my sweet child, you will travel to a place far beyond all space and time."

THE *SOUTHERN SCRIPTURES*

1

This can't be right. As soon as K's rickshaw turns at a corner off the main boulevard, instead of the bustling city streets that should have been there, he finds himself in the midst of a run-down slum. The walls of the buildings increasingly encroach into the narrow side street here, all jammed together to form a cramped labyrinth of brick and stone. Every one of the slum dwellers here gives K pained looks of hunger and exhaustion as they watch him ride atop the rickshaw.

Before long, even the most persistent of the children pursuing K disappear from his sight when his rickshaw dives into a tunnel dug through the side of some building. Emerging on the other side of the tunnel, he arrives at a paved plaza with an odd sculpture in its center. The rickshaw runner stops in his tracks.

"It's over there, sir," the old rickshaw runner screeches.

As he snatches a tattered rag hanging from his belt to wipe the sweat off his brow, he points a finger of his large hand toward a winding staircase across the plaza. Looks like this is the end of the road.

K steps from the rickshaw. After tossing some change to the runner, he pauses to take in his surroundings. Bathed in the bright glow of the afternoon sun, the stone-paved plaza looks hot enough to make one think twice about stepping out from under the cover of the dark shadows. No wind blows. Just dry parched air around the plaza.

"Have a good day, sir," says the old rickshaw man, flashing K a broad, beaming smile.

"You too."

The man keeps his eyes on K even as he picks up his rickshaw from the ground. With just a slight tug at its handles, he pivots and runs off, straight to the other side of the plaza, where a massive wall of hewn stone looms above their heads like an overlooking castle. Basking in the searing sunlight, the walls gleam a bright white glow. K can only afford a brief glance at this wall of light, fearing that just one look at the sheer brightness will burn right through his eyeballs.

The black-roofed rickshaw heads straight toward the wall of light, making no attempt at turning around. Soon, it becomes little more than a black sunspot on the fiery glow of the wall. So black, as if blotting out the very light itself.

What happens next stuns K. Just as a drop of sweat trickles into K's eye, the wall of light consumes the man and his rickshaw. Only the echoes of the rickshaw's rattling remain to fill the empty plaza.

Was K imagining things? No, it can't be. But if this was no mere mirage, then just who was that old man?

What turn of events has brought K to this place? It was only an hour ago that K had climbed aboard the old man's rickshaw. He had gone to City Hall to receive his official notice of appointment. The rickshaw man suddenly appeared while he was at the plaza in front of the building.

K ended up spending the night all alone at the Holy Igitur Monastery after he was left behind to fend for himself. Only when he awoke the next morning did he realize that he had fallen asleep in the empty monastery. Staggering about due to his lack of nourishment, he only barely made it back to the capital, collapsing that night by the city's north gate.

Why had he been left behind without receiving any notice of appointment? What was that strange encounter in the evening all about? As the answers to these questions eluded K, his only hope of getting a handle on what was going on was to visit City Hall again. And so, with his gate pass in hand, he did just that.

Those he spoke with listened to his story. Yet not a single one of them seemed to understand what he was telling them. Everyone just fidgeted about.

What were they all hiding from him?

When he persisted in his questioning, all they offered him were embarrassed looks but no straight answers to his questions. A few even went so far as to try to drive him away with their impertinent words.

"The heat must have driven you mad! Go away and don't bother us!" they told him.

K was completely flustered.

Or to be more precise, something he heard so shook him that he was at a loss for words. All because one of the more mild-mannered administrators finally did listen to K's entire story, only to give him a stiffly askew stare in response.

"This Sacred Exam that you speak of, it did indeed exist a long time ago. But it has long since been abolished."

"What? Abolished? When did that happen?"

"Well, I'm not really sure. I mean, that was such a long time ago."

"Don't be absurd. That's simply not possible. I just passed that exam before heading off to the Holy Igitur Monastery for training to earn my clerical certificate."

"Oh, when was that?" The older man asked in turn, giving him a curious look.

"When? Just half a year ago. I completed my period of training and returned here just last night."

"Hm. Are you sure you're not possessed by some demon or something? This monastery you speak of—it's the temple to the north in the middle of the desert, right?"

"Yes, that's the one. What about it?"

"What do you mean what about it? Pull yourself together, man. That monastery has long been abandoned. There isn't anyone there."

"No way."

K let out a gasp. His shock nearly stopped his heart.

The man gave K a sympathetic look.

"You know, it might be best if you get yourself an exorcism," he said with a shrug.

Well, at least he didn't just brush him off.

K's distress left him unable to do more than stutter another question about the monastery.

"It was in the year 567—not long after the trial of the heretic—that they shut down the monastery."

That meant it happened soon after the Second Papal Conference. That was when they discussed the proper interpretation of Hieronymus Bosch's *The Garden of Earthly Delights*.

"I believe it was the place where the heretic Darko Dachilko was beheaded. After that, his ghost . . ."

"Oh, the ghost? Actually, I saw Darko Dachilko's ghost too . . ."

"Oh?"

The man contemplated K with dolorous eyes. Did he see the ghost inside K too? Just then, the bells marking the arrival of noon rang throughout the city.

"Thank you for your time," K said.

K left the office. He didn't get very far though, ending up sitting at the steps at the main gates of City Hall. He couldn't shake off that feeling of the ground beneath his feet slowly vanishing before his eyes.

The heretic must be toying with me. Was the Holy Igitur Monastery nothing more than the manifestation of a temple from another dimension? What other explanation was there?

So what about the rest of the gang? Hoffman? Mullin? Where did they end up?

Over a thousand candidates took the Sacred Exam. Were they all just an illusion? An elaborate fantasy concocted by that ghost of Darko Dachilko?

Why? Why would Darko Dachilko be perpetrating such an elaborate mischievous game on me?

K would have kept going from one thought to another without coming up with a single satisfactory explanation had it not been for the child who approached K, handing him an envelope from City Hall.

"I was asked by a cleric to give this to you."

Without waiting for K's response, the boy dashed through the plaza, disappearing from K's sight.

K tore open the envelope, finding inside it the official notice of appointment addressed to him.

Was this some kind of cruel joke? Maybe he should just rip this letter up?

Suddenly, the old rickshaw man appeared before K.

"Sir, please get in the rickshaw. It's those bastards in City Hall who are possessed by demons. They know nothing about anything."

2

Now alone in the empty plaza, K has no other option but to head up the stone staircase. Upon reaching a landing halfway up the ascent, the stairs veer left, then right again, continuing up to the city streets above.

K emerges in a narrow street that traces a gentle curve on the ground. It is as silent as a crypt, making the whole place feel like a ghost town. K follows the street, until it eventually leads him to an arch-shaped gate. Beyond the gate, the street widens into a boulevard teeming with throngs of people. Rickety old buildings on the verge of collapse line both sides of the boulevard, where residents have stretched out dozens of cords for drying their laundry.

The boulevard ends at a small park, where an old temple complex stands just slightly off to K's right. An imposing metal sign, ill-matched to the small size of the buildings, stands in front of it. It reads "Planet Bosch Research Center."

"I guess this is the place," K mutters to himself.

K presses the buzzer at the gate. After a few moments pass without any answer, he pushes against the door. The door turns out to be unlocked. Only a brief pause, a passing moment of doubt, precedes K's decision to step inside.

A long and narrow courtyard leads K farther into the interior of the temple complex. Wilted and dried-out plants line one side of the path, while a pool of water surrounds the base of a moss-covered fig tree. The lush greenery dampens the cool air.

Weeds engulf the other side of the path, almost completely camouflaging the presence of another door behind them. Again, no locks bar this door. Just one slight push reveals the dark staircase ascending behind it.

Peering up the steps, K calls out to see if anyone is around. Still no answer. He climbs up the staircase, leading him to a room with some five or so desks arranged within.

K raises the blinds inside the gloomy room, letting the sunlight stream inside. Clearly, the room hasn't been occupied for quite some time. So thick is the dust atop the desks that K has to restrain the urge to trace words over their surfaces with his finger.

"Is anyone in here?"

Standing in the middle of the empty room, K calls out with all the voice he can muster.

A clanging noise from an adjacent room responds to K's call. Soon enough, a shirtless paunchy man walks in while still in the process of putting on a pair of pants.

"What is it? Something you need?"

His words are intemperate. Was he taking a nap?

K hands him the official notice of appointment.

In a blink, the man's attitude completely changes.

"Oh! So you're our new director. We've been waiting for you for quite some time now. Please sir, follow me this way."

He bows slightly, before leading K inside, rubbing his hands together all the while.

After offering K a seat, he calls out toward the back of the room.

"Martha!" he yells. "Martha! What are you up to over there, Martha?"

The cheap screen hanging in front of the arch-shaped entryway flaps open, revealing a young woman behind it.

"Martha, the new director has arrived. Go get him something

cold to drink. No, don't just stand there—introduce yourself to him!"

The slim-figured woman looks at K with a sparkle in her dark eyes, offering him a vague smile and a bow.

"This is my daughter. I am Tantra. I'm the office manager here. We have been expecting your arrival."

"Is there no one else here other than the two of you?"

"Just the two of us. Everyone else departed last month."

"Departed? For where?"

His response is evasive.

"Well, it's really not my place to speak of such matters," he says.

"If there's something you know, you need to tell me."

"Of course, if it is the director's pleasure, sir. I believe that their destination was Planet Bosch."

"I see," says K with a nod.

The truth is that not a single thing has made much sense to K. According to Tantra, five researchers were stationed here. Last month, however, every one of them departed all of a sudden.

"Did the previous director leave behind any messages or instructions for me?" K asked.

"No, nothing in particular, sir. All Mr. Bose asked me was . . ."

"Bose? He's the previous director?" K interjected.

"Yes, that's right. So, all Mr. Bose told me was to await the arrival of the next director."

K looks askew at Tantra in puzzlement. All he can do now is bring to his lips the cold yogurt drink that Martha has handed him.

Later, K takes his place in the director's chair, examining the documents atop the desk. Nothing there seems to be of great importance. What is he supposed to do now without anything to work with?

He's been appointed to the post of director of this institution, so all he can do for now is the work tasked to him. But since no duties have been handed off by the previous director, simply sitting at the desk will have to become his task for the time being, at least until he can come up with a way out of this predicament.

K sits in that dreary room in the research center until evening. Not surprisingly, idly sitting alone in the room turns out to be a truly monotonous task. Not a single phone call reaches him. Not a single visitor stops by.

When Tantra comes by with a pitcher of water, K inquires about the daily routine of the previous director and the other researchers here.

"Well, mostly, they did what we are doing now," he says. "By the way, at what time would you prefer we serve your dinner?"

"What did the previous director do?"

"Mr. Bose usually had his dinner at nine o'clock."

"I guess the same time works for me as well."

More time passes.

Something catches K's attention. A book caked with a layer of dust sits atop the desk. Some reading will at least break the monotony of it all. But a lock adorns the covers of the thick leather-bound book. K searches for a key in the drawers of the desk, eventually finding one in the back of one drawer. When he inserts the key into the book, its covers click open.

Behind the locked cover is an old edition of one of the books of the exalted *Southern Scriptures* that The Holy Igitur left for the people, the famously incomprehensible "Book of the Seed."

K flips through the pages, skimming over the words in the Sacred Euclidean language. Traces of Bose's careful study notes have been left behind in the margins of the book's pages. Perhaps he did not have much in the way of clearly defined tasks either, leading him to pore over this book every day.

3

It takes only a few pages for K to quickly realize that the book left behind by his predecessor is not the standard edition of the "Book of the Seed" from the *Southern Scriptures.* No, this one is a heterodox version of the scriptures, long banned from publication. Rumors of all manner of apocryphal editions of the *Southern Scriptures* not officially sanctioned by the Papal Court abound within the Holy Empire. However, this is the first time K has seen an actual specimen of such a banned book. His surprise soon becomes suspicion. Now he understands why the book is kept under lock and key.

The Holy Igitur left to the people many exalted scriptures, but among them, the *Southern Scriptures* stands out for its exceeding complexity. With its labyrinthine language impossible to translate into any modern tongue, with its employment of a Möbius configuration that layered one theory atop another, no wonder scholars of the text often found themselves thoroughly confounded by it. Indeed, the central issue during Darko Dachilko's trial for heresy in the year 313 revolved around precisely this problem of conflicting interpretations of the scriptures. In the end, Darko Dachilko's position was defeated at the First Papal Conference. However, according to K's friend Hoffman, this defeat had little to do with whether his interpretation was correct or heretical. Rather, it was the political outcome of a factional war within the Papal Court itself.

Understanding the scriptures is an exceptionally difficult task for a young, inexperienced man like K. All manner of strange symbolisms suffuse the entire text of the scriptures, known for its prophetic quality. Although its supposed "Möbius configuration" is a description ascribed to it in retrospect through the work of scholars of the scriptures, it is, in fact, quite apt. Every word of the text embeds a doubling of meaning, an ambiguity between its front side and its back. Moreover, its complex sentence patterns and grammatical features create an even more multilayered text. Misread one small detail and the entire meaning of a passage can change completely. K has to admit that his reading only scratches the text's visible surface, with some sections simply impossible for him to apprehend no matter how much he tries to make sense of them.

Images of vegetation permeate the "The Book of the Seed." One section reads as follows:

> *Should anyone be in doubt, think yourself the seed that rides the gusts of the wind. Or think yourself the seed of the ripened bracken exploding into the air.*

Learn from the dandelion, the maple, the touch-me-not, the jewelweed, and others. When we grasp the various aspects of nature, the secrets of the revelations of Hieronymus will unravel before us.

The Seed is the word of the Lord.

The Seed wanders. Through the great dark space. Through the narrow path to eternity.

The Seed is the word of the Lord, sent to us from the Garden of Eden.

Like the Seed of the Lotus that sleeps for centuries before its flower ripens, keep safe the words of the Lord in times of long sleep, until the great awakening of the time of enlightenment.

Wandering and wandering, around and around every place in the galaxy . . .

K notices that the words *Garden of Eden* have been encircled, with a line pointing to a note in the margins. It reads: "Where is it?" Other notes appear elsewhere on the page: "Ascension X degrees. Declination X degrees. Five hundred light-years from XXXX?" These must be his predecessor's comments.

In the Papal Court's canonical interpretation, the Garden of Eden is understood as a parable, as a mere conceptual device. To treat it as a real thing, as his predecessor's notes seem to hint at, is heresy. This much tells K that his predecessor was already enthralled by the heretic's thinking.

This brings K to the next passage, which captures K's attention. This is the passage wherein The Holy Igitur himself prophesized the existence of Planet Bosch. This is the passage that K must fully comprehend. He silently mouths each word as he tries to make sense of it all.

And so, like a mosquito seeking out the light in the darkness, like the small boats of fishermen seeking out the light of land, the Seed flies in search of a shore to make its destination.

And so, like a billiard ball bouncing from edge to edge of its table, the Seed flies from one center of gravity to another.

Catapulted from Our Lord's Kingdom, from its mother planet, the Seed bursts open like a sorrel, carrying within it the wisdom

*of time immemorial, as though it had become Great Wisdom in
slumber.*

*Perhaps, with the passage of time, a flower will bloom. And the
holy words of Our Lord, creator of all of this great heaven, will be
spread to all the children.*

"The seed is the word of God"—an expression adopted from the
Christian Holy Bible. For a long time, this section of the great
Southern Scriptures garnered only meager attention from Sacred
Service scholars of scriptural interpretation. But for K, it is the
phrase that most clearly shows the miraculous quality of The
Holy Igitur's foresight, of his powers of prophecy.

Still, K cannot shake off the thought that Surim, the astronomical engineer from Yilan who connected the text to a small
discovery in the Sigmen Astronomical Almanac, met a violent
death shortly thereafter. As did Tinguette, the first to set foot on
the planet, who also vanished without a trace soon after returning
home following his marooning on the strange vegetable planet.

The verses continue:

*Oh Providence of the Fates and Reason! From its hidden state of
being, the Seed transforms into Energeia.*

*Watching over this great transformation will be none other
than Our Lord the absolute universal, whose child will bring
about our transcendence as long as we believe in the Word.*

*And this theater of transformation is the Word of the Lord, the
reform of the real into the actual, the proof of our objective being.*

*Now, the Seed faces the shining celestial body before it, bringing
to a close its long voyage across the heavens.*

*Though that be so, the Seed approaches, only to turn another
way.*

Tracing a gentle curve across space, it departs again.

*Like a skipping stone bouncing across the water's surface, once
more it slingshots past the gravity well and begins its eternal
journey anew.*

*Tens of thousands of eons pass, but it blooms and bears fruit
but once. What name shall it be given? There is no name. Like the
pale glimmer of Sirius in the empty sky, it simply sparkles alone,*

since that moment when its mother planet had spread thousands, tens of thousands, tens of millions of Seeds to all four corners of the universe.

What fate awaits all those others that spread across the stars with it?

Of them all, many met their death as they could not bear the cruelty of this lonely universe. Others fell into the stars and met fiery ends. Still others found themselves trapped in the Sargasso Sea of a gravity well and froze alone.

But of course, the Seed will never know what fate awaited its comrades. All it could do was to continue wandering the empty skies of this vast and boundless universe.

And then, a long time passes . . .

Pages upon pages of such verses, which read like epic poetry about a great drama taking place in the vast empty space beyond the distant future, all prophesized by The Holy Igitur. All K can do is try his best to make sense of these prophecies in his own mind.

Among the millions scattered from their mother planet, only a handful find fortune, only a handful escape the merciless cruelty of chance. Just as only a single sperm among millions will find its way to that one egg, the Seed makes its way to a chance encounter with a place that is just right for it to grow.

A solar system with a star not unlike the star its onetime home planet circled. A single planet orbiting a single shining sun. Beside this dark and heavy planet, the Seed splits apart. Soon it takes the shape of a mulberry. It absorbs the energy of the sun, the gravitation, the electromagnetic radiation . . .

Like an aquatic plant floating on the surface of the water, it extends an appendage, an impossibly long root that reaches out toward the surface of the dark planet. Just like that, it floats like a ball of algae in space, vivid green glimmering over its surface. Like an advertising balloon floating in the dark sky, like a strange ball of vegetation attached only by a single root.

And then, pulled by the orbit of the planet, it too begins circling the sun. At times the appendage appears close to tearing, leaving

the Seed to float away. But like a blind man clinging on to some-
thing, to anything, it keeps hanging on.

"Sir?"

Night has already fallen when Martha's voice startles K. He
must have fallen asleep as he was reading "The Book of the Seed."

The windows have been left open, letting into the room the
light from the stars and a view of the crescent moon.

"Your dinner is ready," Martha says.

Martha stands close to K. Too close, their skin almost
touching.

"Thank you," K says, as he conceals his gaze on Martha's lean
body in the darkness of the room.

Already accustomed to the darkness, K's eyes take in every
inch of her pale figure. White skin reveals itself beneath her wide-
open collar. Her breasts swell with her breathing, as if ready to
burst out.

Suddenly, Martha covers K's face with her own. Her soft
breasts press up against him with so much pressure that he can
barely breathe. She giggles when he tries to push her away.

Martha kneels down before K, caressing both of his hands in
hers. A white jasmine flower adorns her black hair, so overpowering K with its fragrance that he nearly succumbs to her seduction.

Somehow, K manages to finally stand up from his seat.

"Holy Igitur!" he whispers to himself as he comes to his
senses.

Desperate to hold off the desire welling up within him, he
steps aside, leaving Martha behind as he makes his way to the
dining room. There, he finds a humble supper awaiting him atop
the table.

4

One day passes, and another begins. Still, K remains disconcerted
and without purpose. Nothing at all has changed, not even when
he returns to City Hall in search of answers.

He locates the room where he was interviewed on that day

he received the results of the Sacred Service Exam. But all he finds is a storeroom, unused for years now. Finding no answers in City Hall, he pushes on to the Papal Court, but he comes up empty there as well.

This peculiar turn of events drives K to lose himself, to suspect that his very hold on this world has become tenuous. He can no longer deny that everything around him has gone out of sorts. So, when did all this go wrong? Out of all the moments in his life until now, is there even any way to tell which one was the turning point?

"To think that the world runs on a single timeline is unnatural. All things in the world are multidimensional, so time too must flow in multiple directions."

Darko Dachilko supposedly uttered such words a long time ago. Now it seems that it is K who finds himself lost in such a maze built out of these structures of time.

Darko Dachilko categorized temporal flows into four types. Just as water freezes into ice when cold or evaporates into steam at high temperatures, time also flows and takes various forms according to the environment it finds itself in. The first form of temporal flow is time as we normally experience it. You might call this the liquid form of time, which itself could be categorized into several more subtypes. While the details of Darko Dachilko's theories elude even K, he does recall that the flow states followed the patterns of fluid dynamics, as subcritical flow, or uniform flow, supercritical flow, or a hydraulic jump. But time could also enter into a "solid state," the time of stillness, which is its second form. Then there is the third form, an extremely indistinct "gaseous form." But perhaps the most interesting of them all is the fourth form of time that Darko Dachilko identified, which he compared to the behavior of a certain type of matter that climbs up the sides of its container against the force of gravity when placed in conditions of very low temperatures. In other words, this fourth form of time was none other than the reversal of its flow.

All this is moot, however, since K has no way of determining if he is caught in one form of temporal flow or another. All he can do is to go with its flow.

And so K sits at the desk, one passing day after another.

On some days, Tantra comes up to his office, requesting his authorization for some trivial matter or another, everything from repairing clogged plumbing to requisitions for food supplies. As far as K can tell, this is the only work Tantra performs. The expenses for these requests are all billed to City Hall. While this is not unusual in itself, what does catch K off guard is learning that their expenses come out of the budget of the Refugee Relief Fund. The fund also covers the salaries for K as the director and Tantra as office administrator. Any additional research costs, however, are a separate matter altogether.

According to Tantra, all the previous researchers received funding by applying to different departments as the need arose. Of course, he knew nothing of the procedures for filing such an application. That would be the director's job. But not knowing what he's even supposed to be doing in the first place, K sees little point to submitting applications for research funding.

What else is there for me to do but wait for orders to come from their end?

K makes up his mind to just sit still for now, even if not knowing what his next orders will be or who will be issuing them frustrates him to no end.

Spending his days doing nothing soon becomes a torturous ordeal for the young K. On those days when he can no longer bear the monotony, he takes a three-hour break in the afternoon to stumble into the old temple next door. The long-abandoned temple has a dome in a style similar to the Holy Igitur Monastery, though the equipment to reflect the light of the stars on the ceiling no longer works.

A cool breeze greets him as soon as he steps inside the stone structure. He stretches out his body on the marble floor, keeping his eyes fixed upwards, gazing at the temple's ceiling. Suddenly overcome by feelings of regret, he stares at the motionless ceiling while keeping his body similarly unmoving. Has he become a fallen angel cast down to Earth from heaven? Has he been wasting away all his precious days of his youth living each day without any purpose?

K has learned to accommodate such self-destructive urges these past few days. No longer are they so despicable in his mind. No, there is no longer any point in refusing to acknowledge the secret desire for debauchery already awakened in him. As if possessed by the spirit of the depraved heretic Darko Dachilko, his corrupted mind can no longer control his growing desire for the body of Tantra's daughter, Martha. Night after night, his fantasies of having sex with Martha bring him wet dreams.

On the tenth night since he was first assigned to this office, Martha sneaks into K's bed. Not noticing her beside him, he continues to sleep at first. But one touch of her skin is all it takes to startle him out of bed.

He gives Martha a harsh reproach.

"Just what do you think you're doing here?"

Still stripped naked, Martha tells him that Tantra sent her there.

Furious, K summons Tantra.

"But, sir, this is how it has always been done, with your predecessor, and everyone else before," answers Tantra, not one bit of remorse showing on his face.

K screams at him.

"You are going against the spirit of The Holy Igitur's teachings! Have you not read the commandments of the *Southern Scriptures*?"

"I have" comes Tantra's nonchalant response. "But are not the officers of the Sacred Service granted exceptions to these commandments? To freely have any woman—is that not one of the privileges accorded to you?"

Tantra lets a smile form on his lips.

"If Martha is not to your liking, then there's not much we can do about that. Of course, my daughter will not at all be happy to hear you say that."

"Why not?" K's confusion was clear.

"As I'm sure the director is aware . . ." Tantra's words overflow with sarcasm. "Your privileges are also your duties. But you are refusing to fulfill your duties. Now, my daughter is entitled to receive your charity. But if that is not something you can grant her, is it not only natural that she would find this hurtful?"

A strange notion indeed. And yet he is unable to find the words to respond.

When K sees Martha the next morning, he finds her on the verge of tears as she cleans the office. Once she sees K, she covers her face with her hands, fleeing to a back room. Martha's feelings elude K's comprehension, but as much as he wishes to pretend that nothing is amiss, he cannot deny that everything about this situation bothers him.

At breakfast, K once again speaks with Tantra about the events of the previous night. But Tantra is not in good spirits.

"You rejected my daughter," he tells K. "There is no greater insult."

"I rejected her. But it was not my intention to insult her." K speaks with a firm tone. "You need to watch your words."

"Understood."

While Tantra does not argue any further, he nevertheless fails to resist the urge to slam the milk jar on the table.

Then, nightfall.

K is deep in slumber when something jolts him awake. A loud scream coming from somewhere downstairs. Quickly, he dresses himself, then rushes down the stairs.

Gently opening the door to the administrative office, he finds Tantra snoring on his own bed. Empty bottles of liquor are strewn about by his pillow. He must have been drinking to help him sleep.

Was that just a dream?

Perhaps it is best to simply head back upstairs. But K feels a thirst, and so he proceeds into the kitchen to get himself a glass of water.

K steps into the dark kitchen. But instead of touching the earthen floor, his feet feel something fleshy. Eyes still unaccustomed to the dark, he feels the ground with his hands.

A body. Martha's body. She is passed out on the floor.

K holds Martha up. After finding a glass of water nearby, he dribbles some into her mouth, continuing until she regains consciousness.

"Martha? What happened? I heard a scream," K asks, still supporting her in his arms.

"It was a ghost. I saw a ghost," she says. "I was so scared. I woke up to go to the bathroom. That was when I sensed something strange over here, so I came in to have a quick look. Someone was sticking his head into the jug, lapping up all the water. For a moment, I thought it might be you, sir, so I said I can pour some water into a glass for you. That was when he turned toward me."

Martha shivers all over her body.

"It's all right, Martha. Whatever it was you saw, it's no longer here."

"It was so frightening. It had a pallid glow and had no head."

"No, that can't be."

Almost reflexively, K blurts out these words. But he knows that it's the truth. Darko Dachilko's ghost was here. But this is no time to panic. He must calm himself down.

"Martha, has this ever happened before?"

"Yes. But tonight was first time I have ever seen it. My father told me before that a ghost sometimes appears in this house. He must have thought it would frighten me, which is why he never said much more about it."

K holds his tongue.

"All right, let's get you back to your room."

"No! Please don't leave me alone. I'm scared."

She trembles, clinging tightly to K's chest.

The scent of Martha's body overwhelms K. There is no longer any resisting its hold on him. A powerful urge beyond his control stirs within him.

As soon as they find their way back to K's room, they immediately get right into bed. Martha takes control of every inch of K's body. Her delicate charm hides an avarice far beyond anything in K's imagination. She finds ways to awaken new and unfathomable desires in the already exhausted K, as if wise to techniques of drawing water from a dried-out well.

Again and again, she cries out in pleasure.

"I want you! I want you!"

////

The next morning, K calls Tantra into his office. Once again overcome by his guilt at breaking the commandments, K initially thinks it will be difficult to face him. But Tantra makes no effort to hide his awareness of the intimate relations between K and his daughter. Now, he takes a wholly different attitude with K, acting overly familiar, overly obsequious with him.

Tantra's attitude annoys K. But he has to bear with it for now. He puts all effort into putting up an unperturbed face for him.

"The ghost appeared here last night," K says.

Tantra's confusion makes itself visible on his face.

"He was in the kitchen, drinking water."

Tantra remains silent.

"You've known about it all this time, haven't you? You don't need to hide the truth from me. A headless ghost does not frighten me. I mean, I have a pretty good idea as to who it might be."

Eyes widening, Tantra stares back at K.

"Do you mean? Do you mean, sir, that you know who the ghost is?"

"Yes, I do. Before I came here, the same ghost made an appearance at the Holy Igitur Monastery. Murdered a man named Abir. But I brought you here, Tantra, because I want you to tell me something. The previous director—Bose—did he know about the ghost?"

Tantra gives K a very uneasy look.

"Yes," he says.

"And the director before him?"

"Yes. I am sure that both of them knew. But is it true? Could it really be the ghost of Darko Dachilko? The man has been dead for seven hundred years."

"I see. So, Tantra, I want you to tell me the truth now. When you told me that Mr. Bose had gone to Planet Bosch, that was a lie, wasn't it?"

"Yes, sir. You are correct."

The pallid color of shock paints Tantra's face.

Things are finally coming together in K's mind.

"Bose was strangled to death by the ghost, wasn't he?"

"You are absolutely correct. How did you know?"

"The victim at the monastery was killed in the same way. Six-fingered hands strangled Abir by his throat."

Tantra leans forward as his face turns pale.

"Just as they strangled Mr. Bose."

According to Tantra, the director prior to Bose also died the same way. Prior to K's arrival, besides the director, there were four other members of the Planet Bosch Research Center. But after the director's death, they all fled, not telling anyone where they were going.

"Actually, both the previous two directors were quite into the study of Darko Dachilko. Could this be connected, somehow?"

"I'm more interested in the connection between this mysterious Planet Bosch and Darko Dachilko. Do you know anything about this?"

"No, I know nothing about that. Even just speaking the name of that heretic gives me the shivers."

Recalling his conversations with the late Abir, K remembers that, just like Tantra, he too was quite frightened about something. But in the end, Abir never got the chance to explain to K what exactly so frightened him. Abir once mentioned that the Papal Court had restricted access to any information pertaining to Planet Bosch, formally designating it all classified. What secrets are they keeping? Is there some connection to the appearances of the ghost of Darko Dachilko?

K contemplates his next words.

"Tantra, I have just a few more questions for you. You told me that the funds for our salaries and the maintenance of this building are taken out of the budget for Refugee Relief. Do you know who is in charge of this program? Where can I find him?"

Whatever doubts or concerns he may have still held, Tantra decides to give K all the information he seeks.

5

Finally, some answers. Just as K suspected, the answers to his questions are to be found in the Refugee Relief Center. When he first comes face-to-face with the person in charge, the man's initial refusal to say anything at all does not surprise K. He already knew that the man has received orders from above to keep his mouth shut. But K presses on, and once he convinces the man that he's already figured out at least some part of picture, he comes about, telling K all he wants to know.

From this man, K learns that the ghost of Darko Dachilko has been on a killing spree, not only at the Holy Igitur Monastery and the Planet Bosch Research Center, but also at City Hall and the Papal Court.

"It seems to target people linked to the research on Planet Bosch in one way or another," he tells K with trepidation. "The authorities understood what a serious matter these incidents were, but they thought it best not to inform the general public, thinking that the ghost of Darko Dachilko opposes the spread of the knowledge of Planet Bosch to the citizens of our Holy Empire."

"Now it makes sense. So, let me see if I've got this right—while we were at the Holy Igitur Monastery, a secret gag order was implemented?"

"That's exactly right. That's why no one at City Hall or the Papal Court would tell you anything. We received a communiqué from the Papal Court prohibiting the discussion of any matter in connection with Planet Bosch. In fact, we even had to clean out all traces of the agency in charge of the research center."

K gives him a puzzled look.

"But wouldn't it make more sense to close down the Planet Bosch Research Center altogether?"

"Yes, you're right, of course. To tell you the truth, this is something I don't understand either. Do you know why they didn't do just that?"

Now it's K's turn to answer questions.

"I wonder. I certainly don't have any answers. Nothing made sense when I went to City Hall. All I know is that once I gave up, some kid came out of nowhere, bringing me my appointment papers."

"Oh, really?"

The man's face lights up as he listens to K's account of recent events.

"Actually, I read your letter of appointment as a part of the approval process for your salary. Everything looked to be in order, so after making a copy, I sent it up the chain recommending approval. Oddly enough, I still haven't heard anything back from them, so it does seem like all of this is being kept under wraps. My guess is that the Papal Court still wants you to secretly continue your research on Planet Bosch, while keeping it all outside the official channels. I mean, with all the trouble with the ghost these past months, that only seems prudent."

The man fixes his gaze on K's face.

That seems to makes sense.

K appears to have found some satisfaction with these answers, at least for now. But this little sliver of insight turns out to be short-lived. Once he gives the matter some more thought following his return to the office, his doubts return, now more overpowering than ever. In the end, all of it is nothing more than idle speculation. The truth he must recognize is that none of this makes sense at all.

For one thing, K has done nothing since he first arrived here other than sit at his desk all day, without any specific tasks to accomplish. If the Papal Court wants him to serve officially as the director of the research center, surely specific instructions should have come by now. But no such thing has reached him. His salary has been approved. That's it. Nothing else whatsoever. And so, once again, K returns to ponder these riddles, still unable to come up with any answers that make sense to him.

A few days later, Hoffman contacts K.

Not once had the telephone on his desk rung since K first arrived here. When it rings for the first time, it takes no time for K to somehow surmise that it might be Hoffman on the line.

"Hi! K? It's me? Do you remember?" Hoffman shouts from the other end of the line.

"Yes, Hoffman. It's been a while. How have you been? Busy at work, I assume?"

"Oh, no, not at all," he replies. "After we parted ways, I didn't end up going to the Sacred Genetics Research Division after all."

"What? Why?"

"I fully intended to go. But on the way there, something seemed off to me. So, I followed my instincts. I asked to be taken to Central Station and boarded a train right away. I went straight home. I've been hiding here ever since."

This news unnerves K.

"What are you talking about? Hoffman, why don't we get a meal somewhere? It'd be better than talking on the phone."

"Sorry, K, that won't work for me. It's been two days since I've been back, but I've been getting a bad feeling about all this again. I only came back to confirm something that had crossed my mind. But now, it's time for me to get out of here."

"Just what is going on? You've completely lost me."

"The incident. Remember, at the monastery?"

"Just as I thought."

"As you thought? Did something happen at your end too?"

"Yeah, the ghost made an appearance over here too."

"Oh."

A heavy silence hangs on the other end of the line.

"Hello? Hello?" came K's impatient words.

"Yeah." Hoffman's voice quivers. "So, I just thought it might be best if I warn you too. I'm calling from the station right now. K, our lives might be in danger. That ghost of Darko Dachilko, I think he's after us. Listen, K, listen to what I'm telling you. Remember all those people at the monastery? No one else is left. Everyone's gone missing."

"Seriously?"

"It's true. Several bodies with their necks wrung like Abir's have been found. All the rest of them must have met a similar fate. Well I should get to my train. Maybe I still have a chance of getting away. But what about you? What are you going to do?"

"Me? I don't know."

"Well, give it some thought. Think up a plan for how you're going to deal with things. Take care of yourself."

Hoffman hangs up the phone.

Stunned, K does not move from his seat. A strange sensation

sweeps over him, as if black curtains drape right before his eyes, increasingly drawing him into their darkness.

A voice jolts him back to the world.

"K?"

Martha stands behind K, jasmine flowers draped around her neck. K's face conveys his relief at the sight of her. No longer is she a mere stranger to him.

"Those are beautiful."

"Can we talk?"

"Of course. Where's your father?"

"He went out. To the market, I think. Probably won't be back until the evening. It's hot in here. Shall we go to the back room? It's much cooler in there."

Martha's eyes glitter with moisture. She holds K's hands in hers, guiding his fingers under her dress, inviting them inside. She is already wet.

The pair step into the dim light of Martha's room. Not a moment passes before they fall into each other's arms. The carnal pleasures of their lovemaking continue until well past the setting of the sun.

No longer can K climb out of the depths of the depravity he has fallen into. Night after night, he devotes himself to his debauchery with Martha. It has become his only relief from his growing fear of the haunting of the ghost of Darko Dachilko.

Still, K remains ill at ease. It's a ghost he will have to face, after all. There's simply no getting around that problem. In fact, more than just a mere ghost, Darko Dachilko has the ability to freely jump the streams of the various flows of time, possessing the knowledge of the techniques to appear and disappear through hyperspatial dimensions. What chance does he have against such a being? Only Martha can be his salvation now. So enchanting, so intoxicating are the pleasures of her flesh that when K is with her, he can leave behind all his fears, even if only for a moment.

No doubt, the growing intimacy between Martha and K must have gratified Tantra. Thinking that K's relationship with his daughter might secure his own position, his persistent requests increasingly become more brazen. Does he think he has K in the palm of his hand? Is that why he repeatedly pesters him for some spending money?

Of course, this annoys K to no end. But for some reason, he finds himself unable to simply shut him down. Perhaps he worries that addressing his problems with Tantra will also damage his relationship with his daughter. No, it isn't worth risking Tantra taking it out on her should he throw a conniption. Besides, the stresses of living in fear of Darko Dachilko's ghost must get to him too, making his behavior more pathetic than anything else. Pestering K for money to buy the bottle of the tequila he so wants, just so he can drink himself to sleep every night—that may be the only thing that lets him momentarily take his mind off this constant fear.

There is no escaping their fate now, no place for them to hide. No matter where they go, the ghost of Darko Dachilko is sure to follow them. This place has now become their prison. But what a depraved prison it is! An administrator drunk out of his mind by the middle of day and a director without any work to do but indulge himself in the sweet charms of a woman's body.

Their lives carry on for a month. Then two months. With the passing of these months, little by little, K realizes just how far he has fallen. This isn't who he was before. The K who completed the Sacred Service Examination now seems like a different young man altogether, one who embraced lofty ideals, one full of ambition and a clear purpose to his life.

Things are different now. I wouldn't even dare say the great name of The Holy Igitur anymore. Innocence and purity are now things of the past, replaced by an altogether different kind of man, a beast of a man.

Depression and disgust at himself fill K's thoughts at times.

If I could at least truly love Martha, then perhaps there could still be some hope for me.

But the truth is that K feels no such affection for her in his heart.

The purposeless passing of each idle day would have surely continued had an opportunity to learn more about Darko Dachilko's secrets not presented itself to K.

One day, Tantra brings back an old book, telling K that he happened to stumble upon it while he was out and about in the market. Just one glance at the title of the book is all it takes for K to know that he wants it. Seeing K's newly aroused curiosity about the book, Tantra tells him that it's a very expensive book indeed. Of course, Tantra is just up to his usual schemes. Knowing him, he would have bargained the price of the book down to nearly nothing when he purchased it. But K cannot be bothered with such trivial concerns now, so he just hands over the money without a word of complaint.

The Enigmatic Heretics, by G. G. Bervera—K recalls hearing about this author during one of the discussions about Darko Dachilko with Mullin and the others at the Holy Igitur Monastery. He gets right to it, examining its pages without delay. Bookworms have chewed through quite a few of the pages of the book, a telltale trace of its age, having likely been published more than three hundred years ago. It's a shame that K does not have the complete text, but still, some two-thirds of it remain legible.

Though it employs a fictive style of narration, much of the content is supposedly based on factual accounts. According to the story, Darko Dachilko once loved a disciple of his teachings, a young woman named Barbara. Quite a stunning beauty, she was the youngest daughter of a wealthy family.

The author Bervera describes the young woman:

> She was such a delicate maiden, possessing the elegance of a fragrant white jasmine. Always, she wore her hair long. Always dressed in white. Always sitting alone contemplating the garden.

Frightening incidents took place when Barbara rejected Darko Dachilko's marriage proposal after having fallen in love with another, younger man. All of a sudden, the life of the delicate beauty was snuffed out by the hands of an unknown assailant. But that wasn't the end of it. Some days later, her body was dug up from her grave.

Grave robberies were not an uncommon occurrence back in those days. Strangely, it wasn't just the many valuables entombed with her that were taken from her grave but also her corpse itself.

While the identity of both her murderer and her grave robber remained a mystery, rumors at the time suggested that it was none other than Darko Dachilko himself.

To this day, the truth of this matter remains a mystery. At the time though, all manner of speculation about supernatural phenomena surrounded Darko Dachilko, so it was easy to draw the conclusion that Darko Dachilko himself stole the young woman's body for some nefarious purpose. Some believe that he had mastered the secrets of life and death, that he was actually over three hundred years old. Some believe that he intended to use this magical knowledge to realize his romantic desires by reviving her body through some strange ritual. He may have succeeded too, as records of his subsequent trial indicated that several eyewitnesses testified to seeing him conversing with a young woman around this time.

The book continues in a style that melds a romanticized story with a critical undertone:

Whispers and rumors talk of Barbara being revived every night at the "House of Osiris" (origin unknown), transformed into an elaborate mechanical doll made to do whatever Darko Dachilko desired. All this happened in a secret room built out of gold and mirrors and equipped with an apparatus that secreted a special gas that could bring the breath of life to those who had passed away. This room had no entrances. Totally cut off from the rest of the world, only Darko Dachilko himself could come and go through his secret mastery of time and space. Only a handful of his close servants even had knowledge of this room.

One time, Darko Dachilko spoke to one of these servants.

"My lover weeps and begs me to let her fall into an eternal slumber," he said without guile. "But I have no intention of doing this, for her great beauty must be preserved for all eternity."

"But, Master, is this not against God's will?" one of his servants inquired. "Is this not in violation of the laws of nature?"

"You are correct," Darko Dachilko answered. "And this is why it will bring about my own tragic and violent end. God will punish me in the same way I punish Barbara now."

"What sort of punishment?"

"Immortality. Even if my body is hacked into pieces, I will find no rest. My own future has been revealed to me. I have foreseen my own fate. Knowing now my true place of birth, I will create a true and proper grave for Barbara. It will be the green paradise that we all seek. It is the place that Barbara had always wanted to see while she still lived. As heaven is a place of our dreams and ideals, its existence is impossible in this world, but as a proof of my love for her, I will plant the seed that will create the place that no one can yet imagine."

"Is it like the brilliant white Taj Mahal that the Indian king took many years to create for his beloved queen?"

"No."

"Then, is it a special tomb for the dead, like one of the pyramids in northern Africa?"

"No."

"Where will you create it?" the servant asked. "Please tell me at least this much."

But Darko Dachilko simply smiled without ever answering the question.

It so happens that Bervera also met a violent end.

6

That night, tragedy strikes the lives of those at the research center.

This is what happens.

Tantra returns home late at night quite thoroughly intoxicated. He must have consumed quite a bit of tequila using the money that he managed to weasel out of K for the purchase of the book. Violent drunk that he is, he starts a commotion downstairs.

Martha flees up to K's room, hands cupping her teary-eyed face. For a long time, she sits by the window saying nothing as she continues to sob.

K finally asks Martha what happened. At first, she refuses to give him an answer. Only when he presses her does she begin to speak.

"Tantra is not really my father," she tells K.

Back when Martha was still a child, the long drought brought many deaths to her hometown, among them, her real parents. Traveling with the throngs of refugees, she ended up finding her way to the capital. But not knowing a single soul there, she came very close to dying of hunger. Only Tantra's intervention saved her life.

At first, Martha thought him a kind old man. But soon enough, she would understand what a rotten soul her stepfather possessed. Tantra raised her and used her as his servant. He also used her in other ways as he pleased.

From a very young age, he made her do all the housework. But things did not stop here. When she became a little older, Tantra demanded far more dreadful things, becoming violent and losing control of all reason whenever he had too much to drink.

"I was just thirteen then, still a child. I didn't understand what was happening. But when I refused him, he beat me to a pulp."

K listens to her story intently.

"You've figured it out, haven't you? Yes, it's shameful, I know. My stepfather was my first man."

Tears again flow from her swollen eyes.

"Whenever he wanted to drink, he would bring strange men to our home. Then, he would let them spend one night with me in exchange for money. Yes, it's against the law. But there is always a way around that. He'd just bribe some city officials with my body. Even this position he has now, he got by using me."

As K listens to Martha's story, an uncontrollable rage burns within him, a rage beyond any reason. He does not direct this hatred to just Tantra's atrocities. No, this hatred, this anger—he feels it for all the filth of all the human beings in the world. That is when it dawns on him that even Martha now disgusts him. What is this rage that consumes him? Is it hatred? Or is it jealousy that he feels?

This woman! She gave herself to not only all the directors of this research center! To countless other men!

K can no longer stand the thought of it. He has no choice but to accept the truth now. He has always hated every single human being in this world.

"Even now, my stepfather, he forces himself upon . . ."

A fit of sobbing cuts off the rest of Martha's words.

"But in the end you let him do it, didn't you? Just like a beast. You screamed howls of pleasure."

Still in tears, Martha nods in response.

"But I couldn't help it! Please! Please don't blame me! I couldn't help it!"

That moment, a sudden pallor sweeps across Martha's face. Her eyes widen, turning almost hollow. A pair of ghostly arms appear from K's sides. They reach for Martha's neck.

K awakens from a deep slumber the next morning.

Officers from the Bureau of Investigations mill about the room of the research center. Noticing K coming back to his senses, they quickly proceed to question him.

"So you're finally awake, sir. Could you perhaps tell us exactly what happened here?"

K repeatedly hits the side of his aching head with his fists.

"It doesn't look like you're quite fully recovered yet. I don't blame you. The administrator and his daughter were both killed last night. We found you passed out here in the kitchen. You looked like you were reaching toward the water jug. Did you see anything last night?

"No, I didn't."

"Well, maybe he got you too."

"He? Who do you mean?"

"The ghost. The ghost with six fingers."

"Six-fingered?"

Hearing this startles K, causing him to look at both his opened hands to make sure he did in fact have only five fingers on each one.

"That's right. Markings from six fingers are clearly visible on the necks of both bodies. I think we can rule you out as a suspect."

Hearing the officer's explanation so overwhelms K with shock that for a moment he thinks he may pass out again.

"Would it be possible to see the bodies?" K asks.

"I guess that shouldn't be a problem. We haven't had the chance to take them away yet. But why the interest?"

"No particular reason, really. Just that . . ."

"Oh, of course you'd want to see them one last time before they're buried. I understand how you feel. Follow me."

The officer guides K to the corpses. Pulling off the sheet covering the bodies to display Martha's dead face, he is almost relieved to see how peaceful she looks. But her beautiful face is frozen in place. A closer inspection reveals the exact same finger marks he saw on Abir's neck clearly imprinted on her skin as well.

The officers briefly question K, but it ends up being a mere formality. In fact, the officer endeavors to communicate precisely this point to him. K's status as a Sacred Service officer must play a part in it. That much is obvious from the officer's attitude.

For the most part, K cooperates with the officers. He tells the inspector everything he knows. Except for that one detail, of course, that one detail he wishes he could just forget, as if it were little more than a bad dream.

Did these events set things back into motion? It certainly seems that way, as soon after a letter arrives at K's doorstep. Written at the top of the document are the words "Notice of Appointment."

"Confirmation of your assignment to Planet Bosch. Please depart within twenty-four hours from Igitur Spaceport—The Papal Court."

7

It is finally time for K to depart this world. He makes his way toward the space terminal that houses the vessels bound for interstellar destinations, located all the way out in the middle of the vast wasteland known as the eastern desert. The Papal Court sends a car around to pick up K. Once the car exits the oasis city of Igitur, it meets a red-brown landscape extending in every direction. Every inch of it glistens under the glare of the severe sunlight, with just a single, lonely asphalt road slicing across the unbroken brown landscape, extending into the distance.

The driver races along the road like a man possessed. In this heat, the engine must be kept cool as much as possible by running the air through it. K spots a weathered ruin on a distant hill, a green flag fluttering atop its structure. Must be the military using the place as a rest stop before continuing on in pursuit of a gang of outlaws.

K sinks into the passenger seat, now drenched in the ceaseless pouring of his sweat. Before him, the sky glows in a cloudless blue. A haze of heat rises above the parched ground.

The previous night was a sleepless one for K. His mind tossed and turned with his recollections of all that has happened, making him slip in and out of consciousness, in and out of dreams. He sees a vision of peeling off a transparent filmy membrane, one layer after another, like a molting cicada casting off its old shell. But with each layer he peels off, the world seems to slip away further. Once one layer comes off, another world reveals itself underneath, only to again lose all color. This ceaseless meaningless repetition slowly drives K toward madness.

The road to the spaceport continues forward seemingly without end. Suddenly, K's car screeches to a halt. After muttering some expletives, the driver pulls a worn-out rag from somewhere, drenching it in water. An engine burnout, perhaps?

K steps out of the car.

Corpulent desert plants still thrive out here. K finds a decrepit human corpse at his feet. All moisture sucked dry by the arid air, the corpse has almost completely mummified. Just a few hairs on its head remain. Nothing else left of the rest of its body but parched skin and bones. Only a matter of time before any living being abandoned alone out here withers and dies, its last few breaths quickly drying up like the little remaining skin on the skeleton.

K twists his face at the sight of the corpse's hollowed-out eyes looking straight ahead into the endless distance. Here, in its final resting place, it sees nothing more of this world.

K's thoughts scatter into so many pieces.

Just where exactly am I going?

After everything that's happened, even Planet Bosch no longer seems all that important to K. No, more than just that, every-thing in this world has lost all meaning to him. If, somehow, he manages to find something meaningful to him, this too will be tenuous at best. So why is he still trying to hold on to whatever fleeting, whatever ephemeral meaning he can find in this world?

Why is that?

When did I start seeing the world this way?

Is it because Martha has departed from this world?

Could I have truly loved her? No, that can't be.

Had the driver not called out to K just then, perhaps his mind would have slipped even further into chaos. Their vehicle is now running again. It is time to continue onward, leaving behind them the corpse slowly submerging into the desert sands. The ground slopes up a hill strewn with dry earth and reddish-brown rocks.

Soon, I will launch into outer space. Soon, I will leave behind all the troubles on this planet Earth.

Rocky hills jutting upwards toward the sky surround the vast area where the space terminal waits. K presents his papers at the gate as they enter the terminal. Turning around, he watches the car double back toward the capital. It speeds into the distance, soon disappearing into the horizon.

K waits for a long time within the steaming-hot inspection area. With nothing better to do, he starts a conversation with a man who has the look of a traveling merchant. The man appears so pale he may as well be a walking corpse.

"Where to?"

"Me? To Loulan. How about you?"

"Farther off. I guess some thousand light-years away."

"Well, that's certainly quite a distance you're going. Is this your first time traveling to space?"

"Yes."

"Same here. It's going to be a lonely journey. It would be great if we were together on the same vessel for a part of the journey at least."

"I think we will be. Until Loulan, that is."

"There are farther interstellar routes beyond there?"

"There is indeed. It's known as the Taklamakan Route."

"Oh."

"It's the route beyond the Space Desert."

A khaki-colored military vehicle finally arrives to pick up K and the merchant. For some reason, the vehicle looks to K like a funeral car.

The terminal's installations glimmer in silver. They go through the routine boarding process, with an officer in a green shirt and shorts checking their papers.

"It's hot, isn't it?" says the officer.

"Yes, it sure is." K answers.

The two of them are the only passengers on the vessel when the shuttle rocket launches upwards, making its way toward the orbital station, much like a giant phallus ready to violate the heavens.

MECHANICAL DOLL

1

The phallus of a rocket penetrates the vulva of the orbiting galactic transport, sending throbbing vibrations throughout the vessel. A buzzer goes off inside the ship, startling K out of his mesmerized gaze at the spectacular sight of the docking procedure between the two spacecraft. He watches from the observation deck as his rocket ship slips its head completely inside the larger vessel's orifice. She slowly envelops the transparent windows of the observation deck fully within the walls of her tunnel, secreting quite a bit of lubricating oil before everything finally comes to a complete stop.

"We have completed our docking procedures," an attendant announces to K and the merchant. "Please proceed to transfer to your galactic transport."

The two release their seat belts. Once they rise from their seats, the officer escorts them to the bow of the ship.

As they make their way to the front, the officer informs K that four flights are scheduled to travel all the way to Loulan every year. It's a considerable trek across space to get there, which is almost five hundred light-years beyond the edge of the solar system.

"Mostly, it's just transporting goods," the tall attendant explains. "We have Karnak-type vessels in service on these routes. Did you see the ship from the observation deck? What a rundown piece of junk! It's probably been in use since the time they first mapped out the Loulan route. No way you can ever get me to travel in these things."

K nods in silence. The attendant is right. The pallid ship does appear rather decrepit. The less said about it, the better.

"You know, that ship does look kind of misshapen," says the merchant.

"Misshapen? Oh yes, of course. But don't you worry. Once she's satiated, she will become beautiful again."

The attendant explains that materials akin to human tissue constitute the body of the ship. She will again expand to her proper shape once she absorbs a full capacity of "cargo." Hence, the pipe attached to the side of the ship, feeding the "cargo" into her womb.

"So what sort of 'cargo' do you feed into her?" asks the merchant.

"Protoplasm," comes the attendant's curt answer.

Not grasping what sounds to him like jargon used only among the crew, K asks for a fuller explanation. But in place of one, all he receives in return from the attendant is a smirk. He says nothing more.

When K and the merchant arrive at the ship's bow, the ship's crew hand them a simple inspection questionnaire to be filled out by all the boarding passengers. Nothing unusual—just the standard personal information such as name and date of birth—but nonetheless required to obtain permission to board the vessel. K makes short work of these forms, then proceeds to the next step in the boarding procedures, undergoing decontamination.

Inspections of the merchant continue for quite a while, leaving the man looking bewildered. As K watches him alternate between shrugging his shoulders and muttering something to the crew, he wonders if he hasn't tried to smuggle some prohibited item onboard.

"See you in a bit," K says as he pushes open the bulkhead door.

K enters the ship's "birth canal," a red fleshy tunnel leading into the passenger cabin, the ship's "womb."

The air is cool and damp inside the cabin. K finds some twenty or so passengers who boarded ahead of him, men and women of all ages scattered about the many rows of seats. Or to be more precise, they aren't so much seats as they are pods in a shape that reminds K of caskets, giving the whole space the appearance of a morgue. A uniformed steward assigns K one of the "seats" while informing him of the vessel's name, *Hades*. Evidently, its sister ship in the class is called *Ghost*.

"Is there no ship by the name of *Heaven*?" K jokes.

The curly-haired and dark-skinned steward can only shake his head.

"No, sir," he says with a very serious scowl. "However, there is a ship called *Soul*."

Every single passenger onboard is bound for Loulan. K asks about his further connection to Planet Bosch. However, he receives only a vague and unhelpful response.

"Beyond Loulan, you will be traveling via the 'Sacred Route.' That's not something we can tell you anything about," the steward tells K. "Ships launch on that route on an irregular schedule, so it's best to look into it after we arrive in Loulan."

The steward's answer disconcerts K. He tries inquiring again, this time with a slight tone of annoyance as he keeps the attendant from going back to his duties. But it is to no avail.

Finally, the chimes ring to announce the ship's imminent launch. Just in time, the merchant rushes into the "womb" in a feverish haste, planting himself in the seat next to K's.

"Please fasten your seat belts and secure your bodies," the attendant tells them.

The other passengers are already buckled in. Following these instructions places them in a position identical to lying in a coffin. Once everyone is in position, the attendant walks through the cabin, shoving something similar to candy inside each passenger's mouth. Its flavor reminds K of fish oil.

The attendant comes around again, this time taking a hand-held canister to each passenger's face, spraying them with some kind of decontamination fluid. All this must have looked like an odd kind of ritual to anyone watching from the outside.

"Do you know what all this is for?" the merchant asks K.

"Not sure myself. The ship will go into Karnak navigation, so maybe it's some sort of safety precaution?"

Of course, this is mere speculation. In truth, K has no clue whatsoever.

The ship begins its voyage, shortly accelerating to a speed a tenth of the speed of light, quickly leaving Earth and its solar system behind it.

2

Since K was secretly looking forward to admiring the view of the cosmos from within his ship, he is quite disappointed to learn that the ship has no windows in the passenger cabin at all. Evidently, Karnak vessels make use of a strictly utilitarian design, entirely lacking in any consideration of the passenger's enjoyment of space travel.

Then again, it's probably the least of their concerns, what with all the complexities of Karnak navigation.

The merchant, looking rather anxious, interrupts K's thoughts.

"Hey, do you know anything about this so-called ghost phenomenon on Karnak vessels."

"Well . . ."

"It's kind of worrying, you know."

"The attendant told me that there's nothing to worry about," K says, pretending to know what he's talking about.

The truth is that the phenomenon known as "Karnak ghosting" is still not very well understood. One explanation—perhaps the most plausible among them—suggests that the phenomenon is an effect of the passage of matter into an incorporeal state during Karnak navigation. At the moment of migration from the corporeal to the incorporeal field, flesh and spirit (normally conjoined in a single being) decompose from each other, effectively allowing the consciousness to separate from the physical body.

Right on cue, piercing alarm bells go off within K's consciousness. While his grasp of the situation is murky at best, he is absolutely certain that this means the *Hades* is now approaching the speed of light.

Here we go!

Between fear and excitement, K steels himself for what comes next. Soon, the *Hades* will exceed the speed of light, thrusting K and every single passenger into an incorporeal state.

Nausea. Blood shooting through his eyes. Objects twisting and turning red before his eyes. Pulse racing. Head aching. Cerebral pressure building. His skull on the verge of exploding. Then, an awakening from a vivid dream.

K's consciousness wrests itself from within, turning him inside out. It emerges from its cocoon, only to lose all substance as it speeds away. A second consciousness hatches within him, then flies off and dissipates. Now, a third consciousness is ready to come into being. And another. And another. This metamorphosis repeats in succession with no end in sight.

Every individual responds to the experience of Karnak forces decomposing their consciousness in their own way. Still seated next to K, the merchant appears to be on death's door, desperately panting and trying to catch his breath. Nearby, a beautiful young woman struggles with what appear to be red flares shooting out of various parts of her body. A married couple stiffen up their bodies so much that they may as well have been petrified into stone. Children's bodies stretch out so much they look just about ready to tear apart. Up or down, front or back—there is no telling anymore. The chaos of the cabin's interior is already beyond any untangling. Time itself loses all meaning. Things that already happened turn around and flow back toward the present. Times yet to come freeze in place, leaving the now hanging up in the air. Total chaos reigns.

The cabin might as well have been a picture of hell.

All of sudden, the fear of breaking apart, of being at once momentary and infinite, disappears. K soon regains his composure. It may be that his now-liberated consciousness is finally adjusting to the experience of incorporeal time.

Relieved, K savors the sensation of fatigue beyond anything he can fathom.

Is time itself disintegrating?

All matter—anything and everything one could think of—has completely decorporealized. Whatever properties they once possessed have now lost all meaning. Only their shadows—traces of things left behind—remain as mere afterimages burning into K's retinas.

What is there to be found on the other side of the barrier of the speed of light? Does objective time, accelerated, still pass there? It no longer matters, for K is now fully under the regime of subjective time, transformed into some kind of ghost, into something incorporeal, into something fully free. He enjoys this taste of an almost ecstatic sense of liberation. Even as his back remains firmly planted in his seat, he lets loose his consciousness from his body, exploring a universe where space and time have twisted inside out.

K watches in fascination the range of different experiences of incorporeal freedom on display in the cabin. The merchant still remains pinned in his seat, his whole body stretching thin, giving him the appearance of a brocade portrait. His shrill mind struggles in vain to escape from his body. But something imperceptible keeps pulling it back in. A woman emits a green aura after having lost her consciousness, which has dispersed into a mist now that her body has entered an incorporeal state. K spots one of her children's projections floating about. In a single bite, he swallows her up, savoring her scent of milk. She must have been the younger of the two charming sisters. K searches for her older sister, quickly pouncing once he finds her elsewhere in the cabin. This time, it's the scent of candy he relishes. He feels completely satiated.

K passes right through the walls of the cabin, finding his way into the ship's cockpit. The pilot radiates green flares of light, his face unseen except for its glowing, hyperspatially distorted outline as he sits before the instrument panel. Is he smiling? Or is he crying?

"Listen closely . . . can you hear it?" says the pilot.

Indeed, K does hear the sound of music.

"That's the music of the heavens. Orion . . ."

"Yeah."

Is the constellation of Orion sending out into space a radio signal of some kind? K loses himself in the melody of celebration. He lets the music overwhelm him until this perpetual present, this endless incorporeal experience of the now, eventually comes to its end.

3

Following a series of hyperspace jumps, the ship finally restores itself to a corporeal state. A sensation similar to a hangover hits everyone onboard, stiffening up their bodies, as if enveloped by a bulky carapace shell. Their minds lose all flexibility and freedom, hardening back into a material substance.

An attendant comes around to check on any injuries among the passengers. As far as K can tell, not everyone manages to materialize completely, leaving the attendants to haul out their bodies for disposal in space. They bring a drink of black liquid for everyone to imbibe, explaining that the drink relieves the "sea sickness."

As soon as the *Hades* begins its deceleration by slowly rolling onto its side, the attendants announce to everyone that they will shortly begin the final approach to Loulan.

K calls the attendant over.

"I'd like to watch our touchdown. Would it be possible to arrange such a thing?"

"Of course, sir. Please follow me to the observation deck."

Perhaps realizing that K is an officer of the Sacred Service, he responds with an air of profound deference. By the time K makes his way up the ladder onto the observation deck, the *Hades* has already begun its gentle descent into a city that glimmers in an emerald radiance.

Although it is the middle of the day in Loulan, darkness nonetheless fills its heavens, with only a few scattered stars visible here and there, faint flickers forming constellations different from those that can be seen on Earth. Only a dim light circles the edge of the massive circular saucer floating in one corner of the darkened sky, shimmering like a total solar eclipse. This must be Loulan's famous black sun.

The *Hades* too is painted black, descending through the atmosphere like a dark raven with its wings extended as it approaches the spaceport. Once more, K turns his eyes toward the dark sky, drawn to it by a deep crack of absolute black in the shape of a woman's genitalia slicing across the heavens.

"That must be the space desert."

K stares at the black rift in the sky, feeling the gap seemingly engulf his very spirit, as if his mere gaze upon it is all it takes to instill in him a deep sense of fear that threatens his existence to its very core.

The Taklamakan Space Desert.

K continues to fix his gaze on the rift, on the border marking the meeting point between existence and its negation.

A deep feeling of shame wells up within K.

All living beings are born into sin.

Why does he feel this way? Is this rift of black, this chasm of negation, the reason?

Bathed in the dark negative energy of this chasm, our sinful ways come to light.

"Upon traveling to Loulan, everyone becomes a philosopher."

K recalls hearing such words, but he can't quite place where he did.

Was it Hoffman who told him this? If only he were here to see this. If only he hadn't gone into hiding . . .

The *Hades* continues its descent through the atmosphere of Loulan, beginning its final approach toward the emerald gleam of the now-visible city.

The sight of the city of Loulan is right before K's eyes, appearing like an underexposed photograph, like a darkened underworld.

Is this the doing of the dark rift above in the heavens? Could it be possible? Could all these waves of negative energy emanating from the other side of the heavens undermine the very foundations of existence on this side of the universe?

K can only wonder.

The question of why matter exists at all is one that's been the subject of much debate within the field of Sacred Ontology. It's not a subject that K himself has mastered, but because it's a foundational field covered in the Sacred Service Examination, he has at least dabbled in its more basic concepts. As far as K understands, one of the field's central premises is the idea that Existence is not something that can be assumed a priori but instead is merely an artifact of phenomenological experience. So, one might say that the negative energy emanating from this darkened rift hanging above the skies of Loulan serves as clear evidence of the theories of Sacred Ontology. Here, objects only have a weak sense of Being. They may still behave as they usually do, but they take on the phenomenological appearance of something akin to flickering images on a screen.

Swimming in the waves of this negative energy, K drowns in feelings of apprehension as his very being is reduced to little more than an incorporeal reflection, to a shadow cast on a wall.

For the first time, K finally makes sense of it all.

In a process known as "negative interference" within the field of Sacred Ontology, fields of negative energy introduce a countervailing force to the field of phenomenological energy. If the phenomenological energy field functions as the plane of existence for the world we perceive, negative energy attempts to counteract it. Caught between these two countervailing forces of Being and Nothingness, those in Loulan struggle within a state of limbo.

4

The *Hades* comes to a sudden stop. Even the faint vibrations coming from the ship's engine room cease, replaced by the buzz of the city from outside the ship. Or to be more precise, it is more like the murmurs of the city, as men dragging shadows that look like disembodied souls scamper about the spaceport to secure the ship's moorings.

The passengers wait inside the ship for some time before the pilot finally issues the signal to disembark. K follows the other passengers as they all alight onto the spaceport. Ramparts sur-round the city of Loulan, and mounted atop them are several large antiaircraft cannons trained upward toward the dark, empty skies.

After undergoing a routine inspection, K steps inside the lobby of the space terminal. The merchant walks with him, con-tinuing to keep him company.

He turns toward K.

"Would you care to stop by my daughter's place?"

The merchant gestures toward the other side of the terminal lobby. There stands a young woman waiting to pick him up.

"That's my daughter," the merchant tells K. "She left some five years ago, and she's been here ever since."

The girl glances at K, offering him a vague smile. She is a beautiful woman, though the heavy makeup thickly layered on her face makes her look almost pallid.

"Welcome to Loulan. It would be our pleasure to have you as a guest in my house."

K nods as he gives the girl a long look.

"My name is Ellen," she whispers in K's ear.

The approach of a slender man interrupts them. He passes K a note while casting a suspicious look at all of them. Oddly, he looks just like the rickshaw puller back at the capital.

K glances at the note. The words on the elegant parchment affixed with an official seal read: "Please accept my invitation—the Lord of Castle Loulan."

K turns to the merchant.

"Sadly, it looks like I must decline your invitation," he says. "The lord of the manor wishes to see me."

"Oh."

Disappointment is written all over the merchant's face. He looks to his daughter.

"Well, then, shall we?"

Ellen glances at K, flashing him a brief knowing smile, before she and her father head off together.

Still standing in place, K lets his eyes follow the girl's lithe fig-ure as she walks away. She pauses right before going through the exit of the terminal lobby. One more turn toward K to meet his gaze and give him another smile. Quite a seductive smile indeed.

Once K comes to his senses, he focuses his attention on the slender man.

"So, will you be taking me to the castle?" K asks him.

"Yep. That's what I do. I'm to bring you to the castle in my rickshaw."

The man hastens to lead K toward the exit. They step out of the terminal to a large plaza surrounded by tall stone buildings. A somber feeling and a strong odor of mold hang over everything. They make their way to the man's rickshaw, whose attached hood casts a faint, long shadow.

Ever since he saw the city glimmering in the color emerald from high above inside the Karnak vessel, he has been looking forward to seeing it up close. But all there is to be seen from the ground is a voluminous mass of black shadows. Perhaps the emerald glow of the city of Loulan when viewed from afar is merely an effect of its surrounding atmosphere. If the beautifully luminous outlines of the craggy mountains visible in the distance are any indication, that would seem to be the case.

The three-wheeled rickshaw is such an old fragile thing it looks ready to fall apart as soon as anyone rides in it. K steps aboard anyway, while the driver sits astride on the saddle and takes hold of the angular handlebars. He lifts his body and begins to pedal, struggling with the weight for a bit, until the street takes a downhill slope.

Walls of buildings block off both sides of the street. Only a few people are out and about. The rickshaw rattles over the street's uneven cobblestone surface as it descends the hill.

The slope steepens. The rickshaw follows the street's counterclockwise curve, continuously veering leftward. Once they clear the wall of buildings, a castle soaring atop the rocky mountains comes into view.

"Sir, that over there is Castle Loulan," the rickshaw man tells K.

Enclosed by high and thick defensive walls, the castle appears jet black, except for its outline, which is traced by the glimmering emerald-green glow.

"By the way," K asks the rickshaw man, "What's the name of the lord of the castle again?"

"Well, I actually don't know. Maybe no one does. Everyone in the city just calls him 'Milord.'"

The rickshaw man speaks at length. He explains to K that, as one might have guessed from his title, the man called "Lord" serves as the ruler of the city. Evidently, he's also been living at this castle as long as anyone can remember.

"Milord built this city of Loulan. Yes, indeed, every single thing in the city."

Unless the rickshaw man is pulling his leg, it seems that this man is a brilliant scientist. Nothing is beyond his abilities. Or so he says.

K notices something strange about the street. Even as the run-down rickshaw continues to speed downhill on the cobblestone street, as far as K can tell, their altitude has continuously been climbing. Even though they should have been descending, K can now catch glimpses of the rooftops of the buildings in the city of Loulan.

That's odd.

As soon as K notices this, he speaks to the rickshaw man.

"Hey! Does going downhill mean climbing up the street in Loulan?"

"Yep."

The rickshaw man gives K an offhand nod without even turning around. But K finds it difficult to immediately take in such unexpected facts. For a man used to the laws of physics on Earth, this phenomenon can only throw his senses into complete confusion.

5

To K's surprise, Castle Loulan is much larger than it appears when viewed from the ground. He wanders inside the castle somewhat dumbfounded by the dingy surroundings. Eventually, guided by one of the castle's stewards, he finds his way to the top of the tower by *descending* the spiral staircase.

"Milord is inside that room," the servant says, pointing toward a small, dome-topped chamber. "He is performing experiments."

"Thank you."

Following the steward, K steps into a room that does indeed appear to be a laboratory, albeit one with an oddly sorcerous quality.

"Milord, your honored guest has arrived," the steward graciously announces.

The Lord of Castle Loulan—an obese man dressed in a deep-blue lab coat—greets K.

"Ah, yes," he says as he raises a flask that contains a liquid that glitters in five colors. "Welcome! After a five-hundred-light-year journey, you must be quite exhausted. Please have a seat."

Looking around, K finds scattered about every part of the room all manner of laboratory equipment. Missing though are any places for him to sit.

But the Lord does not seem to even notice K's bewilderment.

"Please," he urges K, "take a seat anywhere you wish."

With some trepidation, K lowers himself onto a section of empty space. To his surprise, the air beneath him begins to conform to his shape, until some invisible object makes contact with his thighs. His hands tell him that there is indeed a chair there. Reassured, he rests his back on this invisible chair, so soft that it is as comfortable as a woman's lap.

"The banquet won't be ready for some time still, so perhaps you'd like to try this for now."

The Lord offers his flask to K.

"Clara, give our guest a glass."

Suddenly, a pale hand—a woman's hand with nails manicured in an emerald color—materializes in the air next to him. Stunned, K finds himself helpless to do anything but accept the glass. He watches the rainbow colors of the drink as she pours it. It momentarily turns clear as all the colors mix in the glass, only to separate into five colors again. There must be a variation in the density of each layer of color.

K eyes the drink with suspicion.

"What exactly is this?"

"I call it the elixir of longevity," the Lord answers. "Drink one glass and you will be relieved of your fatigue. After the second glass, you'll forget all your sorrows. Drink a glass every day and you're guaranteed to stay forever young. Now, let us celebrate your safe arrival!"

The Lord cheerfully raises his glass toward K. Not having much choice, K raises his own glass as well. After clinking glasses, K brings the drink up to his lips with some trepidation. A scowl forms on K's face when he gets a whiff of the smell of animal blood.

"It doesn't really go down easily at first. But once you acquire a taste for it, it is truly unforgettable. So, bottoms up!"

With the Lord's persistent urging, K eventually manages to down his drink.

"So what is this made from exactly?" K asks with a look of suspicion.

"The fruit comes from what's commonly called the 'Tree of Enlightenment,'" the Lord says. "The tree bears five colors of fruit."

Apparently, this massive tree, which can only be grown within the Loulan Star System, bleeds like an animal and even cries in pain.

K's shock is evident on his face.

"So, is it really a tree then?" K asked.

"Oh, yes, it is indeed a tree. Unlike trees on Earth though, it doesn't grow up or down."

The Lord gazes longingly at his glass, as if admiring its contents, before emptying it.

"If you are so inclined, I would be happy to show you the fruits."

"Yes, I'd appreciate that."

The Lord leads K to the floating garden awaiting them behind the laboratory. No matter which way K looks, all he can see are unfamiliar plants, each one of them exquisitely dazzling. The Lord must be quite proud of his collection, as he provides K a detailed explanation of every single species in his garden.

"This is all quite splendid."

K's response is a mix of simple courtesy and sincere admiration.

"What's this one over here?"

K points at a flower shaped like a rainbow bridge.

"That's a type of giant orchid. Once it reaches full maturity, it will grow even larger than the ship that brought you here."

The Lord squints his eyes, pointing to a flower that looks like a butterfly floating in midair.

"This one's called a 'Butterfly Flower.' It's yet another type of space orchid and can actually fly by moving its flower petals."

He shows K many more flowers, far more in this massive collection than he will remember.

But one plant in particular catches K's attention, a dark-green ball of vegetation secured in a special case in one corner of the garden, as if it were something precious indeed. It is apparently some type of space alga that floats through the heavens, ever so slowly rotating. K's eyes widen upon hearing that the largest ones can grow to the size of a planet.

Finally, there is the so-called Tree of Enlightenment, which floats in the center of the garden, its branches extending out like vines to form a spherical lattice. Oddly, as the tendrils extend outward, their contours fade away into nothingness. But at the heart of the tree, the branches hang low with fruits the size of apples. The fruits come in five colors: red, blue, yellow, black, and green.

"These can be eaten raw. Would you like to try one?" asks the Lord.

K nods, picking out one of the red fruits to take a bite out of it. Its flavor has an acidic tinge. Its texture is akin to chewing beef.

"Delicious?"

K isn't quite sure how to answer.

The Lord also picks a fully ripe fruit from the branches.

"The fruits are certainly a bit peculiar at first," he says. "But once you acquire a taste for them, they can be quite addictive. Quite a few people have become prisoners of their flavor, making it rather difficult to ever leave Loulan again."

"Am I right that this tree has no trunk or roots at all?" K asks.

"Well, you see, it actually has roots. We just can't see them."

"Meaning what exactly?"

"The roots of the Tree of Enlightenment are invisible to the naked eye. But it's not that they don't exist."

K still doesn't get it. So, even knowing how silly his question will sound, he asks it anyway.

"So, do you mean that the roots are transparent?"

The Lord seems happy enough to entertain his queries.

"No, that's not it. Its roots extend into another universe."

"Oh? Another universe?"

"Exactly. Let me put it this way. Thinking about it in the terms of the structures of time-space continuum, you might say that the tree absorbs the nutrients it needs from a parallel world in an adjacent dimension."

The nonchalant expression on the Lord's face tells K that all this is perfectly mundane to him.

"This reminds me, there's something else here even more interesting. Would you like to see it?"

K's curiosity has been piqued.

"Sure, why not?"

"Well then, follow me this way."

The Lord sets a ladder down on one side of the floating garden, preparing to climb up its steps. However, the opposite end of the ladder floats in empty space.

"Come, come. There's nothing to worry about. You won't fall. The space up top has already conformed to the ladder."

The Lord's words confound K, but he does not seem to notice and begins climbing up the ladder before K can even respond.

K follows him to the top. Just as the Lord said, an invisible platform awaits up there. And so he ends up standing side by side with the Lord, as if floating in midair.

The Lord points his finger toward one corner of the garden.

"Look over there," he says.

K does so, seeing what looks like a crack on the wall. Then, the crack opens up, revealing some other place within it. What is he seeing? Another dimension?

Suddenly, something from inside this other world catches K's gaze. A strange creature, a huge shambling mass that's gray in color. K quickly pulls his eyes away from the crack.

"Whoa!" K lets out a little yelp as a wave of nausea sweeps over him. "What the hell was that?"

"Well, to be perfectly honest with you, we're not altogether certain ourselves just what that thing is."

"Is that thing a plant too?"

"Possibly."

"It looks like some kind of alga to me."

"I can see that. Yes, it may just be a kind of alga inhabiting an ocean in the fourth dimension."

K cannot quite shake off his jitters as he peers through the dimensional crack once more. The sheer size of the thing is simply beyond any comprehension. The creature waves several—no, countless—feelers of some sort that extend outward from its body. Just like the roots of the Tree of Enlightenment, the creature's feelers reach out in every direction, vanishing into other dimensions.

"We call that creature a 'Temporal Vine.' As you surmised earlier, we're not quite certain whether we should classify it as a plant or an animal in this world. What we are certain about though is that it feeds itself by absorbing time as a form of nutrition."

The Lord continues his explanation. But he peppers his words with so much specialized terminology—"temporal metabolism" and whatnot—unfamiliar to K that he can barely keep up. As far as he can figure out, the mechanics of its metabolism are perhaps somewhat similar to the photosynthesis of plants on Earth. In the end, the important thing to remember is that the space creature lives by consuming time itself, causing all manner of vexing problems wherever it goes.

"That's why we have to keep it fenced in like this. Otherwise, things get, shall we say, rather complicated."

"I can only imagine," K says, nodding in agreement as he hopes never to encounter such a thing again.

"This one here is the last of its kind. But there used to be many more around in Loulan back in the day. It was quite a task to wipe almost all of them out."

Finally, the two return to the laboratory. Upon their return, they are met by the castle steward, who tells them that the dinner is now ready.

6

To K's chagrin, he learns that having a meal in Loulan does not have the usual meaning of having a meal. You do not, in fact, consume food here. You simply go through the motions of consuming food, mimicking the gestures and acts of eating in a highly formal and ritualized way, hence imbuing the mood at the dinner table with much symbolism.

The plates, bowls, and glasses set on the table before K and the Lord are all empty. Still, when they take their spoons and ladle the soup to their lips, the slight sounds of sipping are discernible. Other sounds—forks plunging into their steaks, knives cutting through meat, chewing—shortly make themselves heard as well. Alongside it all are the splashing sounds of an invisible wine pouring into their glasses. Finally, at the end of the meal, the crunching noises of their bites into the crispy flesh of invisible apples fill the air.

At first, it all bewilders K. But when, emulating the Lord's actions, he follows along with the ritual of a meal, oddly enough, he finds himself feeling satiated in the end. When K thinks on it more after their dinner, the whole thing reminds him of something similar he had heard about, an old custom of setting a meal for an absent person.

Afterwards, the Lord brings K to an exquisite room with rows and rows of fine leather-bound books lining every inch of its walls. With the Lord's permission, K pulls out one of the books from the shelves. Quickly flipping through the pages, he discovers that every single page of the book is blank. Incredulous, K turns to the Lord.

"All the books are like that," the Lord tells him.

"Oh, I get it, all these books are just for appearance, right?" K says.

The Lord responds with a quiet glare, shaking his head from side to side.

"These are memory books. Shall I show you how to properly read them?"

The Lord snatches a volume of an encyclopedia from its

shelf. He heads over to a fine leather recliner, crossing his legs as he sits down. He flips open the book, letting his eyes trace lines across the blank pages as he sinks his back into the chair. After he finishes reading a few pages, he smiles, looking back up at K.

"You see? Just now, I was reading the R volume of the encyclopedia. Now, this is the first time I have read this. But I'm still able to read it back from my memory."

K remains silent as he listens to the Lord continue with his explanation.

"Everyone has a book within their memory. In your case, I wonder what sort of book that would be? An exquisite novel? A superb philosophical treatise? In my case, though, it's this—an encyclopedia."

Having listened to this explanation, K follows the Lord's lead, taking out another book and opening it to its first page. He begins to go through the motions of reading it. It takes some effort for him to clear his head, but with some focus, he slowly learns to put his mind to it, becoming quite absorbed in his reading.

He must have already gone over a dozen pages or so by the time the steward returns to announce that K's room is now ready.

"As you've just heard, your room is ready. Please make yourself at home. You will soon be departing from Loulan to travel through the rift in space, but in the meantime you are quite welcome to stay in my castle."

K expresses his gratitude to the Lord for his kindness and hospitality.

"Thank you very much," he says. "Speaking of my travel plans, I have my orders here, but by any chance do you know when exactly my ship will depart on the Sacred Route?"

The Lord smiles.

"You refer to the ship the *Emissary* returning from beyond to pick you up? Let's see, I wonder when it will return to Loulan. The truth is that no one really knows. It could be tomorrow. Or it could be a long time from now. It's such a capricious thing. Those here in Loulan have all been going about their daily lives waiting for the ship to arrive."

Such cryptic words exceed K's full comprehension. Nonetheless, for him, what matters at this moment is the knowledge that his ship will indeed arrive someday.

"In that case, I accept your invitation to stay here until then," K says.

The Lord gives K a long meaningful look.

"Excellent," he says as he returns his book to the shelf. "In that case, it looks like I'll need to assign someone to you while you're here."

What is he talking about?

Again, the meaning of his words escapes K.

"You will, after all, need someone to take care of your needs during your stay here. There are plenty of choices. Do you have a type?"

"I'm sorry?"

Is the Lord talking about assigning a servant to attend to him? So what does he mean by "type" then? What does that have to do with anything?

Enjoying K's bewilderment, the Lord turns to the steward standing to one side.

"Who would you choose in his place?"

The steward's gaze fixes on K, as if trying to appraise his value.

"I wonder. How about Serena?"

"Good choice. I wonder if she might not be too giggly though."

"Ellen, then, perhaps?"

"I think I may have overdone the snobbishness on her. What about Amalia? I think she's quite lovely. Perfect for him, don't you think?"

The steward tilts his head in curiosity.

"Amalia? Yes, that is an excellent idea. I will immediately make the appropriate preparations and bring her to the guest room."

The steward gives the Lord a deep bow, making a clumsy creaking noise as he exits the room.

K stays in the Lord's parlor for some time after, enjoying his conversation with a man whose breadth of knowledge so thoroughly impresses K.

"You see," the Lord says. "It's not merely a matter of my age. Let's see, when I was about your age—wait, when was that again? It was such a long time ago I can no longer remember. Anyway, even then, I burned with a passion for grasping every single piece of knowledge about outer space that I could get hold of. But a man's life is regrettably only limited. So before anything else, I needed to learn the secrets of immortality, and as a result of all my research, I was lucky enough to end up on Loulan and discover this Tree of Enlightenment."

"Just how old are you, anyway?" K asks with some hesitation.

A hint of melancholy seeps out of the Lord's next words.

"Well, all I can say is that I am old enough to no longer remember my age."

If this man founded the city of Loulan, he must have been born before the year 886 of the Igituran Era, which was when the Loulan Space Route was first developed upon the discovery of the planet with its famous black sun.

"Would you say around 250 years old?" K asks.

The Lord shakes his head.

"300 years old, then?"

"No, it has to be more than that."

"400?"

"No. I have a distinct recollection of being at the courthouse when the heresy trials took place. This would have been around the time of the debates surrounding the interpretation of *The Garden of Earthly Delights*."

But the heresy trials took place in the year 567. This was well before the great leap forward marked by the development of faster-than-light drives. Only after these technologies were in place could the long-distance trek through space to Loulan even become possible.

"That can't be right," K mutters under his breath.

"Indeed," the Lord says in acknowledgment. "Your skepticism does not surprise me. I myself no longer really understand what I am anymore. You see, when you live for some hundreds of years like I have, your brain starts to dull, you start to lose older bits of memory. It can be a real problem sometimes."

The Lord adopts the stance of someone deep in thought. However, it is obviously a mere pose, a gesture for the sake of appearance. Regardless, he insists with absolute certainty that his discovery of the Tree of Enlightenment in Loulan happened in the years prior to the execution of the heretic Darko Dachilko. In fact, he was there to witness the execution.

"That's right. I somehow returned to Earth from Loulan. I was there to witness that man's head shoot up high into the air and disappear in a spray of blood."

This event took place in the year 313 of the Igituran Era.

"That's almost seven centuries ago," K murmurs.

"Indeed. A long, long time ago."

The Lord speaks these words as if he is talking about someone else.

"I heard that every single one of those present at the execution subsequently died facing the wrath of Darko Dachilko's ghost."

"Oh, really?" The Lord displays an exaggerated expression of surprise, making it sound like this was the first time he had ever heard of such a preposterous story.

7

Distinctions between day and night have no meaning in Loulan. All there is to tell time is a single large hourglass sitting in the Lord's parlor. But the golden sand of the hourglass remains still at the bottom end of the clock, not having seen much use for a very long time. A large horned owl perches atop it, watching all with glimmering catlike eyes.

The Lord lets out a yawn, and before K knows it, he has already fallen into a deep slumber while still seated in his reclining chair. A glance at his sleeping face reveals a childlike innocence. A smile forms on K's face as he places a throw blanket over him.

Deciding that it is time for him to rest as well, K steps out into the dark hallway. Only a small bit of light spills out from one corner. K feels his way toward the light, finding his way to a room with the door slightly ajar.

Hearing a noise inside the room, K peers in to find the castle steward.

"Could you tell me which of these is my room? Is it this one?"

"Yes, sir. But could you please wait for just a moment? The room will be ready shortly."

K notices that the steward has brought into the room a chest full of dresses, which he takes out of the open chest to hang in the closet. So many dresses, each one of them cut in a revealing fashion. When he is done with the dresses, he proceeds to fold other items, underwear of every color, shoes, accessories.

Even as he finds it all rather strange, K remains silent, simply letting the steward carry on with his work. In the meantime, he studies the two-room suite. Circular bed at the far end. Ceiling that's somewhat on the low side. Walls painted in a dark-red hue. Multiple mirrors mounted here and there. Floors carpeted with black animal fur. Antique furnishings. The Lord's taste in decor is much too ostentatious for K.

The steward finally finishes his work. He hastily hauls the now empty chest back out to the hallway, only to bring in another chest, this one much larger and covered in leather. He sets it down lengthwise onto the floor of the room. Searching his pockets, he scrounges up the key to the chest. It suddenly dawns on K that this very old chest has the exact size and shape of a casket.

The steward slides the key into the lock, opening it with a single click. Crouching down, he lifts the lid of the casket up, revealing within it a woman with blonde hair and wide-open blue eyes emptily staring at the ceiling.

"What do you think, sir?" The steward asks K. "This is Amalia."

Was this woman, this mechanical doll, what the Lord and the steward were discussing earlier?

K finds it difficult to conceal his confusion.

"Is she to your liking, sir?"

In the face of the steward's subdued voice, K remains silent, gripped with the feeling of facing some kind of diabolical ritual, some kind of spell the steward is casting on him.

The steward presents a frozen glare to K.

"Does she not remind you of someone you know?"

There is no denying the resemblance.

"Please do not worry, sir. We are not on Earth. Indulge in the worst sins as much as you wish. No one will come after you here."

A dim light radiates from deep within the steward's eyes.

"How do you know such things?"

The steward's response is as cool and collected, as full of mystery as ever.

"I know everything about you."

Indolence has fully consumed K's life since that evening when he first met Amalia. Day in and day out, he does nothing else other than hide himself away in the castle. Somehow, he has fallen in love with this mechanical doll.

And yet loneliness tinges this love, a self-love little more than mere empty onanism.

In the end, no heart beats in her chest, no soul breathes life into her body.

The first few days are full of anguish for K. All the guilt he has hidden away returns to face him, haunting him. All because Amalia so reminds him of a woman he killed a long time ago, from another life.

Why? Why did I kill her?

Again and again, K returns to this question, as if to remind himself of what he's done, before his memory of it becomes ever more faint, ever more obscure.

The days pass without end.

In the incessant darkness of Loulan, K gradually loses track of the difference between day and night. The black sun of Loulan rises and sets every thirteen hours—not too different from the rhythms of Earth—but it makes little difference to him. The air supposedly warms up during Loulan's dark daytime hours. At least, that's what the steward says, telling K that the black sun releases rays of heat invisible to those from Earth. He, however, can perceive these rays. K can only imagine how it is that the steward is able to detect such subtle changes in temperature, but perhaps it is because, as the Lord once mentioned, he too is a mechanical doll.

Only twice each day—during the rising and setting of the black sun—does the color of Loulan's sky see a dramatic transformation. From the veranda of his room, K has a view of this splendid sight they call the Loulan Aurora, when the emerald glow of the air is so bright that every so often the inverted image of the city reflects in the sky like a mirage. Other than these moments though, Loulan's sky is constantly shrouded in a curtain of darkness, with an atmosphere so thick it is almost narcotic in its intoxicating quality. Is this what the Lord meant when he told K that Loulan was a sensual city? Is there something infernal, something unholy about the planet's atmosphere?

As long as you breathe this air, you cannot escape from Loulan. Again and again, the Lord idly repeats these words to K.

K once tried to determine the truth hiding behind this mysterious, ageless Lord. But his will to do so has since faded away. Could this too be an effect of the unique atmosphere of Loulan?

Yet deep in the recesses of K's mind is a thought he simply cannot completely bury away, a suspicion that this Lord is none other than the enigmatic heretic Darko Dachilko. Mere happenstance planted the thought in his head when by accident he came across a pair of detached fingers—one left and one right—kept hidden away in a small case in the Lord's parlor. At first glance, they appeared to be made of wax. But a closer inspection revealed that these were artificial fingers that incorporated a highly complex technical mechanism. Seeing this evidence of his suspicions gave K quite a shock.

Could these be the sixth fingers of Darko Dachilko's malformed hands?

All of K's instincts told him that these were indeed the legendary "Fingers of Light."

8

K can always sense Amalia's approach. The mechanical sounds of her gears turning always give her away. The mechanical doll places a bowl of fruit from the Tree of Enlightenment in front of K. Then she just stands there in silence, awaiting his next instructions for her.

"Will the Lord be joining us?"

"The Lord is in his laboratory."

"What is he doing? The usual thing?"

"Yes. The usual thing," Amalia repeats after K.

More sophisticated conversations exceed her abilities, which amount to little more than perfunctory answers to K's questions. Otherwise, she does not speak at all. Nonetheless, there is something unnerving about the authentic, all-too-human quality of her voice.

Day after day, Amalia goes about her business wearing unnecessarily risqué outfits. This time, all she wears as she serves dinner is an apron over her naked body, displaying the exceptional simulation of skin that covers her mechanisms. Although appearing rather tough at first glance, a single touch of her skin is all it takes to reveal a suppleness like that of rubber.

K recalls that the Lord told him once that he constructed Amalia's skin out of some kind of rubber that can only be obtained and refined on Loulan. He also explained the mechanics of how she operated, although K barely understood any of it. Sure, he could grasp the general structure of her anatomy, but the technology that breathed life into her, that part he could not grasp at all.

K was telling the Lord about the perfect proportions of her body that day.

"She's like a goddess in her beauty. Just perfect."

The Lord seemed quite pleased at hearing this.

"You really think so?"

"Yes. I was wondering though—Amalia's body was based off a real person, right?"

The Lord blinked.

"No, not at all. She was based on a generic model," he said.

But K caught a momentary glimpse of hesitation in the Lord, just enough to expose his lie. With probing eyes, he watched for the Lord's expression as he spoke.

"There's this black spot under Amalia's left breast."

"What about it?"

"There's also a birthmark inside her left thigh."

"Your point?"

"If you made the mechanical doll without basing it off a human, why bother to put the dark spot and the birthmark on her? That's what I want to know."

"Well, there's no reason in particular, really."

Their conversation ended there. But K was confident that his suspicions were on the mark.

Later that night, as K holds Amalia's body in bed, these lingering suspicions circle his thoughts, making it difficult for him to find any sleep. He is now almost certain of it. This nameless Lord was none other than the mysterious heretic, none other than Darko Dachilko himself. He has but one piece of evidence, the set of left and right fingers that he found hidden in a case. Yet there is no other explanation that makes sense. These had to be Darko Dachilko's infamous sixth fingers, his so-called miraculous shining fingers.

Could Amalia's model be the girl from that book?

Of course, without any conclusive proof, all of this amounts to little more than K's suppositions.

What was her name again? Barbara. That's right. The object of Darko Dachilko's illicit affections. The daughter of a wealthy family.

Such are the thoughts that distract K as he has fumbling sex with the splayed-out artificial body of Amalia.

Strange . . .

A vague memory that somewhere, a long time ago, he made love with someone like this before.

"Barbara," K whispers to the mechanical doll. "Barbara, what were you up to with the master after the daily gathering at The Orchard?"

"Nothing's ever happened with him, Gilgeas," says Amalia. "Barbara is innocent."

"Don't lie to me."

"It's not a lie, Gilgeas. Please believe Barbara."

"Liar!"

"No, stop it, Gilgeas!"

It all suddenly comes back to K. This girl, this Barbara, she should have been dead for over seven hundred years now. Yet he knows her. He knows her very well indeed. And he burns with white-hot jealousy over Darko Dachilko. The shock of memory overwhelms him.

K flees from the castle, losing himself in the winding, topsy-turvy streets of the city. He wanders without knowing where he's going. By the time he comes to his senses, he finds himself next to the port where the *Hades* was anchored, in an area where several stone structures—warehouses, most likely—quietly line up in neat rows, like headstones in a graveyard.

K ends up in a dimly lit corner inside some shabby-looking bar with only a few customers inside. A man so skinny he may as well have been a shadow approaches K's table, asking for his order.

"Pick something for me," K says, already too exhausted to think.

"Might an Amber Drink be your pleasure?"

"What kind of drink is that?"

"A special drink of Loulan. Sir, I guarantee you that this drink will help you forget all your worries about the world."

"Fine. Let's try it then."

The waiter leaves with a nod. Two girls then approach K, intent on seducing him. But K rejects them without a thought. Prostitutes, no doubt. Their overly revealing clothing tells him that much.

A somber atmosphere pervades the interior of the bar. This is no help at all. If anything, it's only making K ever-more despondent. Nothing makes sense to him anymore.

How do I know this girl named Barbara? Why did I mistake that mechanical doll for her? Why did I try to strangle her?

There is only one answer. K knows this. And yet he refuses to acknowledge its truth.

Feeling as if his heart has been hollowed out, there is little K can do now. He looks around the bar. Various tables are scattered about, shadowy silhouettes of customers clinging close to them like dark specks of dirt. Twisted bottles have been set before many of them. Heated by a small burner at the base of the container, the liquid inside these bottles evaporates into a purple gas that they inhale through a tube. The flames of the burners flicker like lights inlaid onto an altar, lighting up their pallid faces as they suck the gas out of the tubes. Not a single one of them says a word, as if they were all already dead.

K's Amber Drink is equally strange. Several small brown bottles, each one containing a gold-colored metallic substance, are lined up in a row. The flame of a burner turns the liquid to vapor, only for it to cool down as it passes through a complex set of twisting tubes, until it slowly drips into a small, clear glass, accumulating into a drink.

At the server's suggestion, K takes a sip, enjoying the strong, stimulating flavor.

Is this some kind of chemistry lab experiment?

Each one of the bottles has a screw. Twisting these adjusts the mix ratios, changing both the color and flavor of the drink. K fiddles with the apparatus for a while, until a young man close to K's age seats himself in front of him.

"You're not doing it right. Here, let me show you."

The young man moves next to K to adjust the settings with nimble and practiced fingers.

The color of the liquid changes.

"See, isn't that color more striking?"

The liquid flows much more steadily as well.

"Yup. This looks good."

Although the young man is done with his fiddling, he does not leave his spot next to K.

"If I may be so forward, might I ask you where you are from?"

Perhaps he was just looking for an excuse to talk to K from the start?

"I'm from Igitur," K answers.

"So you are from the capital on Earth. Just as I thought," the young man says as he eyes the medal pinned to K's chest. "Oh, are you a member of the Sacred Service?"

"Yes. Yes, I am. And you?"

The young man tells K that he also came to Loulan from Earth a long time ago.

"So, what brings you here?"

More questions for K.

"Just following my orders. I've been sent to Planet Bosch." K pauses briefly, as if deciding whether to continue. "I'm actually waiting for the *Emissary* to return and take me there."

"Oh, the *Emissary,* eh."

A hint of sarcasm hides in the young man's voice. His eyes fix themselves on K's face, studying him as he continues to speak.

"If you're in the Sacred Service, that means you should have read the *Southern Scriptures,* right?"

"Yes, I have. What's on your mind?"

"By any chance, would you mind listening to a theory of mine?"

His request catches K by surprise. Not knowing what else to say, he agrees.

"Sure, I guess I could do that."

K locks his gaze on his counterpart's eyes. Dark beyond description, they somehow remind him of his old friend Hoffman's eyes.

"So," K says. "Tell me about this idea of yours."

The young man speaks slowly, keeping his voice low, making sure to get the words just right.

"The thing is, it's about the 'Book of the Seed,' you see."

As K listens to the young man, it dawns on him that this man must have studied the subject quite closely. K has already read the infamous "Book of the Seed" of the *Southern Scriptures* many times before coming to Loulan, yet much of it still perplexes him. Perhaps it is precisely because of his own inability to fully understand the proper interpretation of many sections of the book that he finds the young man's ideas rather compelling indeed.

According to this young man, the concept of transcription is what's at the heart of the "Book of the Seed."

"So, something like reproduction, then?"

"That's right. The notion of the copy. Photographs and prints constitute the theoretical frame of the text, don't you think?"

"That makes sense. Please, do continue," K urges the young man.

The young man continues in his usual whisper.

"The truth is that I once dabbled in the fundamentals of Divine Genetics a long time ago, despite knowing it was against the law. From what I learned, the notion of the copy can also explain the principle of the heredity of living things. In other words, all the information parents have is embedded into what are called genes, and not unlike the relationship between the matrix and the type itself in movable-type presses, a series of copies of this information can be made. The same thing can be said about us humans. If we were to ask what our ancestors were, the answer would be the early primates, with we humans evolving from them. However—"

K interrupts the young man's rambling.

"Sure. You're talking about the theory of evolution, correct? If I recall correctly, it was a man named Darwin who formulated this theory. His followers subsequently popularized the doctrine, and it became a foundational idea organizing much of the scientific knowledge of the Twilight Era."

"And yet, the field of Divine Genetics flatly rejects the theory of evolution."

K nods.

"Indeed. Current scholarship would have us believe in the notion that human beings descended from God."

"That's right. Not surprisingly, the mission of Divine Genetics was to produce the research explaining the genetic mechanism through which human beings descended from divine incarnations. They used the example of wear and tear of movable-type presses to articulate the phenomenon of gene regression. So, the rough mechanism was already understood, but the most crucial element—concrete evidence that divine incarnations walked our Earth—still couldn't be found."

The man pauses to catch his breath.

Now, K too feels his mind stirring.

"Right," K says. "You're exactly right. And this is why there's so much significance placed on the discovery of Planet Bosch."

For some reason, K recalls the conversation he once had with someone at the cafeteria of the Papal Court.

His interest piqued, the young man begins speaking louder.

"It must be. But what exactly is the connection between this and the theory of evolution?"

This was what K himself wants to know. He listens as the young man speaks for a long time in hushed tones. But whether it's simply his own exhaustion, or the intoxicating effects of the Amber Drink beginning to hit him, K doesn't quite catch several details of the young man's words. Nonetheless, he manages to grasp the central point he wishes to assert. He believes that Planet Bosch is most certainly an exact copy of the images from Hieronymus Bosch's *The Garden of Earthly Delights*.

"But just who is it who . . ."

"I don't know. What I'm sure of, though, is that whoever had the power to make such a thing possible cannot be a mere mortal."

"You mean he's some kind of divine incarnation?"

"Probably. I mean, reproducing himself to create the human, or making Planet Bosch out of *The Garden of Earthly Delights*, you would have to be a being who possesses the highest levels of intelligence to be able to do that."

"But Hieronymus Bosch was an artist who lived during the Twilight Era," K says.

"Yes, I know. That's why I believe that these divine incarnations must have secretly mingled among human beings on Earth."

Just this once, the young man appears quite confident in his statement.

Soon after his conversation, K leaves the bar. With the young man's bold theory still fresh in his mind, K ascends the hill back to the castle, even as the rickshaw he rides makes its way down the slope.

Could Loulan also have been copied from something, just like Planet Bosch?

The memory of another strange painting prompts this thought in K. It depicts exactly this scene before him now, a path ending up on top even as it continuously goes downhill. The name of the man who made this strange painting was M. C. Escher, also an artist from the Twilight Era.

This thought suddenly unsettles K. He raises the roof of the rickshaw, revealing a similarly unsettled darkness in Loulan's sky. Once again, the black rift slicing across the sky draws in his wandering soul.

SPACE CLOCK

1

K slowly grows accustomed to the vague darkness of Loulan. With each passing day, the darkness begins to feel familiar, almost like an old friend, even as Loulan's ceaseless darkness conspires with his own dark thoughts. They fuse together into one, then divide, growing into a mass of darkness nestled deep within him. Resigned to a listlessness that is all too sweet, he can only look on, unable to stop the illicit union between the darkness outside and the darkness inside him.

Yet another day in Loulan idly comes and goes, with nothing for K to do but wait for the appearance of the ship known as the *Emissary*, whose return from beyond is impossible to foresee.

Until one day, during another of Loulan's black sunsets, something happens.

K has made a daily habit of viewing the Loulan Aurora from the terrace of the castle. Twice a day—in the morning and in the evening—he waits for its appearance while reclining against the stone railings. Twice a day, the glorious colors suddenly immerse the sky, only to just as quickly fade away, haunting the sky with the radiance of emerald, with an occasional hint of sullen purple.

K watches as the colors light up the city, projecting its reflection onto the dark sky.

As always, K loses himself in utter fascination at the exceptional beauty of the ever-shifting aurora on this day.

The steward comes in, bringing K the drink he requested earlier.

"Ah, the famous 'Cinema of Loulan.' Enjoying the sights?"

It is certainly unusual for the always-quiet steward to speak to him like this.

"Yeah," K says, taking the glass from the steward.

"Cinema"—well that's quite clever.

"Do you know that the aurora sometimes projects the reflection of a completely different city onto the sky, a city unfamiliar to anyone from Loulan?"

"Really now? How? How would such a phenomenon even occur?"

"I do not know," the servant says, shaking his head. "But look, sir! Don't you think that today's aurora is somewhat different from the usual?"

Only now, when the steward points it out to him, does K notice. It is, in fact, different from the usual mirage he sees.

"Is this not a city that might be lodged in your memory? Over there, look, there's an exquisite garden!"

The steward speaks to him in an oddly roundabout way.

"Yes, you're right! I do recognize that garden!"

K's admission seems to please the steward.

"Just as I thought. So what is the name of this city? Would you be so kind as to tell me?"

"Sure. That is the capital of Earth, the Holy City of Igitur. Wait, no, something's not right."

"Not right? Not right how?"

"Those towers over there—those don't exist in the Igitur I know. Neither does that garden."

"Is that so? Perhaps it is an Igitur from a time that has long since passed."

An odd feeling washes over K.

"I don't understand. Why would the city from the past be reflected here now?"

The servant pours more of the black drink into K's now empty glass.

"Oh? If you want to know the reason for this, there is just one man in Loulan who has been studying this mysterious phenomenon."

"Someone here has been investigating this?"

"Yes. There's a hermit. Do you see the clock tower over there? That is where he lives."

The servant points toward a part of Loulan where a stone tower conspicuously reaches high into the air.

"That one over there?"

"Yes, that tower. The people in town call it the Space Clock. It's a rather strange sort of clock tower."

"Yes, I know," K says.

"Oh, so you've heard of it?"

"Yes. I've been to the base of the tower a few times before."

"Then, sir, you must have seen the clock, right?"

"Yeah, I did. It's an absurdly large clock, or so I thought."

Despite the fact that every piece of the strange clock has been carved out of stone, its face nevertheless has a diameter that's at least twice K's height. More than its size though, its oddity comes from its clock face, which is markedly different from any normal clock K has seen before.

"Do you know what exactly that clock is being used for?" K asks the steward.

"No, I cannot say that I know. I do know what the Lord told me once, which is that each tick of the shorter hand is supposed to correspond to a hundred million years."

If so, this means that the stone clock was created to mark off six billion years in one revolution.

K returns his gaze toward the top of the tower as the aurora's glow lights it up in a green haze.

"Sir, perhaps you should go see the hermit just this once?"

"You may be right."

The steward's suggestion only echoes what K is already thinking.

"You say he's a hermit though. Wouldn't he refuse to see some random stranger?"

"Oh no, not at all. That might be true with others, but he will undoubtedly agree to see you."

There is a curious confidence in the steward's voice.

"And why would that be?" K asks with some skepticism.

"But of course! You are an honored guest of the Lord, so the hermit will most certainly welcome your visit."

A strange smile forms on the steward's face as he offers a courteous bow before going on his way.

2

The almost imperceptible warmth of the slowly ascending black sun awakens K the next day. After washing his face with the basin of water brought in by the mechanical doll Amalia, he immediately sets forth, not even touching his breakfast. For once, K knows exactly where he is going. He is off to see the hermit in the clock tower.

The tower stands in one of the oldest neighborhoods of Loulan, in a part of the city that has nearly emptied out. Cracks have opened up in the outer walls of many of the houses here, leaving fallen pieces of peeled stucco scattered over a wide area of the ground. K follows the road through uneven terrain.

Finally, the road widens into an isolated and deserted open plaza. Abandoned structures on the verge of falling down surround the area, without a single soul to be seen anywhere. At the center stands the clock tower, itself appearing close to collapse, with large pieces of lumber attached with wire clamps supporting what remains of its structure.

K takes his time, standing atop the pentagon-shaped pedestal, looking upwards at the jet-black silhouette of the huge tower rising above him. Only a few stars twinkle dimly against the backdrop of the clear black sky, their constellations hidden by an even darker black gash, by the now familiar black rift cutting across the sky behind the face of the clock tower. Premonitions of ill tidings give K the shivers.

It is no longer the time for any second thoughts. K makes his move, attempting to open the rusty door of the tower. It takes some effort, but eventually K manages to push it open. Stairs descend into a gaping dark passage, waiting for him.

K steps into the darkness. He must have taken a hundred steps, with just his hand on the railing guiding him down. As always, descending leads him up the tower, until he reaches a landing halfway to the top. The arched passage opens into a wide platform with a view of the wondrous interior of the tower. K casts his eyes on it, letting out a gasp.

"Wow . . ."

The sight of the mechanism of the Space Clock leaves K speechless.

Crammed within the interior of the tower is a machine that can record the passage of millions upon millions of years! Just how many components were there in all? Stone gears exceeding the thousands form a complex assemblage. They are as still as the remains of ancient ruins. Around the gears are massive pendulums, hanging massive rocks that swing at such slow speeds that K finds it difficult to ascertain whether they are moving at all.

K locates the hermit squeezed into a tiny room near the top of the tower. Or to be more precise, the hermit is jammed within a crawl space with only a narrow opening and an arched ceiling. Curiously located at the very far end of the chamber, the crawl space lies close to where the teeth of a pair of stone gears—one larger and one smaller—meet one another to form something akin to a staircase. Yet there is a sizable gap between the gears and the narrow balcony extending out from the space, a gap far wider than what K can leap across. Is the hermit being confined here against his will? How long has he been trapped there?

Careful not to slip off the gears, K leans his body forward as far as possible, trying to catch a glimpse of the man within the crawl space. The tiny room has only enough space for one person to lie down within it. Windows have been cut out of three of the inner stone walls, suggesting that the room partly juts out of the tower.

"Hello!" K calls out.

The hermit must have been fast asleep. He stirs in surprise, lifting his head at the sound of K's voice.

"What is it? Are you here to bother me again?"

What is he muttering about?

As far as K can tell, this very old man must be at least several hundred years of age. His face has long since lost any definition, buried as it is in his countless wrinkles. Folded over his body are his arms, decrepit like the branches of an aged tree. The lower half of his body is out of K's sight.

The hermit studies K's face, eyes glazing over.

"Oh, pardon me," he says, his voice weak, little more than the buzz of a mosquito. "I didn't recognize you."

"My name is K. I've come here at the suggestion of the steward at Castle Loulan. I wish to ask you some questions about the aurora."

The hermit coughs as he straightens himself up from his fetal posture. He plants both his hands on the floor, extending his neck to give K's face a thorough examination.

"Well, you're much younger than I expected."

Has he been expecting K's arrival?

"Mr. Hermit, how did you know I was coming?"

The hermit points at the horned owl in the cage next to him. K has seen this bird before. It's the same bird kept by the Lord of Castle Loulan. And also at Clara Hall. Just what is going on here?

"Is that bird . . ."

"Yes, that's right."

On cue, the owl starts yapping.

"I told him! I told him!"

"So, let me get this right—this bird came along to deliver a message from the steward to you?"

Things finally begin to make sense.

The owl's chatter continues as it jumps up and down, wings flapping.

"So you finally got it? Such an idiot! Idiot! Idiot!"

Such an ill-behaved bird! There's no need for insults.

"So, you've met my foul-mouthed friend, I see. It's been flying in from the castle every day to heap abuse on me."

The owl then shrieks like a bird possessed of the mind of a man.

"What was that? What was that?"

"This one here is a spy, you see."

"A spy! You're only alive thanks to the food and water I bring you!"

"Well, that much is true, I guess."

The hermit must already be used to the owl's abuse, as he shows no sign that he pays it any mind. Like a dog coming out of its den, he crawls out of his hole onto the hanging balcony.

"Can you give this old man a closer look at your face? It's been a hundred years since I've had a chance to see another human face. With my failing memory, it's hard to even remember what people look like."

Somewhat stunned though he is, K nonetheless does as the hermit asks, stretching his body forward.

There is a strange story behind the hermit's imprisonment at the top of the clock tower. From what K can gather, it was the enigmatic Lord of Castle Loulan himself who put him here, subjecting him to these harsh circumstances. Uncertain of what to make of the knowledge that the old man has not stepped foot outside the tower for over three hundred years, all K can do is respond with some sympathy.

"Let me get you out of here," K tells the hermit. "I can go find some rope and a ladder from somewhere. Can you still walk? If not, I can carry you out of here on my back."

But the old man refuses K's most generous offer.

"No, that's really not possible. The Lord himself cut off my legs long ago. But, you know, as long as I stay up here, it's not at all a problem to have no legs."

Hearing this twisted logic only deepens K's suspicions and frustrations.

"But didn't the Lord cut off your legs precisely to imprison you in here forever?"

"That's right," says the hermit, oddly tranquil about the whole situation.

"Which is why I'm saying I can carry you out of this place."

But the hermit shakes his head.

"I do appreciate your kindness, but it's really more trouble than it's worth. I mean, what do you think will become of me when I'm out of here with no legs? This place suits me perfectly now."

"If you say so."

K finally gives up. Not surprisingly, though, his frustration does not easily go away. As if reading his mind, the hermit addresses his doubts.

"I told you, even if I leave here with you, what do you think will happen to me? Do you plan to carry me around for the rest of your life?"

"Well, no, that would be a bit . . . well . . ."

K is at a loss for words.

"Besides, you know, my life will never end. It will continue on forever."

"What? What do you mean?"

"I mean that I won't die."

"Are you saying that you're immortal?"

"That's right. One way or another, there's no way out of my prison, my curse of immortality."

"How is that a prison? That makes no sense to me."

For K, the hermit's words go against all logic.

"I mean, if you ask me," K continues, "the fact that everyone is destined to die someday is what leads to suffering. The knowledge that life is limited—that is the prison, the prison of life. So to attain immortality is to find freedom from this terrifying imprisonment. That's what I believe."

The hermit laughs out loud.

"Ha! I used to think just like you when I was your age."

After all that though, his demeanor becomes more solemn as he continues to tell K his story.

3

According to the crippled hermit, he has lived for over 990 years now, having been witness to almost the entire history, the entire

Millennium of Prosperity, of the Holy Empire of Igitur. He possesses an amazing memory of all he has seen through the centuries, telling K about the inside stories behind the seemingly
never-ending North-South War of Two Centuries, the ratification
of the Treaty of Two Worlds in the year 182 of the Igituran Era,
not to mention the establishment of the Law of Five Galaxies and
Sacred Knowledge in the year 223.

"Yes, that's when it was. It was around the time of the First
Papal Conference. The fourth century, I think. That's when I first
met the Lord of Castle Loulan. Oh, we were all still so young then.
Let me tell you something, young man, I was the one who first
mastered the Secret of Osiris. The Lord merely stole the secret
from me."

"I see."

So that's how the Lord of Castle Loulan has managed to live
for several hundred years. Things start to finally make sense to K.
Or, at least, it is starting to dawn on him just how much he doesn't
understand as he continues to listen to the hermit's story. He speaks
at length in a rapid clip without a single pause to catch his breath,
at times making it somewhat difficult for K to follow his words.

But there is no mistaking K's shock upon hearing one detail
in the hermit's account. He tells K that seven hundred years in
the past, a wealthy and influential adherent of Darko Dachilko
once owned a magnificent garden known as "The Orchard." This
adherent, named Ilya, pumped a seemingly endless amount of
investment into the building of this garden over a span of thir-
ty years, which was supposedly modeled on Hieronymus Bosch's
painting *The Garden of Earthly Delights.*

"It was quite simply the most marvelous garden in the land! I
received many invitations to visit it back in the day!"

"By any chance, did this disciple have a daughter?"

K speaks in hushed tones.

"You know the story well. Yes, he had a beautiful daughter
named Barbara."

"And the daughter had a young lover named Gilgeas?"

"She did indeed. The young man was one of Darko Dachilko's
disciples. But alas, Darko Dachilko stole his woman from him."

"So what happened to the young man after that?"

"I wonder. I heard he cursed his father, disappearing to who knows where."

"What? Did you just say that he cursed his father? What do you mean by that?"

The hermit finds K's flustered reaction rather odd.

"Nothing out of the ordinary. Why?"

"Are you saying that Gilgeas was Darko Dachilko's son?"

"Yes, that's right."

"That's the first I'm hearing of it. There's no mention of it at all by Bervera in the book of his that I read."

"I would imagine not. Only a few people knew the truth about their relationship."

"Why is that? Why would Darko Dachilko hide the fact that Gilgeas was his own son?"

"Well, who's to say? I don't know the circumstances between them. My guess would be that it's considered inappropriate to disclose the matrimonial life of a holy man."

Even as the hermit offers only an indifferent response, K cannot be so nonchalant himself. His disturbing dreams suggesting that he is none other than Gilgeas himself now begin to make sense to him. So lucid are these dreams, filling in details of the story of Gilgeas and Barbara not touched on by Bervera's *The Enigmatic Heretics*—could they be more than mere idle fantasies? Could K himself be linked to the heretic Darko Dachilko in some form or another?

Could they be the long-forgotten memories that haunt me every night?

But what does any of it mean?

Do I already know much more than I'd thought? Do I already know the truth?

The young K is unable to hide his trembling.

Afterward, K finally learns the secrets of the auroras from the hermit. He explains that they are not just natural phenomena, not just the refraction of light and color. No, the little-known truth is that they are visions, projections of the grief of some woman from a time long ago. That is why they are known as the Auroras of Mourning.

K recalls seeing the vision of old Igitur in the aurora.

"Who is it? This woman? Did she once reside in the capital of the Holy Empire?"

"That's right," the hermit says. "But now she lives right here, at the top of this clock tower."

"I would really like to see her, if that's possible."

The vague hint of a secret smile flashes in the hermit's eyes, as if stars twinkled deep within them.

"Ah, yes, that's an excellent idea. There's a favor I wish to ask of you. Is that all right?"

"Of course," K says. "If it's within my powers, then please let me know."

"It most certainly is."

"What would you like me to do?"

"That thing that's hanging from your neck . . ."

"Hanging from my neck? Do you mean this Sacred Service officer medallion?"

"Yes. Would you be willing to give me the chain?"

"The chain?"

"Yes. Not the medal. Just the chain."

K hesitates for a moment. The chain can easily be replaced later. It shouldn't be a problem to give it to him.

"Sure, you can have it. But what use is it to you?"

K wavers for an instant, noticing the strange gleam in the hermit's eyes as he watches K's hands detach the medal from its chain.

"All right, I'll throw this toward you, so you'll have to catch it, okay?" K says.

Suddenly, the horned owl stirs from its quiet observation of K and the hermit, once again speaking with alarm.

"Don't give it to him! Don't give it to him, K! K! K! You can't give it to him!"

What the hell?

A strange sensation—like nausea—washes over K. But he pays it no heed. He throws the chain toward the hermit.

The hermit effortlessly grabs it from the air.

"Why thank you," he says.

The hermit smiles, baring his teeth to reveal a pair of sharp fangs. So evil beyond any words is his smile that K cannot help but tremble at its sight. What has he done?

4

Following the hermit's instructions, K jumps from one stone gear to another until he finally makes it to the top of the clock tower, where he finds a hatch in the ceiling. He lifts it open, then climbs up to the rooftop of the tower. Outside, a magnificent view of the black sun hanging low in the sky meets him. The dark day will soon come to an end, only to be replaced by an even darker night.

K admires the 360-degree panorama of the city, a wider view than what's visible from the balconies of Castle Loulan. He takes a deep breath of Loulan's dense atmosphere, savoring the sensual and intoxicating fragrance of the air. But something is different. This is not the fragrance of Loulan's air that K breathes. No, it is the perfume of the woman on that rooftop. She does not notice K's entrance. Standing at the other end of the rooftop with her body leaning over the railings, she looks upon the view of the distant mountains and the city's rooftops as their outlines glimmer in emerald.

K casts his gaze on her slim silhouette. Her long, white dress flows to her ankles, shimmering faintly as if covered in fireflies. When she notices K's nervous approach, she turns around with a look of surprise showing on her face.

"Hello," K says with a bow. "My name is K."

"Oh, dear me, why are you here?"

"I came to see you. Please, tell me your name?"

Just as these words escape K's lips, he suddenly comes to a realization. He knows this beautiful woman. He has known her for a long, long time now.

"Don't you already know?"

"Yes, I do. Your name is Barbara."

"Yes."

How do I know this?

K fixes his gaze on the woman's face. She looks just like that mechanical doll Amalia. His heart races, reawakening with old memories of falling in love.

"Where did you come from?"

"From Earth."

"So far away . . ."

The woman shows him a gentle smile as she returns K's long gaze on her.

"Yes, it all makes sense to me now. I traveled a distance of five hundred light-years, going all the way to Loulan just so I could see you again."

"Oh? But how did you know to find me here?"

"I came here to see the hermit living below to ask him about the secret of the aurora. He told me that you were up here."

The woman's eyes darken.

"Oh, no! Did you meet with him? Did he ask you for some sort of favor?"

"Yes, he did. He asked me to give him the chain from my medallion."

"A chain? Please don't tell me you gave it to him."

"I did. Is there something wrong?"

"This is bad," she says with a sigh.

"Why?"

"There was a large owl with that man, right?"

"Yes. Quite a rude bird, that one. Wouldn't stop yapping."

"Yes, I'm sure it was. But it's a friend of mine. It sometimes flies over here to tell me many things."

"And?"

"The man below lost his ability to fly after his wings were broken. That's why he's been there all this time. But now that he has your chain, he'll find a way to repair the clasps on his wings."

K's shock at hearing this is almost palpable.

"What? Wings?"

"That's right. Do you not know what sort of being that man really is?"

"All I know is what the steward of Castle Loulan told me, that he's an old hermit studying the aurora of Loulan."

"Oh, dear. That's what he told you? That mechanical steward deceived you."

"You mean that it's not true?"

"Oh, no, not at all. That man is the devil."

"What? The devil? What are you talking about?"

"Why would I lie to you? His name is Lucifer."

"Lucifer?"

"That name is from the Bible of the Twilight Era. They say he was a fallen angel banished from Heaven."

"I've heard those stories too, and those in the *Southern Scriptures* that speak of a divine being known as the Dark Wanderer."

"Do you remember that he's also called Dark Wings or the Lord of the Wicked Wings?"

She's right. K remembers seeing such names several times in the massive volumes of the *Southern Scriptures*. The scriptures speak of a Dark Wanderer, a scientist from the time when divine beings walked Earth. But because he possessed evil within his heart, they exiled him from the land of the gods.

"But I thought devils like him have long been destroyed."

"No. He cannot be destroyed. He is immortal."

K shudders.

"There was something he said to me. Something about how he discovered the Secret of Osiris and gained immortality."

"Oh, that cursed magic."

Does she know something that she isn't telling him? K's curiosity gets the better of him. He presses her to tell him more.

"Just what sort of secret is it?"

"It is a type of necromancy, a secret technique for bringing the dead back to life."

With anguish written all over her face, the woman speaks to K about the existence of a revivification tank called the "Sarcophagus of Osiris." The device transmits a tremendous electric charge through a tank filled with a strange gas. Placing a corpse inside the tank brings it back to life within a day.

"But restoring life this way runs counter to the most fundamental laws of nature! Even if you could bring someone back, only their flesh returns. But the soul—that can never be made whole again."

Their time is up.

Lucifer is coming for them. The sound of flapping wings fills the air. K looks up to the now dark skies above them. He gasps at the sight of the giant, bat-like wings swooping toward them. Attached to his back with belts wrapping around him, his wings extend out to nearly twice the size of his stout body. But even more monstrous to behold are his eyes, flickering red in the darkness, fixed right on them.

Lucifer dives toward the top of their heads, leaving in his wake a reeking stench so foul it makes K and Barbara gasp for air.

K tries to fight back atop the cramped rooftop of the tower, doing all he can to place himself in front of Barbara as Lucifer lunges for her. But he is no match for Lucifer's ferocity. He circles above their heads, seizing any opening he finds, pouncing from every direction.

K falls, then gets up. He falls again, then gets up again. But in the end, his bravery is all in vain. Tiring of K's stubborn refusal to stay down, Lucifer lets loose a plume of flame out of his mouth. The fire singes K's hair and back, unleashing the noxious stench of burning sulfur. Yet despite the haze and nausea increasingly overwhelming him, K still does not stop fighting.

But Lucifer's attacks on K are relentless. Finally, the stench overcomes K. As soon as he falls to the floor, Lucifer grabs hold of Barbara's body. He carries her off, flying away toward Loulan's black sky.

Still fighting to stay conscious, K calls out Barbara's name. Again and again, he screams, until his voice goes hoarse. But Lucifer's dark shadow has already flown far beyond his reach. He has already disappeared into the dark sky.

5

K awakens to a sky already blanketed in the deeper darkness of night. What happened? The hair and the clothes on his back should be burnt. But there is no trace of fire on them. His ears ring, and his head aches, as if it were slowly being emptied out.

Was I dreaming? Did the devil attack me in my dreams?

Yet all that happened remains far too vividly etched in his memory.

K descends from the top of the tower. Nowhere else to go now but return to the city. Once again, K aimlessly wanders through town. Once again, he ends up back at the harbor where all the docked starships slumber.

Thoroughly exhausted, K slips inside an empty waiting room in the terminal building. He plants himself down on one of the benches. His ears continue to ring.

K hears a voice in the distance calling out to him.

"It is you!"

Languidly, K looks up. The young man K met at the bar some days ago stands before him. As usual, his face is dark and dismal. Nonetheless, he makes an effort to offer a weak smile.

"Not a nice night, is it?"

"Not really."

It's the only response K manages to muster. For a moment, the thought that this young man resembles his old friend Hoffman crosses K's mind. But it was a long time ago, back on planet Earth, when they parted.

"You don't look too good. How about we go get a drink to make you feel better? If you wish, I can take you to another bar."

K briefly hesitates, knowing that his invitation means that all the costs will be paid out of his pocket. But it doesn't take long for him to change his mind.

"That's certainly a thought. Sure, let's go."

The young man brings K to a dilapidated area not too far from the harbor. Hidden behind the mountains of rubbish strewn around the area is a secret entryway to a place that's little more than a cramped hole in the wall. Not much space to go around in this place, with parts of the ceiling already collapsed and bits and pieces of the walls crumbling away around them.

With a tone of familiarity, the young man orders something from the bartender. The bartender's surly look and gray robes give him the appearance of a monk. With rough hands, he sets out two glasses for them, pouring their drinks from a pitcher.

"This must be your first time," the young man says with a proud flourish. "This is the drink that Loulan is most famous for."

K draws his bulbous glass close to his face, peering inside.

Numerous tiny larvae swim within the clear liquid.

"Am I supposed to drink this?" K asks in disbelief. "Just what is this?"

"Those are the larvae of the famous butterfly flowers of Loulan."

With these words, the young man brings his glass to his lips without a moment's hesitation.

"So these are the larvae of the flowers that float through the air?"

K remembers seeing such flowers in the floating gardens of Castle Loulan.

"Give it a try. It's delicious."

The young man empties his glass. Wiping his mouth with the back of his hand, he turns to the bartender.

"That was most excellent! Quite fresh!"

"Yes. They hatched the day before yesterday," the bartender curtly replies. "Another?"

"Oh, yes, please."

The young man speaks as if he's quite flush with cash, despite the fact that it's K who will pick up the tab in the end.

K observes the larvae swimming in his glass. Growing to a length of about a finger up to its first joint, the larvae swim about at dizzying speed, propelling themselves with a single flagellum extending out of their bodies.

"This is what the egg looks like."

The bartender brings them a strip of paper, much like an egg card of a silkworm.

"You first immerse them in alcohol. After three complete days, you warm them up to hatch the larvae."

K finally empties his own glass. Might as well just get it over with. The young man eagerly eyes K, watching for his reaction.

"So? How was it?"

"I don't know. I can't really say I found it to be all that great."

"Really? But the sensation when it goes down your throat is quite something else, isn't it?"

"Well, I just drank it all in one gulp."

"Then, you must have another."

At the young man's urging, K steels himself for another try of the drink. This time, he takes his time drinking it. The young man is right. K does feel an odd slippery sensation as the drink goes down his throat.

"You should start feeling the alcohol soon," the young man says, placing his hand on his stomach. "Right now, they're desperately struggling right in here, but soon enough they will burst open."

The young man explains that the bodies of the larvae contain some sort of alkaloid, which mixes in with the alcohol as their bodies burst open. It is indeed a strange kind of intoxication, markedly different from what you find from any Earth drug. That is not to say that it's a pleasant sensation. For K, it feels as if his very being were splitting apart. At first, he figures that the experience differs from one individual to another. But when he asks the young man how he is feeling, he describes similar symptoms to what K feels. Whether one takes these symptoms to be pleasant or not though, that is another story altogether.

"A magnificent feeling, isn't it?"

"Well . . ."

Somehow, the drink's effects remind K of the unpleasant sensations he experienced when he first traveled to Loulan, when his starship entered Karnak navigation.

"Everyone feels funny at first," the young man tells K. "Maybe the narcotics work at the level of the unconscious? Anyway, you should indulge yourself. Come with me."

The man leads K to the back of the bar, into another cramped room. Pulling aside the hanging curtains separating this room from the front, the young man takes K inside. There, they find a space without any tables or chairs. Instead, plush carpets rest directly atop the bare earth.

"Why don't you lie down for a bit?"

No longer able to walk straight, K finds the young man's suggestion quite attractive indeed. He drops down to the carpets so quickly he might as well have just fallen off his feet. The young man tends after K, first loosening his clothes, then bringing out a leather pillow from somewhere to place behind his head.

"How do you feel?" he asks.

"Not too bad," K says, taking the time to study the young man's face once more.

Just as he had thought, he does look like Hoffman, almost like a twin. Could it be? Or is this just another of the effects of imbibing the butterfly-flower larvae? To K's eyes, the young man appears to be wearing a mask of Hoffman's face. Or is it Hoffman who's put on this young man's face for his mask? In the end though, does it really matter which is which?

K's mind is still in the midst of this confusion when he finally dozes off.

6

A large crowd gathers around K. He does not notice them until the sounds of their heavy breathing enter his dreams, awakening him from his inebriated slumber. He opens his heavy eyes, scanning his surroundings. Throngs of people now fill every inch of space, every single one either sprawled out on the ground or crouched down without a single care for the world. A few pass around a joint among themselves, each one taking a drag in turn, empty expressions on their faces. Among them is a young girl staring at the ceiling as she holds her knees, looking rather unbalanced.

Young and old, men and women—there must be more than ten people inside this cramped room. The young man who brought K here cuddles with a sullen-looking older woman in the opposite corner of the room, appearing to be deep in conversation with her.

Another familiar face, the merchant K met in the Karnak vessel, also mingles among the people here, along with a younger woman, his daughter.

What was her name again? Ellen or something?

Her eyes are red, as if she has been crying for quite a while.

Has every single woman here been crying? Why is everyone dazed or frightened all of a sudden?

Something isn't right here.

Feeling somewhat rested, K rises from his rug, turning to the middle-aged man in some sort of work uniform seated next to him.

"Did something happen here?" he asks.

"What do you mean did something happen? Just who the hell are you?"

The middle-aged man glares at K with a weary-looking face. Without a word, K retrieves his Sacred Service medal from a pocket of his clerical robes, flashing it to the man.

"Oh!"

The man's attitude flips in a single heartbeat. As if frightened by his very presence, he shuffles away from K as fast as he can.

Watching the man's behavior only confuses K further. Shrugging his shoulders, he sits back down, holding his knees just like the woman sitting across the room.

"What a depressing night! It always gets like this whenever it visits," someone mutters.

"Not a soul left in town now."

"Of course not! Nights like these call for narcotics! Only way to forget the doom and gloom!"

The bartender walks through the curtains from the other room, bringing in his hands a five-sided tray, atop which stand numerous triangular glasses and a square blue bottle.

"Everyone! Please, feel free to have a drink! These drinks are on him!"

The shouts come from the far end of the room. It's the young man who brought K here, pointing toward K. K has no recollection of agreeing to any of this.

"Oh, that's wonderful! Thank you! Don't mind if I do!"

"Come on! Pass around the glasses!"

For a moment, some semblance of cheer returns to the people gathered here. It looks like they've accepted K as one of their own. The beautiful woman whose gaze was affixed to the ceiling earlier hands K the first glass, pouring a drink for him. K winces when he catches a whiff of the liquor's strong aroma. But once it touches his lips, all that matters is its sweet flavor on his tongue.

"Will you drink to my happiness? Cheers!"

She reminds K of the woman at the bar where Hoffman took him once.

"Sure," K says. "So, what's your name?"

"Who cares about names? Just call me whatever you'd like."

"Fine. Your name is Serena."

After clinking their glasses together, the wild beauty slips her body into the narrow space next to K.

"So, Serena. Everyone, even you, has been acting rather strangely. Would you mind telling me what exactly is going on?"

"You're an odd one, aren't you? Aren't you coming onboard too?"

What is going on here? Will someone please just tell me?

"Serena, what are you talking about? Could you please tell me? I'm not from around here. I really have no idea what's going on right now."

"Oh my God. You're really not joking, are you?"

She does not even try to hide her surprise. Lowering her voice, she pulls K close to whisper something in his ear.

"It's the *Emissary*."

"The *Emissary*? You mean the ship headed for Planet Bosch, right? So what about it?"

"It's returned."

"Where?"

"Just outside the harbor."

"Really? When did it arrive?"

"A couple of days ago."

"What? How? I didn't see anything at all."

"Unbelievable. Sacred Service officers these days really know nothing. Nobody has ever seen the true form of the *Emissary*."

"What? You can't see it? So, how do you know it's here if you can't see it?"

"Of course you can tell. You can feel its presence."

K tilts his head, taking another sip of his drink.

"That's why everybody's in a funk. That's why we've all gathered around here like this."

"Okay. I still don't quite get why people are so depressed about it though."

"Of course people get depressed. When you know that the *Emissary* is out there beyond the harbor, there's no point in going anywhere. All you can do is either sit at home quietly or in a place like this and wait to see if it's your time."

Nothing makes sense to K anymore. Not even his drink.

"What do you mean exactly?"

"If your time has come, that means you've been summoned," Serena says, looking close to tears.

"Every time the *Emissary* arrives in Loulan, it sends out its summonses. No one knows who'll receive them. It could be for fifty or sixty people. It could be two hundred people. It changes every time. Until you hear them, no one can tell how many summonses will go out."

"How then do you receive the summonses?"

"Only those who receive them will know. The order to board the ship comes directly into your mind."

"So what happens if you refuse the order?"

"No, you can't do that. It's simply impossible."

"Why?"

"It's just not possible. A call from the *Emissary* is absolute."

The words make her tremble as she presses her soft body against K.

7

How much time has passed? Midnight approaches, and soon they will cross the boundary separating today and tomorrow. Little by little, the momentary cheer of the bar's back room returns to its previous gloom.

Noticing this, K once again addresses the crowd.

"Shall I get another bottle for everyone?"

However, not a single one of them says a word.

Grave expressions smear everyone's faces. All await the important decision to come down from high above. Now, even K himself begins to sense the cruel and melancholy force coming through the entrance, approaching him.

The middle-aged man seated next to him before the woman he named Serena sidled up to him approaches K. He leans down to speak, telling K that those summoned by the call of the *Emissary* will never again come back home.

"But hasn't the space route to Planet Bosch been designated as a Sacred Route? Doesn't that mean it's closed to the general public? So why would all these people be traveling on it?"

All this is quite odd indeed.

"I hear that you'll be traveling on that vessel as well?"

The man tries to keep his voice low.

"Yes, that's the plan. That's why I traveled all the way to Loulan from Earth. I've actually been waiting for this ship to return all this time."

"I see," the man says with a nod. "So I take it that you're already aware that the ship that services the Sacred Route is a Nirvana-class vessel."

"Oh? It's not a Karnak-type ship?"

"You didn't know? Must be why you have so many questions. Now it all makes sense. Anyway, Karnak-type vessels have a maximum operating range of only around 160 light-years before needing to refuel. They can't be used on the Sacred Route, with its distance of several hundred light-years."

"Do you mean to tell me that the ship will fly through the Sacred Route in a single jump without any stopovers?"

"That's right. You know that there's the Space Desert in between here and there, right?"

"Yes. I heard that it's a gap in space where there isn't a single fixed star."

"Right. That's why only Nirvana-class ships can service the Sacred Route."

"Just what sort of ship is a Nirvana-class vessel?"

The man turns pale.

"It's a cruel ship," he says.

Much of the true workings of Nirvana navigation employed

on the Sacred Route are a mystery. But what K can gather from the grievous words the man speaks is that this type of ship uses the power of the human mind to hurtle through the deepest reaches of space.

"So, let me see if I understand. You're telling me that this so-called Nirvana drive uses the unconscious as its fuel? Is that correct?"

"Yes, that's right. We used to actually call the jump of Nirvana-class ships a 'dream jump.'"

K does not even know how to respond.

"So, are you, by any chance, a spacefarer?" is all he can say.

"I used to be" comes the man's answer.

K learns from that man that the workings of the Nirvana navigation system have been classified top secret under the laws of the Papal Court.

"The only reason I'm telling you any of this is because you're a Sacred Service officer," the man says in a faint whisper.

K recalls that Karnak vessels used cargo loaded through a large pipe as their fuel.

"Yes. That cargo is ground up into a protoplasm that functions as a catalytic agent."

Nirvana-class vessels also have their version of "cargo." Finally, it dawns on K why the ship known here as the *Emissary* has to load up with so many of Loulan's people before it can make the trip all the way to Planet Bosch. Still, the specific mechanism at work in their conversion to the energy powering the space drive to traverse a distance of several hundred light-years in a single jump eludes K. Not that there is any need for him to have any understanding of this.

A total silence now hangs over the place as all wait for the appointed time.

Suddenly, a young woman stands straight up. It's the daughter of the merchant. It's Ellen.

Has she received the summons from that thing?

"Ellen! Ellen!" says the merchant as he desperately tries to hang on to her body like a madman. "Please! Someone! Please help my daughter!"

His face covered in tears, he turns to every single person in the room. His eyes then make contact with K's.

"You're a Sacred Service officer. Can you not stop her? Please help! Please help my daughter!"

But Ellen has already lost all capacity for reason. With incredible force, she easily brushes off her father's grasp on her.

"Ellen!"

The merchant's cries go unheard. Ellen exits the room as if possessed by some evil spirit. Every single person in the room is as silent as a rock. For a long time, they remain still, not moving a single muscle.

8

K steps outside into the darkened city.

He just barely hears the whistling of the wind from somewhere far away. As he follows the road toward the harbor, more and more people who have been summoned like Ellen appear around him.

They form a line of sleepwalkers. More show up at each crossing, until the line becomes a full-blown crowd. All of them march toward the harbor's boarding area, beyond the designated waiting rooms of the terminal building.

K looks up. If not for the deep black rift that slices across the dark heavens, K would only see clear skies above him.

It is a hectic night for the workers at the spaceport. They arrange the arriving people into rows, leading each one aboard awaiting barges. One after another, each barge then flies out upon filling up, only to then return to the harbor empty.

The sight of the waves of flying saucers filled to capacity with passengers lifting off against the glittering emerald-green light transfixes K. Every one of them veers toward one particular spot in the night sky. K focuses his eyes on that spot. He sees it. Something jet black in color, its shape indistinct, floats there. Difficult though it is to tell with the darkness of the background, he nonetheless manages to make out the outlines of what looks like a primordial creature with appendages extending out in all directions.

K stops a passing spaceport worker.

"Is that the Nirvana ship?"

"Yes."

"It sure looks disgusting."

"Indeed. I feel sick every time it returns here," he says. "Wait, who are you again?"

K retrieves the medal from a pocket of his clerical robes.

"I'm supposed to get on that thing. Could you tell me what I need to do?"

"Oh, I take it you haven't checked in yet?"

"No," K says.

"Please hurry up then. The office is straight down this way, inside the terminal building. The ship will be departing soon."

"Thank you," K says.

With hurried steps, he heads to the terminal building but finds nothing that looks like a room, only a dark hallway.

Here we go again. What is going on this time?

K mumbles to himself as he gropes his way down the dark hallway.

At the end of the hallway, in the triangular space underneath a staircase, a single candle lights up a desk. A man's silhouette sits behind the desk. He wears black clerical robes, hood pulled over his head as he continues to examine the documents in front of him.

"Excuse me," K says, approaching the desk. "Could you tell me where I can find the check-in counter for passengers headed to Planet Bosch?"

The hooded man looks up.

"Right here," he says in a low voice.

"I'd like to do so then."

"Do you have your notice of appointment?"

The man is completely nonchalant.

"My notice of appointment? Yes, I do."

K remembers a distant memory. It was right about the time of his departure from Earth that he first received his notice. Ages ago. The papers have been all crumpled up.

The man unfurls the wad of paper with a nod.

"Everything appears to be in order. Any luggage?"

"No."

"You're all set, then."

The man scribbles something at the bottom of K's notice of appointment with a quill pen, affixing his signature at the end. He then takes a stamp next to him, pressing it hard onto the paper.

"Please proceed."

All too simple.

"That's it?" K asked.

"Yes. Please present your notice of appointment to a member of the spaceport staff. Good day."

With these words, the man closes his book of documents. With the book under his arm, he stands up to leave, picking up the candle.

"It's you!"

For an instant, the candle lights up the man's face. But just as quickly, he blows the flame out. There is no longer any way to verify K's suspicions. Not that he needs it. He is already positive that the man is the Lord of Castle Loulan.

Shortly after, a jet-black, single-seat flying saucer lifts straight up to the sky with K aboard it. For some reason, the shape reminds him of a flattened funerary urn used for burials. Once he is high enough, a view of the entire spaceport opens up below him, with a bird's-eye view of all of the city of Loulan tinged with the color of emerald in the background. He cannot see above though. The enormous blackened body of the ship blocks his view.

One section of the black ship's body opens up, radiating the glow of a white ray of light. K's flying saucer follows the light's path, until it approaches close enough to be swallowed up by the body of the Nirvana ship. Once inside, the Nirvana-class galactic transport screams a silent roar as its body trembles, before vanishing in a flash of light.

A single hyperspace jump that traverses 450 light-years!

An ocean of dreams stretches out between here and there.

SACRED ROUTE

1

No alarms of any kind warn K before the Nirvana ship enters its dream jump. Only the sensation of his whole body dissolving before his very eyes informs him of what is happening, until he can no longer recognize his own physical being, until all of his body dissolves to the point that he can become pure consciousness in itself.

Outside the ship, the Space Desert expands in every direction around them. Total darkness fills this vast expanse of space. In this empty sea where no light exists, no longer is it possible to fathom existence itself, as the total absence of light robs all matter of any tangible quality. All that remains now is the absolute solitude of K's consciousness. Mind unmoored from body, spirit freed from flesh, his consciousness expands out to the universe, wandering back to some place and time back home, as if guided by the great will of space itself.

Time loses all meaning, no longer flowing from one moment to the next. Is this eternity? Or is time simply standing still, utterly unmoving? Consciousness itself becomes one with this limitless expanse of time. Does the very idea of "thought" even make sense in such an instance? That is an open question.

No words can ever be adequate to describe this sensation. After all, without the sequential flow of time from past to future, words cannot be arranged next to each other to produce any meanings. All that is certain now is a vague, almost indiscernible sensation of enlightenment. But it is more than just a simple sensation like a pain or an itch. No, it is a ripple forming in one's consciousness, like ripples that reveal the water on the surface of a lake so smooth and mirrorlike it reflects back the lakeshore scenery when a gust of wind blows over it.

Finally, K understands everything.

Human consciousness is akin to the surface of a mirror. The surface does not in itself exist. All the mirror can do, all that defines a mirror, is its capacity to reflect back the object before it. Just as the mirror cannot reflect back its own surface, human consciousness—whose sole function is to perceive the world as phenomena, to turn objects into observable occurrences—cannot perceive itself. The purer the consciousness, the less of its own surface can it see. Human beings are aware of themselves not because the consciousness recognizes itself, but because it perceives something other to itself. Only indirectly do we know our own being.

This is what it means to sense a ripple in the consciousness. Only through the distortions of these ripples over the mirrorlike lake surface is the existence of a consciousness revealed to the consciousness. Entombing one small part of the grand cosmic consciousness—the consciousness in a state of purity—in the corporeal existence of the flesh adulterates it with impurities, which has the perverse effect of giving the consciousness an awareness of itself.

Is this what we call God? Is God this cosmic consciousness, this totality, this pure consciousness of all the cosmos? If God is the surface of a cosmic mirror, then insofar as God is pure, there can be no awareness of himself as God.

K's consciousness soars across the 450 light-years of the Sacred Route.

Soon, K's consciousness, K's soul, begins its return to the prison of material existence. As his ship approaches the end of its route, bit by bit, it rematerializes, restoring itself to flesh. It is a sickening experience, nothing less than hell itself, as K witnesses a vivid display of the truth of Nirvana navigation.

K trembles in fear at the sight before him. The interior of the Nirvana-class vessel has become as chaotic and colorful as the circular world of a mandala, with the souls of all the people who were loaded aboard at the port of Loulan floating within the cabin. An insatiable hunger consumes him, making him chase after these other souls, engorging himself on them one by one as he tries to satisfy his unbearable hunger. But there can be no satisfying his cravings, this primordial hunger.

Is this the fate of all souls? Is this the hunger that utterly burdens all souls? Could it be that this primordial hunger is the will that governs all of the great cosmos?

K's soul grows bigger every time it devours another, even as he cannot forget who these souls he consumes used to be.

2

K finds himself in a grassy meadow, as some kind of beast with a mane fluttering in the gusts of wind.

A nearby herd of deer trembles at his presence.

His raw hunger urges his hind legs forward.

Pounce! His prey is the space merchant's daughter, Ellen. She puts up a violent resistance to his strike from behind. But before long, the smell of warm blood drifts in the air. K's fangs dig deep into the bone.

K's long dream finally ends.

But waking brings K no comfort. All he finds is the horror of the interior of the *Emissary* devoid of anyone else but him.

Did all the other passengers disembark while he was asleep?

K pushes his body up through the cabin of the vessel. He appears to be inside some kind of cavernous holding tank filled with a viscous liquid.

This must be the protoplasm that fuels the ship. Still in a

daze, he extends his limbs from their fetal position. He swims in the direction of a light. That has to be an exit.

The exit appears to be a tubular tunnel that resembles a drainage pipe. Along the way, he encounters several valve locks, each one operating automatically, opening for him as he swims from one chamber to the next. With each chamber he swims through, the volume of salty liquid thins out, until he makes it to the final chamber, which is filled completely with air.

K has found his way out of the Nirvana ship.

Looking back, K sees the black ship behind him engorged with air. It appears to have crash-landed on a grassy meadow. A fence made of a strange thorny wood surrounds the area, continuing down the rolling hills beyond his view. A herd of domesticated animals grazes in the distance, but K has never before seen such green beasts.

This was no spaceport at all. Not one sign of a single structure or piece of equipment—or, for that matter, any people—that you would expect from such a facility. Not much choice but to make his way up to a nearby hill. At least, maybe, he'll see something from up there.

A warm, pleasant breeze blows over the meadow. Walking up the hill, K could easily be mistaken for someone going on a picnic. Once he makes it to the top, he turns his gaze back on the *Emissary*. Even from atop the hill, the ship still appears enormous, looking like a gigantic balloon that tumbled onto the field. It astonishes him that such a flimsy-looking vessel could have traveled across vast reaches of space spanning several hundred light-years.

K watches as the Nirvana ship belches, spewing out the liquid inside it into a small stream that flows down the slope in the pasture, until it is all absorbed into the ground. Right before his eyes, the ship's exterior begins to deflate.

Almost as soon as the ship flattens out, it begins to inflate anew. Once it is fully inflated, the wind tumbles it along the field until, suddenly, it launches itself into the air. Now fully transformed into a balloon, the Nirvana ship steadily climbs upward into a boundless sky serene in its brightness, with every bit of it awash in clear blue, as if it has become a soul lifted up to heaven.

Struck dumb with amazement, K can do nothing but watch as the ship slowly disappears from his view.

It takes some time for K to come to his senses. As much as he might want to wallow in despair at being left all alone in the universe, he can't just linger about atop this hill forever. He decides to head down the narrow trail on the opposite side of the hill. Surrounding him is a picture of tranquility. Birds sing in the distance, but none are visible to K. Perhaps it is pretentious to think so, but there's something oddly mythic about the atmosphere of this place. Stagnant, yet seemingly governed by a time that stretches for all eternity.

K arrives at a fork in the road. Though uncertain of which path to take, in the end he opts to follow the road that goes farther down the gentle slope, spiraling down the hill. K walks without stopping to rest. But the path doesn't seem to go anywhere, just continuing on without end.

Or so K thought. After walking across seven or eight hills, he comes to a turn in the path. Right there stands another man. So abrupt, so unexpected is this event that K is taken aback for a moment.

This other man is quite old indeed. He wears a bulky cloak with a hood over his head. Oddly, the man seems to have been expecting K.

"It really is a pleasant day. Just perfect," he says. "I was just about to head off to pick you up. You were on that black ship, right?"

"Yes." K nodded.

"What's your name, son?"

"My name is K."

"I see. My name is Parnassus. Where do you wish to go now? Or would you prefer to follow my lead?"

Not seeing much choice, K tells the man that he will follow his lead. The old man turns on his heel, leading K back up the road he came from.

K walks side by side with him.

"The thing is, I was on my way to Planet Bosch," K says. "But it looks like my ship had to make an emergency landing here."

The old man Parnassus gives K a knowing look, as if he no longer needs to hear his story. Indeed, he makes it seem like he's already heard it all before. Yet he explains little to K, only giving roundabout answers that entirely miss the point to any of his questions. All he tells K is that he is alone on this unnamed planet.

"So just what have you been doing here all by yourself?" asks K.

"It's my job to take care of lost children like you," the old man answers, laughing.

"Oh? Does the black ship make emergency landings on this planet every now and then?"

"It does indeed. There are plenty of planets just like this one around this part of space. And each one has a caretaker just like me. We all take care of any lost souls."

"So, how many are there?"

"You mean in this star system?"

"Yeah, I guess," K says. "Do you mean this planet orbits a star? What is this planet called?"

"There is nothing of the sort."

"Just as I thought, it's a planet without a name."

"Well, if you must call it something, then you can call it by the name of Planet Nirvana."

"Planet Nirvana."

K gives Parnassus a sidelong glance.

"Correct. And the central star of this system is the Nirvana Star, so called because the star is composed of the same substance as the souls of you travelers."

The old man's words confound K.

Seemingly reading K's mind, he points to the zenith of the sky, toward an orb of white light shimmering against the clear blue sky. Circling around the larger orb are smaller soul-stars, whose numbers must have been in the thousands, even the tens of thousands. Even the old man has no idea how many there are in all. It reminds K of the structure of an atomic nucleus, with so many small satellites orbiting a central nucleus, each tracing its own orbital path.

"So, the large soul-star above us is like the sun of this system," Parnassus says. "This soul-star you stand on now is also one of the planets in the system, revolving at the farthest of orbits. One day, you too will return to the Sacred Star."

Lips loosened all of a sudden, the old man explains to K everything he knows about the spiritual astrophysics that govern this star system. Much of it escapes K's understanding, but one detail that leaves an impression on him is the fact that this star system, located at the very edge of the Taklamakan Space Desert, was the point of origin for all life in the entire universe.

"So, the thing is, I have orders to travel to Planet Bosch. Parnassus, do you know how I can get to Planet Bosch from here?"

However, the old man has fallen silent. K looks at him, but he simply stands in place, unmoving.

"Hey! Are you there? Is Planet Bosch far from this place?"

Parnassus still does not answer. That's certainly odd. K peeks under the man's large hood. He sees the old man breathing in and out as he sleeps, even as he remains standing.

3

Night falls on the planet. As the large soul-star circles to the planet's far side, the smaller soul-stars hidden by the afternoon light now give off a pale glimmer. Worlds both large and small flit about the night sky, looking like countless fireflies.

K sits down on the side of the road, watching the still-sleeping old man. He does not look like he's about to move again any time soon. Not a single twitch of movement, not even a breath, as if he had fully petrified into a fossil. Frozen while still in the midst of walking, his pose strikes K as rather precarious, but oddly enough he does not fall down.

Without any idea of what to do on his own, K doesn't really have much choice but to wait for the old man to awaken. It would be an entirely different story if others happened to live on this planet, but since only this old man here can guide him, there's not much else for K to do.

K turns his gaze to the sky, watching the smaller soul-stars flickering out there, reminding him that this place is another world altogether.

It's certainly been a long road from Earth.

How long has it been? Leaving my hometown, journeying to the capital city of Igitur, taking the Sacred Service Exam—all of these feel like happenings from another story, from another lifetime.

Such recollections of things past overflow in K's mind, making him feel increasingly more alone in the universe.

What is going to happen to me now?

All these things that have happened simply beggar belief. K passed the Sacred Exam. He trained in the monastery in the middle of the desert. He received the official notification to go to the Planet Bosch Research Center. He received another notification to depart from Earth. He traveled to the strange emerald-colored city of the void. Finally, he boarded the ship to traverse the great distance of the Taklamakan Space Desert. Things seem to be happening far beyond his control or understanding.

What is going to happen to me now?

K repeats these words over and over. Ten times. A hundred times. But there is no answer.

No one tells K anything at all! Not about his journey. Not about his destination, the Planet Bosch. Why has all information about this planet been suppressed? What is the purpose behind his journey? How is he supposed to know what to do without such information?

Is such a thing even possible?

Frustration builds within K as these thoughts circle around his mind.

Argh!

K screams out to the sky, though it comes out more as a cross between a yawn and sigh of lament than anything else. As if responding to his call, the smaller soul-stars floating in the night sky tremble.

K lays his head down on the grass, using picked grass as a pillow. The comfortable softness of the grass surprises him. It may as well be a top-of-the-line bed as far as he is concerned. Somehow, this relaxes him, calming the anger that welled up inside him just moments ago. His face starts to look even blissful.

When you think about it, human beings are born into this world, then die. To what end? Who's to say?

There's a famous dialogue between the heretic Darko Dachilko and his disciples that's relevant here:

"Where do people come from and where do they go?"

To this question, Darko Dachilko gave this answer:

"My beloved disciples, why human beings are born into this world, then live their lives, then die—we do not know the fundamental reasons for this."

"Master, please tell us!" The disciples all persisted.

Then, Darko Dachilko answered:

"Human beings come from the one and only place and return to the one and only place. An eternally repeating cycle."

"Where is the one and only place?" one disciple asked.

"It is a place where all life is born and where all life returns upon death."

"Is it in the Great Heavens?"

Darko Dachilko answers:

"It is the womb of all life and at the same time the tomb of all life."

"Master, do you know this place?"

"I know the place. I have been to this place and seen this star. Do you all doubt this?"

"No!" the disciples shouted in unison. "But, Master, how did you come to know of this place? How did you come to see this place?"

Thus Darko Dachilko spoke:

"Are you all demanding to see proof from me?"

Darko Dachilko's retort was quite harsh. And so the disciples fell silent.

But among them, the one known as the Dark Disciple suddenly stood his ground and shouted back.

"Yes, Master. We do demand such a thing from you."

Sad eyes accompanied Darko Dachilko's next words:

"So we have a traitor in our midst. Telling you all the facts of the matter will only bring me sorrow. And my sorrow will become your sorrow. But I will step forward and tell you all. For once you know how I came to know of this place, once you know the facts of the matter, you will believe that the teachings I have preached are the truth.

Sadly, in the edition of the collected dialogues that K read—officially banned, of course—the crucial section that follows had been redacted. All that remained of it was a short phrase, which read, "This is because I am a XXX."

The story goes that Darko Dachilko's revelation of the truth caused a stir among all the gathered disciples in The Orchard.

Soon after, the Dark Disciple betrayed Darko Dachilko to the Papal Court.

And so Darko Dachilko was arrested and brought to the infamous trial for heresy. All sorts of crimes were included in his indictment. Finally, the verdict came down—execution. They say that his confession—the truth he purportedly told his disciples in the redacted part of the text—was the single decisive factor in the determination of this verdict.

4

K falls asleep.

He awakens to the large soul-star rising from behind the horizon beyond the hill.

It looks like Parnassus had slept standing through the night. His eyes snap open as soon as K rises from his grassy bed.

"Oh!" the old man says. "I slept quite well."

"Do you always sleep like that?" K asks.

"Yes. I always sleep at sunset and awaken at sunrise without fail."

He takes a couple of steps forward, proceeding tentatively as if testing his feet. Once his body fully returns to normal, he turns to K.

"Shall we go on, then?"

K dusts off the grass from his clothes.

"Sure, all right. But first, could you tell me where we're going?"

"Where? Didn't you say you were going to Planet Bosch?"

"Yeah."

"Then, follow my lead."

"All right."

The pair return to the road, walking along hills and even more hills in every direction. It begins to dawn on K that this road will continue on and on without end. He snaps.

"Parnassus!" he shouts from behind him.

"What's the matter? Tired already? Shall we rest for a bit? Time is one thing we have plenty of."

"No, nothing like that," K says. "I'm just wondering if this road continues on and on without end."

"Why do you think so?" the old man asks without turning around.

"I don't know. I guess it's just a feeling."

"Oh, is that right?" says the old man, his voice almost mocking.

"Wait! Aren't you supposed to be the only man on this planet?"

"That's right."

"Then shouldn't you know exactly where this road will take us? Shouldn't you know if there's actually a destination at the end of it or whether it just goes all around the planet, taking us back to where we started?"

The old man's face goes dark as he shakes his head, his earlier mocking confidence all but vanished.

"The truth is that I don't know myself. It's been hundreds of years since I first came here. Or has it been thousands? It's been so long I no longer remember. But I still have no idea whether this road will ever end somewhere."

Rocking his head back and forth, the old man speaks about his life on this planet, telling K that after all his walking, he can say with certainty that this road circling around the base of the largely featureless hills of this planet never crosses paths with any other roads.

"But it doesn't really seem like such a huge planet," K says, obvious disbelief written all over his face. "I mean, you can even see the curvature of the horizon."

"You are absolutely correct," the old man says. "This planet isn't all that big."

"My guess is that following this road for three days or so should take us back to where we started."

"You would think so, but I must have walked this road many thousands of times, and yet never have I returned to where I started."

Hearing this disturbs K, though there is still a part of him that wonders if this old man isn't just trying to play him for a fool.

"So, what you're saying is that it doesn't matter how long we keep at this. In the end, I'll never find my way to Planet Bosch, will I?" K says in frustration. "You told me to follow you, and so I did. I thought you would take me to a spaceport where they dock the ships bound for Planet Bosch."

"A spaceport?" says the old man. "I've never seen such a thing in my life."

"Then, why did you tell me to follow you?"

"I have no recollection of ever ordering you to follow me. I just asked what you wanted to do. Besides, instead of just standing on the street waiting for nothing, walking along this road at least gives us something to do. Anyway, going on is all we can do. In the end, it's at least a good way to kill time."

In the end, this is all Parnassus is doing.

"Do you really think there is much to gain from just walking?"

"No, not really," the old man says, seemingly indifferent to it all. "In fact, I'm completely bored with this scenery. It's just hills upon hills as far as the eye can see."

"And yet you keep on walking?"

"That's right. What else am I supposed to do? You never know, maybe there's something beyond the next hill I just haven't come across yet. I haven't lost hope quite yet."

"Sure. But hope alone won't really get you anywhere."

"You may just be right. My thinking was just like yours in the beginning. Just like you, I thought I'd quickly get tired of all this walking and just quit. But even if I stop walking, it's not like there's anything else I can do. So I might as well just keep moving forward even if only to kill time."

"I guess so."

"That's when I had a realization. Hope, you see, is something that will never disappear. It's just something you can never exhaust. As long this road continues going beyond another hill, and another hill, then so too will hope persist forever."

"And you're satisfied with that?" K says. "You've lived on this planet for a while, so that might be enough for you! But I'm someone who needs to get myself to Planet Bosch!"

"I know that. But there is nothing we can do about it."

"No, that's not good enough! I'm not going to keep doing this. I'm going to get off this road and go climb that hill until I'm standing at its summit. Maybe I'll spot something from up there. Maybe the ship that left me behind here will have returned, or maybe another ship will arrive for me."

"Oh, no," the old man says, his voice trembling, deathly afraid. "Please don't go off the road."

"Why not? You have no right to stop me."

"This is true. But if you go off the road, I will cease to exist."

Lines of anxiety form on the old man's face, not that K has any understanding of what he's saying.

"Don't be silly."

The old man becomes desperate. He starts to cry.

"Oh, please stop! Please stop!"

But K pays him no attention. He steps off the road. He cuts across the grassy hills to make a run for it.

Finally, K again awakens from his dream. This time, for real.

5

So it was just a dream.

K remains inside the cabin of the jump ship traveling through hyperspace.

What an odd dream!

When did his dream begin? When he woke from one dream,

did another one continue in its place? Had he woken up inside his dream? This must be an effect of the ship's distortions of time, letting such sequential dreams take place.

I can't even trust my own senses.

K has to face his own personality.

A dream, a dream and a dream of a dream. A dream of a dream of a dream.

And so this topsy-turvy world continues on forever.

What if everything I've experienced thus far has all just been a dream?

Was any of it real?

What exactly is reality? Is it even possible to tell apart dream from reality?

Perhaps nothing truly exists in this world. Perhaps existence is nothing more than phenomenological appearance. Something may look like it exists but in reality it does not. It is a mere mirage, a shadow of something. Is all the world just an illusion?

K is alone inside the cabin of the ship, so dreadfully, so absolutely alone that he starts to think that loneliness is the fundamental essence of the universe.

No matter how much you recognize that there's no guarantee of its absolute truth, it is nevertheless quite easy to grow accustomed to a world wherein the inescapable flow of time follows a strict order, moving in one direction, from past to future.

Nearing the end of its journey, the Nirvana-class jump ship undergoes a metamorphosis, changing the form of its black hull into the shape of a stingray as it glides down the dense atmosphere for landing. The ship has arrived at Planet Sola, the last inhabited planet at the frontiers of the Holy Empire of Igitur, located near the very edge of the Taklamakan Space Desert.

"Welcome to Planet Sola."

Only a single member of the ground staff operates the spaceport. Somewhat stilted though it may be, he nonetheless attempts to present an affable smile to K. After giving K's documents a quick glance, he sends him on his way.

"Everything looks to be in order, sir. Please proceed."

K retrieves his documents.

Looking over his surroundings, K finds a spaceport that amounts to little more than an empty field. What facilities they have consist of little more than a small section marked off by wooden poles stuck through the ground at four corners with a straw rope going around them.

As far as K can tell, he is the sole disembarking passenger. He assumed that at least a few crew members had been piloting the ship, but it seems like he guessed wrong. Just to be certain, he inquires with the member of the ground staff who met him, who confirms his suspicions.

"Yes, sir, that is indeed the case. You are the only one who is arriving. The ship is fully automated, operated solely through your own willpower."

Yet another feature of the black Nirvana ship no one told K about.

"Were you born on this planet?"

"Well, yes, in a manner of speaking. Or to be more accurate, I guess you can say that I was constructed on this planet."

"Constructed?" K says, uncertain of how to take the man's statement.

"It means that my flesh was made out of the soil of Planet Sola, but my soul was brought in from Loulan and breathed into me."

"So, you're a robot?"

"Not exactly. We all call ourselves Haniwa. Terracotta Clay Dolls, in other words."

Dumbfounded, K's mouth hangs open for a while.

"Is everyone on this planet . . . ?"

"Yes, we are all Haniwa."

"Just how many of you are there?"

"Well, quite a few. I can't really give you an exact figure."

A thought crosses K's mind.

"So wait, is the Nirvana ship constructed in the same way as you?"

"No, sir, that's not the case. That ship is completely different from us. It's actually a crow living in this area of space."

"What? A crow? That ship?"

"Yes. They call it the Space Crow. It's also sometimes called a Soul Bird, since it devours the souls of living beings. Others also call it the Night Bird."

"Impossible!"

"It's the truth. Of course, the wild ones are quite lazy and useless. But, as you've seen, when they're well trained, they're able to transport people across vast distances of space."

K cannot believe what he's hearing. If this Haniwa officer is to be believed, two such trained Space Crows ply the Sacred Route. He's heard enough. There are more important matters on his mind right now.

"In any event, as you have seen in my paperwork, my instructions are to travel to Planet Bosch. Everything has the proper signatures from the Papal Court. Could you please arrange a connecting flight to my destination?"

The gentle face of the Haniwa officer contorts into a big smile.

"Yes, of course. If I am not mistaken, the next flight to Planet Bosch will depart the day after tomorrow."

"Is Planet Bosch far from here?"

"No, sir. It's only fifty light-years away."

"Oh, really?" K says, quite relieved to hear the final destination is now just a stone's throw away. "In that case, please make the arrangements for me . . ."

"Understood. In the meantime, please do let us know if you have any particular needs while you are here on Planet Sola."

"No, there's nothing really that I need right now."

"In that case, please make yourself at home during your stay here. As you can see, this is little more than a frontier planet. People traveling from Earth may find it to be rather disagreeable."

"No, that's all right. If it's only a couple of days, I can put up with pretty much anything. So, is there any place I can spend the night?"

"No, we don't have any such places prepared for you. Well, we might as well just say there is no such place here. But if you head into town, you may find something."

The officer claps his hands twice, signaling to two men crouched on the ground nearby.

6

One man is a rotund giant, the other an emaciated dwarf. The emaciated one appears to be in charge, sometimes slapping the rear end of the giant as he continues to sluggishly plod along without so much as a wince. The giant carries K on a seat strapped to his back.

Despite all appearances, the dwarf turns out to be quite helpful, providing straight answers to all of K's ever-present questions arising from his usual curiosity.

According to the dwarf, while Planet Sola isn't particularly large, its gravity is almost as strong as that of Earth, in part because of the high density of the planet's core.

"They say that there's a solid core," he explains. "Although no one has seen it, obviously."

Indeed, it is a small planet. The planet's featureless terrain extends as far as the eye can see, making the curvature of the horizon clearly discernible even to the naked eye. No mountains or hills to obstruct the view. No oceans, lakes, or rivers, either. None of that at all.

"This place looks to me like an accumulated chunk of clay," K says.

"You're right, sir. Planet Sola did indeed form out of coagulated dirt."

"But how does clay form on this planet without any rivers? Without water penetrating through rocks, there's no way for clay to form."

"That the master has many questions is only natural," the dwarf says. "The truth is that Planet Sola was created by the same man who breathed life into us."

K gives him a puzzled look. It doesn't sound to him like this story is merely some mythic origin story.

"So, this creator is your god then?" asks K.

"Yes. The God without a head. Even now, he returns to our world every so often."

He explains that their God, the creator of these clay dolls, reappears to breathe new life into them. He always comes right around the time when they have almost forgotten about him.

So Planet Sola is an artificial planet.

Learning this fact amazes K.

"What is the name of this God of yours?"

"Our Lord Darko Dachilko."

"What?"

K's shock is almost palpable, indeed, very nearly traumatic.

So the heretic is indeed still alive!

"Oh, does the master know of Our Lord Darko Dachilko?"

"Oh, yes. I know of him. But, you see, he was supposed to have had his head chopped off hundreds of years ago. He's supposed to be dead."

"Oh, no, he is not dead," says the dwarf, walking tall as he speaks. "In fact, his last visit to our planet happened just recently. It was he who ordered us to prepare the grounds for the spaceport."

So all the strange tales surrounding Darko Dachilko must be true. Make no mistake, the legend of his immortality, and his time-traveling abilities, they all really happened. His wealth of knowledge about the secrets of the hyperspace pathways of the universe has given him the power to traverse time and space at will.

Right before K is the clear proof of all this.

It is hard to call the one and only settlement on Planet Sola a town at all, seeing that it is little more than a bunch of smaller paths intersecting the main street. A few houses constructed out of clay line these paths, every single one of them lacking any roof.

Several Haniwa clay dolls linger in the heart of the town, all of them looking idle and dazed.

K's guide, the emaciated dwarf, stops the giant at one cross intersection.

"Sir, this is where you can get off."

"Sure, thanks!" K says. "By the way, do you know of any good place to stay tonight?"

"You can stay wherever you like," answers the dwarf, echoing the rather curt answer K got from the officer at the spaceport.

The man urges the giant on by striking his whip, leaving K standing in the center of the town.

The planet's sky displays the approach of sunset. With time on his hands, K decides to walk around the settlement. Three hundred steps are all it takes before he reaches the end of the town. From the edge of the settlement, the featureless clay landscape presents a desolate sight as it extends all the way to the horizon. He turns around, retracing his steps back to the center of the settlement.

On his way back, K realizes that every single one of the townsfolk wears a face constructed with a permanent smile. Rather than making them appear amiable though, it gives them a crazed look. Their faces coupled with the ponderous manner of their movements make them quite a strange sight. And when they stop moving, they become indistinguishable from statues.

The sun begins to set while K continues to wander about the town. Having returned to the intersection he started from to catch his breath, he once again runs into the dwarf from earlier. The dwarf approaches him, calling out his name.

"Sir, are you done with your sightseeing?"

"Yes, all done."

"Have you decided where you'll be staying?"

"Actually, no, I haven't."

"Of course. I mean, with everything so dirty, you just don't feel like sleeping anywhere, right?"

"No, that's not what I mean."

K tries to say more, but his words fall on deaf ears.

"Shall I take care of finding you lodgings and a woman, then?" asks the dwarf.

He whistles without waiting for K's response. It must be a signal, as the giant immediately appears from out of the darkness, standing beside him.

"Let's go!"

K does as the man suggests, riding the giant's back once more. They walk through winding roads in one area of the settlement, as K sways from side to side. Finally, they drop him off in front of one of the houses.

Leaving K by the doorway, the dwarf enters the house. Almost as soon as he goes in, he comes right back out.

"Everything's ready," he says.

K had thought that he would be sleeping outside tonight, but it looks like things will be unfolding differently, so he won't have to prepare for the worst any longer. K offers his sincerest thanks to the dwarf.

K steps inside the house, finding a room with a hearth built into its center, where black, tar-like coal smolders. Five Haniwa clay dolls—a family, by all appearances—live here. One is an older man, who appears to be the grandfather. Another pair of them look like a married couple. Beside them is a child sprawled on the floor. There's something off about how he looks.

"Is everything all right with him?" asks K.

"He's sick," the clay husband answers.

The clay husband tells K that the spirit is draining out of his child. K brings his face closer to the child but finds nothing out of the ordinary about it.

"He's probably just stopped moving."

This whole thing is ridiculous. Is this planet of clay and its animated dolls of clay just some plaything that Darko Dachilko made on a whim? Making Planet Sola may be a massive undertaking. But in the end, it is a child's toy. Although these animated clay dolls have been built at a life-sized human scale, they are, in the end, little more than dolls.

Leaning his back against the clay wall of this clay house, K can see that this is really the inside of some kind of giant dollhouse. Like all the other houses here, no roof protects this house above. Looking up, he sees unfamiliar constellations glittering against a rectangular slice of the night sky. He senses among them the watchful gaze of invisible eyes from far above the heavens.

Are you watching us from above, Darko Dachilko?

The clay wife sits before the hearth making rice cakes. A closer look reveals them to be made out of a white clay that looks like porcelain. She rolls them into balls, skewers them, then roasts them over the coals of the hearth. Helping her is their other child, a clay doll playing the role of their daughter. She carefully places more pieces of tar-like clay into the hearth.

After a few minutes of roasting, the rice cakes harden into white ceramic balls. They hand over the ones that are ready to K.

Eating them is clearly out of the question. But out of curiosity, K nonetheless asks about it.

"Like this," the clay husband says as he dusts off the ash from the rice ball, bringing a piece close to his mouth. Just as K suspects, he does not actually eat it, instead merely mimicking the gesture of eating even as he declares it to be delicious.

Ludicrous! Like a child playing house! But what choice does K have? It's far less trouble to just follow their lead. Might as well just go through with it. He brings the still searing-hot rice cake near his mouth, careful not to burn himself.

"This is delicious!" K also says.

"Isn't it? Please, have some more!"

The husband looks very pleased, continuing to push more rice cakes to K. There's no way he can refuse him now. Soon, the rest of the family joins in the meal, turning the scene into a dinner party. The sight of everyone devouring these rice cakes as they repeatedly proclaim them to be delicious must be quite humorous.

After the meal, the family readies themselves for bed. The married couple occupy the best part of the room. The child does not move. The old man heads outside the house.

"You, go to the back room and sleep with our guest," the clay husband orders his clay daughter.

With widened blue eyes, the clay daughter looks toward K with a slight reddish blush showing on her cheeks. K hesitates. Her parents though have no such compunctions. They immediately engage in their conjugal relations right there for all to see. With her body stretched out on the floor, the clay wife takes in her clay husband, making a squeaking noise that grates on the ear each time their bodies come into contact.

No longer able to watch this exceedingly absurd spectacle, K decides to make his exit from the house. But the clay daughter stops him, instead taking his hand in hers to guide him into the back room. To K's surprise, the room is not all that bad, properly furnished even if every single piece is made of clay.

K sits down on a clay chair. Next to it, a small bookshelf leans against the wall. K picks up the thick decorative tome made of clay sitting within it. Squinting his eyes in the starlight reveals the words *Southern Scriptures* engraved on the book's cover. Of course it was only decorative, impossible to flip open and read. Returning the book to the shelf, he turns his eyes to the clay daughter, who loads coal-black clay into the fireplace.

The room brightens up as soon as the fire is lit. Finally, K gets a good look at the clay daughter's face. He gasps in stunned surprise, as if stricken by some magical spell.

"What's your name, girl?"

"It's Barbara."

It's the name that K hoped to hear.

Suddenly, the entire room is transformed in a flash.

The clay walls and clay furniture have vanished. The chair K has seated himself in changes into a seat tinged with the texture of velvet. The rest of the furniture becomes fine pieces made out of rare wood. From the filthy room of the muddy clay house, they are transported into the arbor of The Orchard clearly etched within K's memories. The clay dress of the clay doll is no more, replaced by the serene blue dress of sheer silk that Barbara wore at the time.

What is going on? Has a strange form of magic unveiled memories locked within this clay world?

"Barbara," K calls out the woman's name.

"Oh, I've been waiting for you so long, Gilgeas."

No longer a clay doll, Barbara stands before K in the flesh.

"Barbara, please tell me. Who killed you?"

"Oh, Gilgeas, you don't need me to tell you. I forgive you."

"Who was it who dug your grave?"

"Your master."

"Him?"

"Yes, that's right."

"But what is my relationship to him?"

"You know this already."

Perhaps I do.

"I don't have much time left, Gilgeas. I will be waiting for you there when you arrive."

"Where?"

"Planet Bosch, of course."

"Tell me, just what sort of planet is it?"

"It's Paradise. Of course it is."

Her voice cuts off. The spell has lifted. The room has become clay once more.

THE GARDEN OF
EARTHLY DELIGHTS

1

The cosmos constricts at its center. Twisting into an hourglass shape, all the world converges into itself. Time is no exception.

In that instant, time turns into something else.

The turmoil of the vortex of a vast dream envelops K, a vortex dreamed up by all the world, a vortex at the very heart of the universe.

What lies at the bottom of the vortex? K's mind falls endlessly toward darkness, as if funneled down a narrow tube out of his very being. Consciousness now unsullied, pure as the polished surface of a mirror, immaculate as an infant completely free from the prison of being.

Swathed in this new experience of time, dwelling within time itself, K begins to transform into someone else, something else, a whole new form of being altogether.

Now, he sees everything. He sees right through every single thing, through all creation itself. Sentience is no more. All that's left is perception. K has become vision in itself.

This form of being—is this what we call by the name of God?

God is not a being that can be seen, perceived. Perhaps God is a state of being, of dwelling in the reversal of time. That is why

God manifests in any place and any time, traversing the spatial and temporal fabrics that weave through the universe.

No further explanations are possible. You must awaken to it. A great awakening. This is what K finally learns at the end of his dream.

By the time K awakens from his dream, Planet Sola is already far behind him. He finds himself seated within the cabin of a lotus-shaped ship, tranquil in its flight through space. Not a large ship. Nor does it have a crew aboard. He remembers that the ship is called *Pilgrimage*.

K cannot tell if the ship possesses any kind of propulsion system at all. It simply travels through space, flying without any noise, without any vibration.

"Just keep praying."

K recalls the words of the officer at the Planet Sola spaceport. K does just that. Does this mean that this lotus-shaped ship flies through space powered by prayer? Does the *Pilgrimage* draw its energy from K himself as he sits cross-legged in its center? Or perhaps K himself is some kind of circuit, channeling some form of energy that pervades the universe?

The ship continues to fly K on the final leg of his route.

How much time has passed around him? That is impossible to tell. K must focus his attention on his prayers, must devote all his mind to concentrating on one spot on his forehead.

Until suddenly, his destination zooms right before him.

Planet Bosch!

A planet! A green globe floating in the blackness of space! This must be it!

I've made it!

K is filled with sheer joy.

The sun blazes before his eyes, giving off a resplendent glow against the dark background. A G-type star, not all that different from Earth's sun. K first assumes that Planet Bosch revolves around this star. But as his flying saucer approaches closer, another dark planet comes into view. Several times larger than Planet Bosch, approaching a size similar to Earth's moon, it also revolves around an even larger planet close to the size of Earth. So, this dark rock is the satellite. Planet Bosch, therefore, is the satellite of a satellite.

K's mind swells with burning passion as he observes the system of three celestial bodies from his ship. No doubt, these bodies must exert complex gravitational forces on one another, generating complex movements in turn. Watching these bodies in motion, K realizes that some sort of vine connects Planet Bosch to the dead moon. This must be the chain of Pleiades that the astronomer Surim discovered. As far as he can tell, Planet Bosch extends its roots toward the satellite, absorbing all the nutrition from the soil of that moon. Multiple passages describing such a planet appear in the *Southern Scriptures.* He never thought he would have a chance to see precisely what those passages from the scriptures describe.

Some believe that Planet Bosch once revolved around Earth's moon like this a long time ago, until it broke away, floating off like a giant ball of algae in space, much like the one K saw back at Castle Loulan.

But this one is far more massive.

His eyes widen at the sight of this massive ball of green algae, now grown to the size of a celestial body.

Finally, *Pilgrimage* enters orbit around the planet. K's journey to this sacred land will soon come to an end. Up close, the verdant glow of the green globe visible from the window of his ship is even more stunning than he expected.

The ship wanders close to the planet's umbilical cord, the tubular stem, beautiful and green, linking it to the dead moon. K peers through a telescope, searching for the end of the stem. He sees the stem split off into countless root branches, spreading across the surface of the moon like a tight mesh. K shudders at the sight of the indistinct remains of what must have once been a civilization where one of these root branches burrowed beneath the surface. The appendages of Planet Bosch must have destroyed it, devouring all its natural resources, leaving the host moon barren beyond belief, its desolate rocky surface presenting an image of hell.

K's ship makes a smooth landing. An electronic foghorn

sounds as the *Pilgrimage* completes its docking procedure with the Tower Station Terminal Ring. A voice, sounding almost synthesized, speaks to K through the speakers, informing him of the procedures for disembarking.

"Welcome, K. We have been waiting for your arrival. My name is Basen, and I am in charge of this base. Right now, you will need to take off your clothes and sterilize them."

The inspection procedures at the station are unusually strict, requiring that K go from one decontamination dock to another, until finally ending with a shower in an aqueous solution and ultraviolet light.

Tower Station is suspended five hundred meters above the surface of the sacred Planet Bosch. Traveling to its surface requires a long trip down a lift. Only a single shaft supports the whole station, while three branches constructed out of a hardened high-tensile polymer extend downward from the primary shaft at sixty-degree angles. Fitted at the tip of each branch is a heavy metal spindle. K is familiar with this structure. Known as the Balance Toy Structure, this system supports its main structure by coordinating and adjusting the angles of the branches through a precise gyroscopic horizon connected to a computer. Although it may appear ready to topple over easily, in fact, it is quite a dynamically stable structure.

As instructed, K proceeds down a narrow hallway in search of the sign identifying the atrium. All of the Sacred Service staff on this planet must be elsewhere, using the common facilities above or performing inspections below, as this part of the complex is completely devoid of activity. K locates the atrium without too much trouble. Sliding open a dividing curtain, he arrives at a rather small, but nonetheless clean and efficiently planned, fan-shaped room. And he certainly can't complain about the view. Curved panoramic windows line the whole surface of the outer walls, opening up to a magnificent view of the verdant terrain of Planet Bosch.

Pulling one of the hover chairs to the window, K lounges for a little while. More than he could have ever imagined, the lush landscape almost glows with a fresh green hue. Looking as if they were blanketed by a thick carpet, the plains extend all the way out to the horizon. Scattered here and there are various sizes of vesicular structures of vegetation that appear to be settlements of different shapes and sizes.

2

Could this truly be the planet that The Holy Igitur once prophesized? Before K now stands a city, not man-made, but one that grew organically. And as much as its structures appear to have been arranged in advance, anticipating the coming lives of its future residents, as far as K can tell, there is no one here.

K recalls a widely known section of the *Southern Scriptures,* the "Law of Unplanned Nature." Igitur taught that "this Nature itself only exists as it is. You give it purpose yourself. But your pride comes in and ends this state of being. You too will likewise be ended." This teaching has since become a fundamental tenet of the Holy Empire of Igitur, calling for a spiritual way of being as the sole path to coexistence with nature. Igitur teaches in the "Book of the Body" that "this Body of yours is nature. This is where your error lies. You must return this body to nature. To possess a body is not good for the spirit." Scholarly commentary has since traced the philosophical basis of the "Ten Prohibited Desires" to these passages of the *Southern Scriptures.*

But the heretic Darko Dachilko directly challenged these teachings, declaring in his "Treatise on the Pleasures of Nature" that God's nocturnal emissions created the universe, that all the world is God's sperm. He wrote: "The single reason for all of creation, the phenomenon that has made this world appear as this world, is precisely God's pleasure. Thus, what we experience as the phenomenological world is none other than the discharge of God himself, the result of the process of God's nocturnal onanism."

K relaxes in the comfort of the hover chair as he spends much of his first day since arriving gazing out at the vivid colors of the sunset on Planet Bosch.

The next morning, K wakes early in the day to prepare for his first descent onto the planet's surface. The first step is to review the rules to observe while on the surface. These regulations are nonnegotiable. Next, like a hotel guest heading to the pool, K wraps a bath towel around his naked body and makes his way to the descent lobby on the lowest floor. Ultraviolet light and X-rays illuminate every inch of the room, permeating the air with the smell of ozone. The low grumbling of the air-filtering system gives the room an incessant clamor. Upon his arrival, he receives a card with the allotted time printed on it from the registration desk. He then steps inside a chamber, where he is to sit on a bench, giving him the impression of entering a sauna.

Once he completes these procedures, K steps into the lobby, where a few others seeking to descend to the surface stand waiting for the lift to arrive. K briefly considers starting a conversation with one of them but then decides against it. There is just too much of an age difference between them. So everyone remains silent, until eventually, the lift comes up for them.

The lift descends through a transparent shaft. It does not take long for K's excitement to build as they slowly approach the surface. Unable to contain this excitement, he jumps out of the lift compartment before anyone else as soon as it touches the ground and the doors open. The fine green fuzz covering the surface of the ground caresses the backs of his feet with a touch akin to velvet. This carpet will never wear out. It will always be new, always be fresh, always be alive.

K opts to walk on his own, apart from the other researchers who descended with him. It takes no time for him to face the same sense of disbelief that Tinguette—the first man who returned to Earth from this planet—had experienced when he first saw the planet.

Everywhere around K, thickets of pod-shaped structures of vegetation in all sizes sprout from the ground. The larger pods grow to the size of the cargo containers at the spaceport. The smallest among them are about the size of a human hand. Most of the pods, however, are just large enough to house a few people within their hollow interiors. Evidently, these pods are organic, growing in size with age, so all that distinguishes the smaller ones from the larger ones is their place in the developmental stage. According to Tinguette's book, close to the equator, these pods can grow magnificently gargantuan. Closer to the poles, however, their sizes are much smaller on average.

It's just like standing in the middle of the beautiful garden, reminding K somehow of his lost memories of The Orchard. The magnificent forests extend beyond what his eye can see, enshrouding the whole planet with a faint fragrance that's quite intoxicating. For K, there is simply no resisting the urge to wander around this landscape without a single care in the world.

K's sole possession is a compass he carries around his neck. He carries nothing else, roaming the land just as primitive humans would have done. No other animals, never mind any predatory animals, are to be found on this planet of vegetation.

K reaches the opposite end of the open field, where he finds a dense forest of the pod-shaped plant formations. A smattering of unusual pods, otherwise identical in shape but in colors that remind him of outcroppings of coral, mingle within the vast sea of green.

Tinguette explained all this in his famous report: "Although I have considered a number of possible explanations for the existence of these pink pod formations, my hypothesis is as follows: Not unlike the agar-agar of planet Earth, red algae can photosynthesize energy from radiation at longer wavelengths. I am certain that the red pods work the same way. The long history of the growth of Planet Katavolos may have included a period of parasitism on a red dwarf star, and traces of this time have remained coded in the genes of the vegetation, leading to the occasional birth of a red pod."

K emerges from the forest into another open field. Crossing the field brings him face-to-face with mounds of the pod formations piled atop one another to form the walls of a twisting pathway. Without a moment's hesitation he steps inside, losing track of how much time passes as he navigates its labyrinthine path. When he emerges into a clearing on the other end of it, his empty stomach begins to growl.

The entire area of the clearing is slightly sunken, with a mirrorlike surface waiting in its center.

"A pond!"

This joyous discovery quickens K's steps. He recalls no mention of any such pond in Tinguette's report. Otherwise, he would have been honored as the man who discovered the Pond of Planet Katavolos.

Where does all this water come from? K squats by the side of the pond, scooping some water with his hands for a taste. Pure water though it is, it nonetheless has a sweet fragrance akin to tree sap.

K plunges himself into the water, which goes no higher than his waist at its deepest point. His bare feet feel the smooth touch of a carpet-like covering of moss at the bottom of the pool. He wades toward the center of the pond until it is deep enough for him to swim. It's been a long time since he quite thoroughly enjoyed a swim. And in such an ideal natural environment to do it too, surrounded by the quiet green of the pod forest. Only when he's thoroughly savored the experience does he emerge from the pond, lying down beside the water.

K basks under the refreshing warmth of the sun, overflowing with feelings of joy.

It takes him some time, but K eventually does find the source of the water on the opposite end of the pond, where it flows out of a small channel. Less than a hundred steps from there is another pod, which secretes the water from its skin, as if it were sweating.

Every single thing here comes from nature itself. Not a single man-made thing in sight. Truly, Planet Bosch is a living planet, a ball of algae grown to the size of a planetoid, grown to a size large enough for inhabitants to land on its surface. Even though K knew the stories about the wondrous beauty of this planet, there was no way he could have imagined just how much of a paradise it truly is.

Like Marimo moss balls floating in water, this ball of space algae drifts through space, balancing between the forces of gravity and the speed of its revolutions. Unlike Marimo moss balls though, it produces its own water. Estimates drawn from a geological assessment suggest that multiple pockets of perched water—literal inland seas—hide beneath the planet's crust. Deeper into the planet's core—that is, the heart of this giant globe of algae—unbelievable amounts of dense mineral deposits are packed together in plasma form.

It is well past time to head back to the Tower Station. But K is in no hurry. Even if night falls before he can make it back, he can always find a suitable pod for shelter, just as an insect in the woods or mountains might snuggle inside some plant to hide itself from the evening dew.

This is indeed what K decides to do. It does not take him much effort to find a complex pod formation made of four pods layered atop one another. He quickly locates the opening that Tinguette describes in his report toward the rear of the formation, where the other pods close in on each other to form a narrow pathway. The entrance has the shape of a flower petal, which folds itself closed when night falls. Light, changes in humidity, and some sort of mechanical stimulation also allow the petals to open and close on command.

Tinguette believed that these pods evolved from insectivorous plants. He writes: "Even though they function as perfect dwellings for humans, for other less developed animals, the pods of Katavolos are a deadly trap. Their nectar emanates a sweet fragrance that surely seduces any animal, compelling it to slip inside the pod through the flower petal entryway. Engorging themselves on this nectar hypnotizes them into a deep slumber. But as for me, all this was a charming lullaby."

K slips inside the pod's main hall, which is a step lower and covered in a grassy fuzz. Unlike grass on Earth, this fuzz does not feel damp to K's feet and resembles more the texture of the fur of an animal. As he expects, the walls of the two smaller rooms attach to the main hall with more flower-petal entryways. K marvels at the sight before his eyes. The light of the setting sun passes through the dome-shaped ceiling, gently illuminating the interior through a translucent green curtain, with the veins running along the leaves creating netlike patterns that remind him of stained glass windows.

At the center of the hall stands a raised pedestal, nectar flowing out of its concave top like a water fountain. This must be the plant's pistil. K recalls Tinguette's description of this nectar: "I bent down on my knees and took a sip of the exceedingly refreshing water, letting its sweetness penetrate every part of my body, as if it were some kind of elixir of eternal youth and immortality. I remembered a verse from the old Christian Bible: *'John's clothes were made of camel's hair, and he had a leather belt around his waist. His food was locusts and wild honey. I followed in the footsteps of John the Baptist, the prophet of the wilderness.'* Matthew 3:4."

K too tries a taste of this "wild honey" of Planet Bosch. He takes a sip of the viscous oily fluid, savoring its delicate, almost milky flavor. Tinguette compared it to nectar, but its texture is actually closer to oatmeal. K places his mouth right at the rim of the bowl and laps up this nectar until satiated.

Now, the darkness of the night falls upon K.

The roof of the pod complex proves to be an excellent screen. Rays of light from the unfamiliar constellations above the skies of Planet Bosch pierce through the dome and are scattered, their brightness intensified a dozen times over. The splendor is just too much for K, taking his breath away.

K spends the night in one of the smaller chambers connected to the main hall of the pod complex. It is a quiet and cozy semicircular space of less than seven feet in radius. It almost looks like a green yurt of vegetation. Like the main hall, it also has a planetarium-style ceiling, letting the light of the stars shine into the smaller pod. But when his body grazes the walls by accident, the ceiling folds shut, concealing the night sky. Evidently, these pods react to mechanical stimulation, much like the leaves of the mimosa on Earth. How magnificent it must be to incorporate the mechanical sensitivity of these pod formations into architecture! Such structures go beyond merely holding human beings, becoming faithful servants that serve those who reside within them with all devotion!

K lays his body down on the soft green fuzz. In turn, the pod displays its devotion, folding up the roof to conceal the constellations above him while lighting up the walls of the pod itself with a soft green glow. Enzymes within the cells of the leaves store energy from daylight like a silicon battery, only to release this energy as bioluminescence in response to K's touch. A few gentle strokes on the plant walls adjust the brightness of their glow.

Quite frankly, Tinguette's words fail to capture the magnificence of the bedchambers within these pod formations.

"In time, as I lay down, I entrusted my body to the delicate sensations of this bedchamber. I was able to experience with my own body the actualization of Katavolos's vision of organic architecture. Could it be an effect of the nectar? It must have something in it that is able to awaken long-forgotten sensations in me. I had a melancholy hallucination. It was still in my memory when I woke up the next morning. Far too vivid to be something I dreamed up."

Papal censors have redacted a section of Tinguette's writings. Although no one knows why, undoubtedly they considered something written within this section detrimental to the interests of the citizens of the Holy Empire. Rumor has it that in this redacted section Tinguette wrote about a kind of forest sprite, a gurana—a name purportedly mentioned in an unpublished "secret book" of the *Southern Scriptures*—appearing before him. The guranas are supposedly manifestations of the Holy Spirit, the same Holy Spirit that impregnated the Holy Mother to conceive Igitur.

3

Other than a nightly prayer in the middle of the evening, everyone is free to do as they wish on the station. By far, K is always the most eager of all the researchers to descend to the surface. Day after day, he continues to return to the planet, making careful observations and keeping close records of the various features of the pod formations. But as these days of monotony and perseverance pass, K increasingly detects a whiff of heresy within the station, manifesting as expressions of sloth and tedium. Although the other Sacred Service officers behave devoutly while roaming the surface, every now and then, he smells the odor of Darko Dachilko's influence in their words and actions.

K feigns calm for now, making an effort to suppress his suspicions. Before he can act, he needs to figure out what's going on here, to get the others to trust him. There's still something about Planet Bosch that he's yet to fully grasp, a secret he's yet to uncover.

The secret begins to unravel when K discovers that the man in charge of the station, a man named Basen, is the same man who interviewed him back on Earth, when he first learned the results of the Sacred Service Exam. Perhaps it is only to be expected though. After all, Basen did tell him offhand, on the stone steps of City Hall as they were leaving, that he too would be assigned to Planet Bosch. Now, here he is indeed.

But there is an even bigger shock in store for K. One day, he catches sight of the supposedly dead Abir in the cafeteria. He can't help but stare at the old art professor as if looking at a ghost. But that isn't even the end of it. The roster of trainees from the Holy Igitur Monastery—most of them, at least—have also gathered here.

Shouldn't they all be dead?

K shivers, remembering Hoffman's news about their fates.

Even Mullin, the most intelligent of all of them, is among those here.

"Hey, where's Hoffman?" he asks K. "Wasn't he supposed to come here with you?"

"No," K answers. "Since the monastery, I have spoken to Hoffman only once, over the phone. He sounded terrified of Darko Dachilko's ghost."

"Really?" Mullin says.

He strikes K as oddly cold and uninterested as he quietly walks away with an enigmatic smile on his lips.

Not just Mullin, but all of K's former acquaintances are similarly standoffish to him. That's not quite right. Further observation makes it apparent that they don't treat him any differently. No, they're just as reserved with each other, always speaking in hushed tones everywhere in the station, as if this place too has now become a monastery. K suspects that they are all waiting for something to happen.

Indeed, something does happen. One evening, Basen calls a midnight gathering in his room. Everyone on the station has already assembled there by the time K makes his entrance.

K has learned since his arrival on the planet that Basen is apparently the leading authority on Hyperspace Theology. Not only is he in charge of the operations of this base, at the same time, he's also the intellectual leader of all the researchers on Planet Bosch, who look to him for approval.

When K arrives at the gathering, he notices the sweet fragrance of a Loulan narcotic permeating the room. The gaseous substance has the effect of "liberating" all these men, and along with them, K too is instantly "liberated." Just a moment ago, everyone was behaving as if they were all already dead. Now, they're in high spirits.

"I am Bose," says a man who approaches K.

"You were my predecessor, weren't you?"

Bose was the director of the Planet Bosch Research Center, until K took over the role.

Shouldn't he also be dead?

That's certainly what Tantra had told K, if he is to be believed.

"Oh, no. Tantra too has been resurrected, and he's also here now."

"Him, too?"

"Yes. But he's already gone ahead of us."

"What? Gone ahead? To where?"

"To the south."

"What is in the south?"

"*It* is in the south."

Clearly, Bose takes for granted that everyone on the station already knows what he's talking about.

Bose asks, "So has anyone told you about Professor Basen yet?"

"No."

The surprise registers plainly on Bose's face.

"Oh?" he says. "Well, I better let you know now, then."

A haze already starts to form in K's mind. Nonetheless, he makes every effort to focus on Bose's words.

According to Bose, Basen and everyone else in the station are all members of a heretical Christian group that existed in the fifteenth century of the Common Era. It was a secret sect known as the "Homines Intelligentiae" or the "Brethren of the Free Spirit."

Bose continues to speak, though K's mind has almost completely clouded over, and he can barely understand or articulate any words.

"So, all of us gathered here—that includes you—are to become brothers," he says. "The truth is that Hieronymus Bosch, the artist from the Twilight Era, was supposedly also a member of the sect during his time."

"But what sort of teachings does this secret sect profess?"

"A distinct characteristic of this secret sect is that its followers believe in praying to God through sex," Bose answers. "Does this surprise you? They say that Darko Dachilko founded this church of the naked body."

K does not know what to say.

"Later, he linked the interpretation of the *Southern Scriptures* to this secret sect from the Twilight Era. He said, 'There is clear evidence that The Holy Igitur was himself also a disciple of the Brethren of the Free Spirit.'"

"Impossible. There's no way I can believe that."

"I don't blame you."

Bose gives K a sympathetic look.

His mind now thoroughly addled, K ends up listening in on an exchange between Basen and Bose while in a trance. He can barely make sense of what he hears.

Antichurch. Anti-Sacred Service. Heretic. Hieronymus Bosch. Millennium of Prosperity. Red. Pineapple. Talking Owl. Garden of Earthly Delights. Noah's Floods. Dried Weeds. Garden. Temptation of Saint Antoine. The seed. Is God's Word.

No one else remains in Basen's room when K awakens from his deep, muddled sleep.

Not only that, every single person in the whole station has disappeared.

No one else is here anymore.

There's something eerie about the emptied-out station. K descends to the lowest level. Fresh graffiti in bold letters stains the walls at the entrance to the lift:

As a cloud vanishes and is gone, so he who goes down to the grave does not return. He will never come to his house again; his place will know him no more.

— Job 7:9

The lift is at the surface level. It takes its time to make its way back up. As soon as it arrives, K leaps inside. He flicks the switch.

The lift begins its descent.

Straining his eyes to look out over the planet's surface, K catches sight of a group of people disappearing behind the curvature of the horizon. Just where are they going? Where?

Once K reaches the surface, he finds footprints left behind on the earth. They head in the same direction as the people he saw earlier.

K follows these footprints.

Many days pass. After, many more days pass again.

The planet is abundant in food and drink. For food, fruits hang from the pod formations that are all over the planet. They taste like a blend of meat and vegetables. For drinks, plenty of sunken patches of earth filled with endless reserves of spring water dot the landscape. There must be some strange substance in the water, for a single sip is all K needs to fully reinvigorate him.

But this trip on foot does not make much progress. K frequently gets lost in the labyrinthine pathways in between the pod formations. Still, he presses on. One thing is certain—he must continue going directly south.

With every passing day of this trek, the pod formations K encounters become increasingly larger. More red pods begin to appear among the green ones, until the ratio between the green pods and the red are just about half and half. Finally, after a few more days of walking, every single one of the pods before him has become red.

By the time it happens, K has already lost track of how long it has been since he started this journey. Something startles him, a creature, white and moving within the dense layers of the coral-colored forest. K's pulse races. It's a naked woman. She must be a forest sprite, a gurana. Like a startled deer, she flees the scene. The realization finally hits K. Soon, his long walk will be over. The commotion of a nearby crowd tells him as much. K runs toward the commotion, shouting in joy. He emerges out of the forest, appearing before a clearing with a pond at the center of it.

The Bosch painting!

K screams.

A large pond lies in the center of the wide clearing. Directly on the other side of it stands a bright pink tower constructed out of a misshapen pod formation. Countless numbers of naked men and women have gathered here, filling every space of the clearing, frolicking and dancing.

There can be no doubt about it. The scene before K is none other than Bosch's *Garden of Earthly Delights* re-created in the flesh.

K finds himself at a loss for words.

Suddenly, two naked women run toward him. They take his hands, leading him toward the strange scene, drawing him into it.

4

A strange garden with winged men and winged fish flying in the sky.

Just what does it all mean? The men from the station K tracked here are all present, singing, dancing, playing, clamoring, laughing, and whimpering. All are lost in a large crowd of naked bodies, making it difficult to tell who is who.

The two naked women who led K here chirp like birds. Although he does not understand the meaning of their songs, their gestures and expressions communicate to him a welcome to the garden. Throngs gather around piles of fruit the size of people—pineapples, berries, apples, and grapes. Couples soak together in pools of water. Masses of naked bodies strike various poses and mingle with grotesque hybrid beings.

Such awesome hedonism! Sexual congress all over the place! The spontaneous atmosphere of this bizarre anticosmic garden swallows up K, devouring all his powers of reason. Enchanted by the sight before him, he slowly slips and falls into the depths of madness.

The forest sprites must have quickly gotten bored with K's body. Leaving behind only their birdlike chirping, they go after another. A robust, ox-like man pursues them in turn. Their three bodies tangle with one another, all falling to the ground with loud guffaws under the shadow of a red plant pod.

For a while, all K can do is watch it all while still in a daze. But when he finally regains his wits, he begins to wander around. Though still half-stupefied, he steps into the scenes unfolding before him.

A woman with a blue fruit for her head seduces a man lying on his belly. A half-pig man and woman stick their faces into a bell-shaped flower as they exchange secret whispers between them. Two lovers sit together inside a massive piece of fruit.

Mingling among the men and women is Abir, who earnestly attempts to make a move on a dark-skinned woman. They sit atop the back of a giant aquatic bird. Noticing K, he grimaces in embarrassment for an instant but quickly goes back to what he's doing.

K also spots Mullin, who is attempting to persuade a reluctant blonde woman to listen to him. Their two bodies make a splash when they fall into the water. The woman swims out, fleeing. Mullin pursues her.

Who's that conversing with a gorgeous woman with a sophisticated air about her? It's Bose. The woman stands proudly, paying little attention to his words.

Tantra looks completely out of it as a massive duck feeds him a piece of red fruit.

K catches his breath under the Tree of Knowledge of Good and Evil, just as a fruit-man with a huge owl over his head begins performing a wild dance.

She must be here somewhere. Among all these naked frolicking bodies has to be the woman he's been searching for all this time. This is the one thing K is absolutely certain about.

"Here, have some."

Another gurana seats herself beside K, offering him an

apple—no clothes at all on her naked body as she draws herself close against him, trying to seduce him. She seems to feel no shame whatsoever at exposing herself to him, even as she spreads her legs apart, showing him her golden pubic hair and the slit of her genitals.

A realization strikes K when he looks again at the center of the Garden of Earthly Delights. The rounded shape of the pond resembles the female genitals. Around it, horses, deer, camels, pigs, bears, and all manner of other animals carry people on their backs, circling the pond, almost as if they're staging a performance symbolic of the cyclical character of the cosmos.

Still eating the apple, the gurana persists in her attempts to couple with K. He refuses her, leaving the spot under the tree to cross the central pond, making his way to the towers rising behind it.

Another, much larger pond waits over on the other side. Five towers surround it. Someone from inside them must have seen K's approach, as another gurana meets K, inviting him to the tower farthest to the rear. K follows her toward the tower's entrance, where a stream of water flows out into the pond.

This tower must be what the pod formations become at their full maturity, fully developed and transmogrified into a complex system. Its cavernous internal passageways connect to a central chamber with a rounded ceiling. Small, spiraling tubular corridors gradually ascend to the top of this chamber. All of it glimmers in coral pink under the light of the sun.

As the forest sprite guides K into one room, a sense of trepidation, a premonition, creeps within him. There's someone here he's supposed to meet. Soon, the truth of all that's happened will finally be revealed to him.

He hears a tinkling voice, a voice still vivid in his memory.

A woman. White robes embrace the gentle curves of her body. Soft eyes. Flowing golden hair.

Finally, he meets the shining beauty.

K's next words are barely audible.

"What name should I call you?"

"I am the same Barbara that you've always known," she says, smiling as she takes K's hands.

A narrow spiral staircase ascends from the coral-pink chamber. Hand in hand with Barbara, K follows her up this staircase. K hears the bells of a clock tower ringing twelve times in the distance.

They enter a small room at the very top of the tower. Barbara's bedchamber? A sweet fragrance enshrouds the bright-pink chamber, giving it an atmosphere much like the inside of a fruit.

All the secrets of the world will be revealed in this chamber. Drawn all over the ceiling, the walls, and also the floor are countless paintings. No, that's not right. These are no mere paintings. They show various animated views of the world outside, shifting and changing with every moment. The images appearing on the ceiling show a different world altogether. Take one step inside to be transported right into that world. And then there's the rounded wall on one side, displaying the scene of The Orchard from a long time ago.

"I have been waiting for you," Barbara says. "You've finally made it."

A deep grief shows in her eyes, eyes that have seen everything in the world.

"Yes," K says. "It took me a very long time to get here."

Somehow, K made it here. Only now does he realize the gravity of what he's accomplished.

"I didn't understand anything at first. But along the way, it dawned on me why I had to come to Planet Bosch."

Barbara offers K a faint smile.

"You came for me, right?"

Indeed, K has come here for Barbara, leaving Earth, traversing a vast distance of a thousand light-years, just so he could make it all the way here.

Why? Why did I need to see Barbara?

Finally, K remembers. Barbara is the woman he has always envisioned in his mind. She is the woman who has dwelled in his heart all this time.

"Yes. I have been dwelling in your heart for a long time."

She smiles, as if reading K's mind.

"I've had that feeling for a while now," K says. "That's why we meet again so many times, right?"

"Yes, that's right. We first met in the previous life."

"Hundreds of years ago?"

"Yes, hundreds of years ago. In this previous life, you were Gilgeas."

Just as K has long suspected. He is indeed Barbara's old lover, Gilgeas.

"Yes. But the two of us died without having consummated our love."

"That's right."

The rounded wall inside the tower displays the scene, a reenactment of their previous lives. The gazebo in The Orchard comes into view. K and Barbara both stand within it, facing each other, having just exchanged their final vows in this world.

The K within the screen whispers to Barbara as he gazes deep into her eyes.

"Ready?"

Barbara returns his gaze.

"Yes."

K extends his arms toward Barbara's neck. His fingers tighten their grip. He strangles Barbara.

Six fingers on each of my hands?

Lost in a daze, K continues watching the images on the wall. They show his deformed hands picking up a nearby vial of poison. As he watches over Barbara's dying face, he removes the cap from the vial.

Barbara speaks.

"Just as we promised each other, you took the red poison. But then, with his own hands, your father dug up my body under the cover of darkness and gave me back my life."

"You mean the heretic Darko Dachilko?"

"Yes. He placed me within the Sarcophagus of Osiris to raise me from the dead. That's why I did not die. We were supposed to die together and be forever joined as one. Instead, we were torn apart, separated between this world and another world for several hundreds of years. Until now."

As K listens to Barbara's story, he finally begins to understand all he's done, all that made no sense at the time. Darko Dachilko was Gilgeas's real father. And Gilgeas was K in a previous life. Like Darko Dachilko, he too had six fingers on each hand.

"I understand now," K says. "Gilgeas has been within me all this time. His curse became mine."

"Yes. But we've now fulfilled our centuries-old promise to each other."

Barbara's words resonate with clarity.

"But the Gilgeas within me killed poor Martha."

Poor Martha. Daughter of the administrator at the Planet Bosch Research Center. She loved K.

"I know. But you have nothing to worry about. Martha is here too. See?"

Barbara points toward the pond beneath them through the window. There she is indeed, locked in the throes of passion, squirming underneath the weight of a large, pot-bellied man.

"Darko Dachilko resurrected her. Like me, she was placed inside the Sarcophagus of Osiris. Then he brought her here to Planet Bosch."

"What about my mother? Is she here too?"

She was the beggar woman who went by the name of Eva. She was the woman who offered K her milk in his time of need.

"You mean Lady Piponoclara? Of course she is here! Over there!"

Looking to that direction, K sees her on a white boat just as it crosses the pond right below them.

"Who is the man on the boat with her?"

"That's your father, of course."

Looking over his parents as they appear to enjoy each other's company gives K a strange sort of feeling.

The beautiful woman who introduced herself as Piponoclara at dinner that night at the Holy Igitur Monastery was once a

Sacred Courtesan in her day. That same salacious hall where K lost his virginity—Clara Hall—was once, a long time ago, her own hall.

"She too can travel across the boundaries of space and time. She must have appeared before you," Barbara says.

"But why?" K asks. "There must be some reason she offered me her milk. It can't just be the simple expression of a mother's love toward Gilgeas."

"You're right, of course. The milk she offered you was for the poor Gilgeas locked within you. But that's not the only reason she appeared before you. Lady Piponoclara needed to save you from starvation so that you could pass the Sacred Service Exam and make your way here to this planet."

Her milk did have a strange power to clear my mind.

"But to what end?"

"It was to ensure that everything could return to what it once was. Just like the old days, so you and I could be together again."

Little by little, the story begins to make sense to K. Of course, everything unfolded according to Darko Dachilko's plan. First, he appeared before him in the form of his master. Just as he once suspected, Hypocras truly was Darko Dachilko in disguise. But he was also the pope. The first day's questions at the Sacred Service Exam must have been created by Darko Dachilko just for K.

No wonder I was able to answer them without too much trouble.

Barbara explains to K that the Sacred Service Exam was held for the sole purpose of bringing K to Planet Bosch, of selecting that one candidate from all over the Holy Empire who can fulfill Darko Dachilko's will.

Outside, K's mother, Piponoclara, has revived her old romance. Having rekindled the affection of Darko Dachilko for her after it was once directed at Barbara, she looks very happy indeed on the boat in the middle of the lake.

Still . . .

Just one last thing that K has yet to understand.

5

So Darko Dachilko has the ability to take on many different guises. He did not appear to K just as Hypocras or the pope but also as a guard at the Holy Igitur Monastery. He also received K as the Lord of Castle Loulan. Finally, he even appeared in K's dreams as that strange old man Parnassus while he was aboard the Nirvana ship.

Even that old devil living in the massive Space Clock tower— could he have been another one of his incarnations?

Such a powerful man is this Darko Dachilko that at once he plays the role of both saint and devil. His split personality sometimes manifests as a great man of conscience whose power and influence make him a leader of the people. But at other times, he turns into a cruel man, a man who would make Barbara the object of his illicit desire.

"Barbara, do you remember when you were confined in the tower of the Space Clock by that devil? What was that all about?"

"Let me explain it to you," she says. "His imprisonment there was his punishment for confining me to that tower."

"Is that why that devil—that incarnation of my father—could not take even one step outside the tower?" K asks.

"Until you handed him the chain from your medal."

"Yes. The devil used the chain to repair his own wings."

A cold chill runs up K's spine as he recalls the eeriness of all that happened then.

"It didn't matter whether you knew what you were doing. What you did was an important symbolic act. You, as his son, forgave the devil inside of him. That's why the devil brought me from the dreary darkness of Loulan to this paradise."

"What happened to him?"

"The incarnation of the devil inside your father lost all its power."

K's questions to Barbara continue.

"So who was it that meted out this punishment on the devil?"

"Of course, that would be Darko Dachilko himself. No, that's not right. It would be more accurate to say that it was yet another incarnation of your father. It was The Holy Igitur."

Truly, these words astound K.

"What?" he says. "The Holy Igitur was my father?"

"That's right," Barbara says, her voice as serene as it can be, clear and without a single hint of darkness. "Darko Dachilko is none other than The Holy Igitur himself."

And so the mysteries of the universe begin to reveal themselves. The Millennium of Prosperity that was the pride and joy of the Holy Empire of Igitur—Darko Dachilko built all of it. Was it his very own ideal world that he had dreamt up? Or was all of reality in this Holy Empire simply taking place within his dream?

But why would my father seek to bring me to this planet?

"Within me is Gilgeas, his rival in his affection for you," K mutters.

"Well, K," Barbara says. "That's because it's your turn now. At long last, he's going to pass everything on to you."

None of this makes sense to K.

"What do you mean?"

Does Darko Dachilko intend to give back Barbara to his son, Gilgeas?

Barbara continues: "I think he has grown tired of living. I mean, he's lived more than one thousand years. I guess if you've lived that long, you might come to know too much about the world, such that your very reason for being in the world disappears. He often said, 'After all, this world is nothing more than a dream—to live in this world, even if it lasts for more than a thousand years, is still to live an empty life.' K, you're still young, and so you probably wouldn't understand, but I think that I do, in a way, understand what he means. I mean, I too have lived many centuries through the magic of Osiris."

Upon speaking these words, she raises her hand, waving as if stroking the empty air. Every single one of the images of the various worlds displayed on the walls disappears all at once.

Finally, the two embrace one another. They lay their bodies

down to perform a ritual of love before a single altarpiece. The painting shows scenes much too familiar, much too similar to the paradise on Planet Bosch. No doubt, this is the Hieronymus Bosch painting from the Twilight Era.

But K does not think to ask how the painting managed to find its way to this planet. It vanished from the Papal Art Gallery following the inquisition of the year 567 of the Sacred Era.

It is a partitioned triptych altarpiece. They say its images represent heaven on the left side and hell on the right. And in the center of it all is this Garden of Earthly Delights.

6

"My son."

A booming voice comes from beyond the window.

"Gilgeas, answer my call."

The great garden falls still and silent. K rushes to the window. K spots the giant of a man standing tall in the center of the pond. This man must be none other than Darko Dachilko himself.

He raises both hands and looks toward the tower that K is in.

He is a great man with a pitch-black body.

The Melanosized Messiah—the man appears just as he had been described by The Holy Igitur in the *Southern Scriptures*.

Barbara stands next to K.

"He is calling to you," she says. "Go and answer his call."

K nods.

"I am here!" he shouts.

"My son."

Once more, the black heretic calls K as he stands waist deep in the water.

All those frolicking just a moment ago stop whatever they are doing, standing silent as they watch things unfold.

"At last, he intends to complete the Jump into the White Light," Barbara whispers to K.

"The *ablutio* is complete," the man says, "Thus, my body will perish. My *nigredo* flesh will be purified. My son, perform my *baptisma*."

Somehow, K understands exactly what he means.

Several pages of the *Southern Scriptures* cover matters of Alchemical Marriage, recording three forms of purification toward the stage of *albedo* following the destruction of the flesh. The *prima materia* of the flesh will perish by either *sortio, separatio, or putrefaci*, becoming *nigredo*. This death is then followed by a purification that proceeds step-by-step along three stages.

The first stage is the *baptisma*.

The second is when the *anima* escapes the flesh, then reintegrates into the dead body to raise it from the dead.

Finally, the third stage passes through the *omnes colores* or *cauda pavonis,* the phase of many colors, uniting all these colors to bring about the *albedo.*

K addresses Darko Dachilko with his own booming voice.

"Why do you seek *baptisma*? You are able to return to the flesh of this earth and be resurrected through the magic of Osiris, are you not?"

"My son, indeed it is possible for me to be resurrected into this world, just as Barbara was. But it is time to complete the Magnum Opus. And so, my son, grant me the *baptisma*."

As Darko Dachilko wishes, K grants him the *baptisma*.

And so it begins.

Once more, the man in the pond begins to speak.

"People of the world! Hear me! The *anima mundi* has been trapped in the material world. What is salvation? It is the *Opus* of freeing the long-suffering spirit of the cosmos. I have devoted myself to the salvation of such suffering spirits of this world and all the cosmos. You are the chosen ones. Now it is your turn to save others. No longer will you be the ones who need saving."

His voice overflows with confidence, as if the will of the cosmos itself speaks through him.

"God took the form of his son and hid himself inside Mary, within her virgin land, within this purest manifestation of the *materia*. It was then that the history of the Savior began."

K listens intently.

"I myself did the same as Jesus Christ. The ground on which you stand, this very planet, will soon cease to exist. But this is not the punishment of God. Nor is it the will of the cosmos. All this, all of nature, came into being through the Great God's nocturnal emission. The world is no different. Because all of the universe manifests within God's dream, its end will begin with God's awakening. And so you have all been saved and brought to this planet by my hand. But now, I must return you all to nothingness once more."

As his thunderous preaching continues, he begins to ascend from the pond.

"Look. The purification has begun," Barbara says, pointing toward Darko Dachilko.

Indeed, as if he were being thrust into another dimension, his putrefied naked body washes away before all their eyes.

He hovers in the air for some time, twirling his hands as if he were about to lead one final prayer. And then just like that, he is gone.

Barbara sighs.

"It's over."

People start to leave. No, they start to vanish into thin air, becoming one with the Holy Spirit.

After the ceremony, the garden returns to silence.

"Now, we have to cut the chain of Pleiades," Barbara says.

Something must have been readied ahead of time. Barbara gently presses a spot on the wall. Immediately, the planet begins to undulate like a ship whose anchor has been cut.

"Now, it's time for us to sleep."

Barbara guides K to press their naked bodies together.

As they hold one another, everything around them begins to take on the quality of a dream. K knows what will happen next. If he falls asleep now, he will cross over to the other side of his dream, awakening to an entirely new, entirely unfamiliar world.

Only a miniscule—if such a word even still has meaning— amount of time flows past them before Planet Bosch transforms completely. In an instant, everything dries out like a desert. The transformation is as rapid as an egg's growth after fertilization.

"The time has come for us to go."

"To where?" K asks as he caresses her white bosom with his lips.

"To the new Earth. We will travel there to become the seed of the creation of the world."

Planet Bosch explodes.

It happens quickly, as if its very existence had always been right at the threshold all this time.

The planet scatters its seeds, countless seeds that will wander through the darkness of space.

Perhaps, with the passing of time, everything will be reborn. Perhaps one of these seeds carries the spirits of Barbara and K. Perhaps one day it will reach some star in some galaxy, just as it was foretold by the allegories of the "Book of the Seed" in the *Southern Scriptures*.

"Thus, once more will God desire in this great dream, and a moment of joy in his dream will be inseminated among the people. And so the Millennium of Prosperity will begin anew."

TRANSLATOR'S ACKNOWLEDGMENTS

I am indebted to many individuals whose support at various stages made this translation possible. Foremost among them is Thomas Lamarre, who stewarded this project from beginning to end, giving me not only the initial opportunities but also valuable guidance and feedback throughout the process.

Initial work on the translation was supported by a postdoctoral fellowship from the Social Sciences and Humanities Research Council (SSHRC) of Canada.

Many thanks go to the University of Minnesota Press, especially Jason Weidemann and Erin Warholm-Wohlenhaus, for continued commitment to the project despite delays along the way. Takayuki Tatsumi facilitated contact and communication with Yoshio Aramaki. Kazuko Behrens's initial work on Aramaki's novel was an important starting point for my translation. My wonderful colleagues at the University of Minnesota (Suvadip Sinha, Christine Marran, Jason McGrath, Travis Workman, and others) made this work all the more worthwhile. My wife, Denise, offered patient support through many late nights.

Finally, let me express my appreciation to Yoshio Aramaki, who kindly entrusted his work to me. I only hope that I have done it justice.

CHRONOLOGY OF IGITUR'S
MILLENNIUM OF PROSPERITY

Year 182   North–South War of Two Centuries ends. Treaty of Two Worlds ratified. The Holy Empire claims the right to engage in missionary work within the southern celestial hemisphere up to a distance of one thousand light-years.

Year 223   Establishment of the Law of Five Galaxies and Sacred Knowledge

Year 288   Discovery of the Field Theory of Hyperspace Navigation

Year 313   Beheading of heretic Darko Dachilko (First Papal Conference)

Year 323   Pope Algol I designates the Holy Disciplines of Sacred Inquiry. Beginning of the Sacred Service Examination system.

Year 420   Pope Algol IV broadcasts Temperance Proclamation

Year 567   Interpretations of Hieronymus Bosch's painting *The Garden of Earthly Delights* declared heretical (Second Papal Conference).

Year 640   End of civil war that began in 567. Devastation of the realm.

Year 708   Hyperspace jump navigation implemented.

Year 886   Development of the Loulan Space Route. Expansion of the realms of the Holy Empire.

Year 900   Discovery of the Taklamakan Space Desert

Year 975   Planet Bosch Research classified as a Holy Discipline

Yoshio Aramaki is a prominent writer of the New Wave of science fiction in Japan in the 1960s, which explored "inner space," and his early fiction is known for its surreal and picturesque imagery and fantastic metaphysical narratives. He has written the novels *Shirokihi tabidateba fushi (Departing on a White Day, Immortality), Sei shutefan jiin no kane no ne wa (Listen to the Bells of St. Stephen's Cathedral),* and the *Konpeki no kantai (Deep Blue Fleet)* series.

Baryon Tensor Posadas is assistant professor of Asian languages and literatures at the University of Minnesota. He studies the doppelgänger motif in modern Japanese film and fiction, as well as Japanese science fiction, empire, and the imagination of futurity.

Takayuki Tatsumi is professor in the Department of Humanities and Social Sciences at Keio University. He has written many books, including *Full Metal Apache: Transactions between Cyberpunk Japan and Avant-Pop America* and *New Americanist Poetics.*